AGAIN AND AGAIN

SUSAN JOHNSON

AGAIN AND AGAIN

BRAVA

KENSINGTON PUBLISHING CORP.

http://www.kensingtonbooks.com

BRAVA BOOKS are published by

Kensington Publishing Corp.
850 Third Avenue
New York, NY 10022

All Kensington titles, imprints and distributed lines are available at special quantity discounts for bulk purchases for sales promotion, premi-
ums, fund raising, educational or institutional use.

Special book excerpts or customized printings can also be created to fit
specific needs. For details, write or phone the office of the Kensington
Special Sales Manager: Kensington Publishing Corp., 850 Third
Avenue, New York, NY, 10022. Attn. Special Sales Department. Phone:
1-800-221-2647.

Brava and the B logo Reg. U.S. Pat. & TM Off.

ISBN 1-57566-805-X

First Kensington Trade Paperback Printing: May 2002
10 9 8 7 6 5 4 3 2 1

Printed in the United States of America

Chapter

1

Yorkshire, November 1821

The snow had been falling since morning but the coachman had pressed on through the storm only to have the horses brought to a halt by impassable roads on the outskirts of Shipton. Unlike several of the passengers who grumbled about their altered schedules, Caroline Morrow was more than happy to descend from the cold, cramped coach and stumble through the drifts toward the welcoming warmth of a nearby inn.

Once inside, she shook the snowflakes from her cape, threw off the hood, and moved through the press of travelers in the small entryway toward the parlor where she stood as close to the crackling fire as prudence would allow. Holding her hands out, she basked in the comforting warmth. The heavenly possibility of actually sleeping in a soft bed gave her further reason for gratification.

Lost in her reverie apropos of the pleasures of a real bed and a hot meal, the familiar voice at first went unattended. But the deep, distinctive tones eventually insinuated themselves into her consciousness and she lifted her head to listen for a moment before discounting the absurdity of such a coincidence. The buzz of conversation suddenly swelled when several other passengers moved into the parlor and the curious voice from her past disappeared from her thoughts.

She ignored the sound of footfalls behind her a short time later, not wishing company, but she couldn't ignore the fragrance drifting into her nostrils, nor the impact the pine-scented cologne had on her emotions.

She spun around.

"I thought it was you."

He stood no more than a foot away: large, powerful, more handsome than she remembered, his dark hair damp with melting snow, his caped riding coat black like his eyes—and his heart.

The color momentarily drained from her face, but even as she drew in a fortifying breath her gaze turned chill. "A pity it's such a small world," she said coolly.

"More like my good fortune it's such a small world."

"Allow me to disagree."

"As usual." His smile was impudent. "What are you doing here?"

With her initial shock receding, she managed to speak in as dégagé a tone as he. "Taking refuge from the storm like you."

"I meant where are you bound?"

"None of your business."

He tipped his head in amused deference. "Have you missed me?"

"Not in the least."

"I, on the other hand, have missed you terribly."

"I'd hardly think that possible with your busy schedule. Do you still receive twenty *billets-doux* a day? Or has the number risen since you've become an eligible duke?"

"Who says I'm eligible?"

"Are you married then?"

"No."

Her immediate sense of relief annoyed her. "Then you're eligible regardless of your disreputable life," she noted tartly, correcting her brief lapse in judgment.

"Don't snap at me, darling. You were the one who ran off and married."

"I'm not your darling and I didn't run off. I simply considered it foolish to wait around until you were ready to give up your profligate ways."

His nostrils flared for a moment, but his voice was bland when he spoke. "Has married life suited you?"

"I'm divorced."

His eyes widened; divorce was rare—and expensive. He knew her financial status and as he recalled, her émigré husband had lost his fortune in the Revolution. "I'm sorry." When he wasn't. When he felt an elation he hadn't felt in years.

"You needn't be. I'm quite content."

"You disappeared five years ago. No one knew where."

"I left for the Continent."

"Do you live in Yorkshire now?"

"Yes." She didn't precisely yet, but once she reached her new employers, she would.

"May I call on you?"

"No." She wasn't about to tell him she was reduced to the status of governess, her small inheritance dissipated.

"Surely you don't dislike me so."

She took a deep breath and the sudden blush on her cheeks wasn't from the heat of the fire. "I don't dislike you, Simon. We just have never suited, that's all."

"I disagree. We suited very well, as I recall." His voice was velvety and low.

"Sex isn't enough."

A dozen gazes swivelled around at the provocative word and she turned beet red.

Simon Blair immediately cast his cool, ducal glance on the curious bystanders. "This is a private conversation," he said, his voice like the low thunder of distant artillery, and within moments everyone had backed away. Returning his attention to her, his mouth curved into a faint smile. "You were saying?"

"I don't frighten so easily."

"You don't frighten at all if I remember. And sex may not be enough, but it's a damned good start, Caro, and you know it. You shouldn't have run away."

"I'm not a patient person."

"Did I ask you to wait?"

"Somehow I got that impression. And after finding you in bed with my maid," she pointedly added, "my interest waned."

"You never let me explain."

"I imagine you would have had a very good story."

A tick appeared high over one cheekbone. "You were damned busy with suitors, too."

"But not actually in bed with any of them. I believe there's a difference."

"It wasn't what you think."

She shrugged. "What's the point, Simon. It all happened five years ago. I wish you good fortune in your life." Taking a side step, she began moving around him.

His hand closed on her wrist, his grip gentle but confining. "Have dinner with me." He glanced at the frosted windows, the icy tattoo of pelting snow a stark reminder of the storm outside. "Neither of us are going anywhere tonight. Tell me what you've been doing, where you've been these last five years. Pass the evening with me." His voice dropped to a murmur, a conciliatory warmth shone in his eyes. "Like friends. You can't say we weren't friends . . ."

She couldn't, even if she'd wished to, when they'd known each other from childhood, when they'd been friends long before they'd become lovers.

"It's only dinner."

She hesitated still, a flood of painful memories coming to the fore.

"If I annoy you, leave at any time. The inn is crowded with people. You're perfectly safe. You'd be safe even without the others," he gently added.

She was no longer an innocent, if she'd ever been, her years with her husband the ultimate in harsh reality. Surely she could handle a simple dinner with Simon. "I *am* hungry. Just friends, now."

"Whatever you want."

"That's what I want."

"Fine." His grin was boyish, achingly familiar. "Sit here by the fire," he offered, pulling up a chair for her, "and I'll bespeak us some dinner. Do you still like white clarets?"

"Anything will do."

"If you have a choice."

"A white claret would be very nice."

He not only bespoke dinner, but also a private parlor with a cozy fire on the hearth, silver candlesticks on the table, a host of wine bottles displayed on the sideboard, along with a sumptuous array of food. As he escorted her into the small paneled room that had been heated to a balmy summer temperature, she looked up at him with a tight smile. "You're still persuasive, I see."

"The landlady remembered my father," he blandly replied, showing her to a table set before the fire.

She cast him a suspicious glance. "And that's why we're the only ones with a private dining room?"

The innocence of his smile couldn't have been improved on by cherubs on high. "Apparently she liked him a lot."

"I'm not in the mood for a seduction," she warned.

He nodded as he sat opposite her. "Agreed. I just preferred conversing with you apart from that rowdy crowd outside." Deftly uncorking a wine bottle, he poured a small measure into her glass. "The landlady actually had some Chateau de la Bréde claret. Remember when we drank it that day on the Thames? Let me know if it's improved in five years."

She wasn't able to immediately reply, memories of their sensuous picnic near Richmond evoking an intense spiking pleasure. Lifting the glass, she examined the fine golden liquid, needing a moment to compose her emotions before taking a sip. Her voice when she replied was deliberately bland. "It's perfect as ever."

"I'll take that as a good omen." Grinning, he filled his glass and lifted it to her in salute. "To our future friendship."

"What are you doing here?" she abruptly asked, not capable of so cavalierly contemplating a renewal of their relationship. She was no longer naive and gullible.

"I'm on my way north to hunt with some friends. The storm drove me off the road—a happy coincidence I might add." His gaze above the rim of his glass was genial. "Are you hungry?"

"Very much." She glanced at the sideboard. "The stage stops don't offer such sumptuous fare."

"Then let's eat. I've been riding since morning."

She didn't need a second invitation with the savory aromas wafting their way to the table, and together they filled their plates from the numerous dishes. Over a dinner of pigeon pie, veal cutlets, steamed potatoes, peas with butter sauce, salad, plum tarts, along with a goodly portion of excellent wine, they conversed in an easy way, concentrating on impersonal subjects—the weather, the state of the roads, the king's splendid and expensive coronation, the prime minister's gaffe over the Sumner affair.

And much later when they'd both finished their second serving of plum tart along with an excellent Tokay, Simon pushed his plate aside, leaned back and fixed his dark gaze on Caroline. "I'm glad you're divorced."

More relaxed after several glasses of wine, pleasantly full and strangely content, her mouth quirked in a small smile. "So am I."

"Why did you do it?"

"Lord knows; it was a long time ago."

"I tore the city apart looking for you."

"Because you don't like to lose."

He grimaced. "Maybe . . . or maybe I needed you."

"You never need anyone for long, Simon. I was just more practical than you." Her brows rose in derision. "Surely you're not going to tell me you've pined for me in my absence."

He didn't answer for a moment and she said, "There. You see? Consider what would have happened if we *had* married five years ago. You would have been unfaithful within a fortnight; we would have quarreled incessantly and both of us would have been abjectly miserable."

"Maybe."

She wrinkled her nose. "Fortunately we didn't marry on such wavering ambiguity."

"And yet your marriage failed."

"Louvois found a rich woman."

The umbrage vanished from his eyes. "I'm sorry."

"It turned out for the best. She was French like Louvois and I discovered in my travels on the Continent that I was more English than I thought. I was pleased to return home."

"Did he leave you funds?" Aware of Caroline's family background, Simon's concern was genuine.

"I'm managing very well, thank you."

"Should you ever be in need . . ."

"I'm not—really."

"You're sure?" He took in her unfashionable gown, her lack of jewelry, and recalled her red cape that had been out of style these many years.

"I'm sure. You have no need to care for me."

"But I may wish to."

"Sorry, Simon. You relinquished that opportunity years ago."

"I was mistaken," he said softly.

She made a small moue and waved her hand in the direction of the wine. "Pour us both another glass and desist from talking nonsense. I'm not some young ingenue you can charm. I know you too well. And I'm not the same woman you were acquainted with five years ago. Let's simply enjoy a convivial evening and forgo any undue sentiment. I find of late, I prefer less emotion in my life."

His gaze held hers for a penetrating moment and then he grinned. "So shall we just get drunk?"

"I'm not sure a lady is allowed to actually reach that vulgar state," she murmured archly, "but I'd be in favor of enjoying another glass or two and seeing if I can still beat you at piquet."

"You never beat me."

They'd played since childhood and as her father's daughter, she had a rare talent for cards. "Do recall who taught whom, my dear Simon."

Although he was older by three years, she'd been a child prodigy. "I believe I may have overtaken you, darling Caro. I've had considerable practice these past years."

"Do you think I haven't?"

His gaze narrowed. "Have you fleeced all the unsuspecting men on the Continent?"

"On occasion." A sudden bleakness touched her eyes, quickly replaced by a brilliant smile. "One must survive after all."

"I warn you, darling." Amusement colored his voice. "I'm far from unsuspecting."

"Good. I prefer a challenge."

"Just so," he said softly.

"Not that kind of challenge, Simon. Acquit me of your habits."

He laughed. "So you've given up sex?"

"For the moment."

"Perhaps I could change your mind."

She shook her head. "Not a chance, darling. Your reputation precedes you. Once burnt, et cetera, et cetera..." she said brightly. "Now shall we say a guinea a point?"

"A guinea it is. And should you lose?"

"I shan't lose." She couldn't. She only had five guineas to her name.

And she didn't.

Despite the fact that they played far into the night, her talent was fascinating to observe even for a man who prided himself on his expertise at the tables. He never lost by much, but she managed to always have the edge and he gave her high marks for improvement since he'd last seen her.

"What happened to your money," he said, several hours later as she gathered the last of his guineas into the pile before her.

She didn't pretend not to understand. "He took it."

"I should call him out."

"He's not worth your time. Are we done playing?"

"You cleaned me out tonight, Caro, darling. If you'll take a chit, we can continue."

"I'm not sure you truly lost or let me win."

"I'm not that generous. You won. And need I say, I'm impressed."

"Thank you. Now if only Papa could have drunk less, his talent for cards wouldn't have gone to ruin along with his estates." Sighing, she pushed away from the table. "If you'll excuse me, I'm suddenly very tired. Hopefully there's still a room available for me."

"First door at the top of the stairs."

A flicker of suspicion illuminated her gaze and then she said, "Thank you again," in a tone of politesse that could have been used to address a stranger.

"I won't bother you."

"I know you won't. I intend to lock my door." She stood, gathered her winnings and slipped them into her reticule. "I enjoyed the evening, Simon. Very much." Her voice this time was warm. "I'd forgotten . . ." Her words trailed off and she smiled like she had so many times in the past.

"I'll see you in the morning."

She nodded and walked away.

He watched her in her outmoded gown that failed to diminish her glorious allure, her beauty still capable of silencing a room and he recalled nights in the past when she'd not walked away from him. An auburn curl, come loose from her coiffure, lay on the plain blue serge of her shoulder and he wished that he could tuck it behind her ear like he had so many times before. It took enormous effort to restrain himself, to remain seated as she exited the room.

The sound of the door softly shutting should have put period to his restless desires. Any man of conscience would adhere to a lady's wishes.

And he did for the time it took to drink another bottle.

Chapter
2

She was sleeping, but she heard the key turning in the lock as if she'd been waiting for it. As the door quietly opened and closed, she sat up in the large curtained bed in the fire-lit room. "You must have wakened the housekeeper for the key," she said to the man leaning against the door.

"She didn't mind."

"Perhaps I do."

"I thought I'd find out."

"You haven't changed."

Who did? he thought, but he was on his best behavior. "Do you like the applewood fire? I told the housekeeper applewood was a requirement."

"Thank you. Now, are we going to pretend you're not here for all the obvious reasons? Are we going to discuss the weather too?"

"I thought we did that rather thoroughly at dinner." His smile flashed white in the dimness. "But if you wish . . ."

"What I wish apparently makes no difference to you. I expressly said I'd be locking my door."

"If you want me to leave, tell me."

"I'm not sure you'd leave even if I wished it."

"I see." Neutral, noncommittal; a man who had no intention of leaving.

"No, you don't. Your focus, as usual—as always—is only on what you want," she said sharply.

"I don't want to fight." He didn't say he had no answer to such a blanket condemnation. "Tell me what you want me to do and I'll do it."

His voice was deep and low, velvety with suggestion. Whether consciously or unconsciously, he was offering her what he offered every woman. And that was the crux of her dilemma. Whether she wished to requalify as one of his legion of lovers. She frowned. "How many times have you offered a woman carte blanche?"

"Lord, Caro, you're prickly. Never. All right?"

"Liar."

He shrugged. "Twice, then. How's that?"

Or pick a number, she thought, half-rankled, half-enticed— and unfortunately—wavering. She wished he didn't look the way he looked: too handsome, too available, too sure of himself.

And she wished she didn't feel the way she did . . . hungry for him, or maybe for any handsome man offering her what he was offering.

"Don't fall asleep on me, Caro," he murmured as the silence lengthened. "Tell me what you want."

Problematic, dangerous words. She took a small breath, opened her mouth to speak, then closed it again. Was he sincere? Maybe. Did it matter? "I haven't had sex in a year," she blurted out.

"Really," he said, quelling his shock beneath the mildness of his tone. "A year." He hadn't had sex in forty-eight hours, but it might be counterproductive to mention it now. "That's a very long time," he said politely.

She couldn't help but smile, not only at his tact but at his nonchalance. "So as long as you're here, you're thinking."

A smile tugged at the corners of his mouth. "You have no idea what I'm thinking."

"Well, *I'm* thinking I might as well make use of you." There. No more flustered uncertainty.

His teeth gleamed perfect and white. "At your service, ma'am." He pushed away from the door.

She laughed. "So compliant, Simon. I hardly recognize you."

He slid his dark jacket off and tossed it on a chair. "After five long years, darling, I'm more than willing to be conciliatory . . . or as you put it—used." His voice lowered to a silky murmur. "What would you like first?"

Perhaps a year really had been too long. Perhaps she'd always been rash with Simon. Or maybe now that she'd crossed that irrevocable line, there was no point in pretending. "What I would like," she murmured, echoing his silky intonation, "is no preliminaries and that," she pointed at his obvious erection, "inside me."

He grinned. "Talk about people not changing."

"Is that a problem?"

"Not if it isn't for you."

A small warning perhaps. She leaned back against the pillows, spread her arms along the cushiony tops and slowly surveyed him. "It definitely isn't at the moment."

"Because you haven't had sex for a year," he murmured, thinking her breasts were splendid, thrust out like that with her arms raised.

"The most compelling of impulses, I admit."

"So anyone would do," he said, the sudden thought disagreeable.

"Acquit me of your democratic tendencies, darling. I've always been more selective than you."

He frowned faintly. "You sound like a courtesan." She looked like one as well with her indolent pose and bold gaze, her plain, white nightgown notwithstanding. Even sackcloth would fail to conceal her flamboyant, lush curves.

"Don't tell me you've become prudish. Have you given up courtesans?"

"What the hell does that mean?" How *had* she supported her-self after the divorce?

"It means have you given up courtesans? I believe a simple yes or no would answer the question."

"You're beginning to piss me off." Although his resentment may have been spurred by something other than her impudence.

"Oh, dear. When I thought you'd be staying."

"I'd forgotten how irritating you could be," he muttered, unty-ing his cravat and sliding it off, dropping it on the floor.

"I, on the other hand, haven't forgotten how faithless you could be."

"Don't start, Caro. I'm not in the mood."

She glanced at his swift unbuttoning of his buff and blue striped waistcoat. "But apparently you're in the mood for some-thing."

"I thought you were interested in ending your year-long celibacy." His tone was as mocking, his gaze insulting. "If that's even true."

She suddenly sat upright and pulled the sheet up to her chin. "Everyone's not a liar like you. Get out. I've changed my mind."

"Too fucking late." His waistcoat joined his cravat on the floor.

"Are you some barbarian who would force his unwanted atten-tions on a lady?" she sneered.

"Give me a minute and we'll see about the unwanted part," he muttered through the linen shirt he was pulling over his head.

Her voice turned waspish. "You always were arrogant."

"And you always were one hot little piece as I recall," he drawled, tossing his shirt on the bed. Balancing on one foot, he leaned over to pull off a boot.

Caroline tried to suppress the flutter of excitement racing through her senses. But the startling width of his shoulders was too near, the taut sweep of his back too familiar, the powerful muscles rippling across his torso and arms too graphically male. "Simon, I want you out of here!" she said fiercely, as though the force of her words might bolster her uncertain resolve.

He glanced at her over his shoulder, demonstrably untouched

by her vehemence. "Are we giving orders? Then take off that nightgown."

"I most certainly will not."

"Sure you will." He stood upright. "Or if you want to wait until I get these trousers off, I'll do it for you."

She trembled when she shouldn't—when she should hold such brazen insolence in contempt. But not yet lost to all sanity, she managed to speak in a level voice. "You forget, I'm not one of your tractable females. You won't be touching me. Simon. I forbid it."

He shot her an amused glance. "You should be on the stage."

His casual dismissal reminded her of another night when he'd brushed off her recriminations, when her feelings hadn't mattered. When the pain he'd caused had changed her life forever. And hadn't she just freed herself of a man who thought only of himself? "You should be using your charm on someone more susceptible. You're not having your way this time, Simon. I mean it."

"I'm bigger," he murmured.

"And I can scream louder. Get out."

He continued his unbuttoning.

"Don't say you weren't forewarned," she murmured, and opening her mouth, she let out shrill, high-pitched cry capable of waking up the entire inn.

In a flashing second, he lunged, clamped his hand over her mouth and a second after that he captured her flailing arms at the wrists, his grip bone-crushing. Hauling her to the edge of the bed, he leaned in close and bent his head to meet her furious gaze. "Play your prick-teasing games with someone else," he whispered, his eyes hot with temper. "Understand?"

And then he waited as though he expected an answer.

"Go to hell."

The sound was muffled, but audible.

"We could go together," he said grimly, easing his hand from her mouth, one brow cocked in warning.

She knew better than to cry out, but her gaze was chill. "I've already been to hell with you."

"Remember who shared your trip. That fond memory aside," he added, caustically, "make up your fucking mind about sex. First you say you want it, then you don't . . ."

"I don't want it."

He exhaled in a long rush of air. "Fine. Have it your way."

Rising to his feet, he swiftly buttoned his partially undone trousers, and moved to the door. Undeterred by his lack of clothes, he walked out, shut the door, then opened it again to reach around and pull out the key.

This time the door slammed shut with a bang.

She heard the key scrape in the lock, followed by the sound of his footsteps growing faint as he walked away.

Was she a prisoner?

It seemed an overdramatic word considering she knew Simon so well. Although, five years could account for a great many changes in a person's life. Hers certainly had altered drastically. She was divorced now and alone . . . literally—locked in this room—not unlike a scene from a bad farce. She smiled at the droll thought. This would be the point where she'd put her hand to her forehead and bemoan her fate. Or better yet, devise a plan of escape. If she'd been less fatigued, she might have had the energy to formulate such a plan as would any self-respecting heroine on the stage. But she was bone tired, it was very late and after days of travel, her bed felt more enticing at the moment than her freedom.

She'd think about escape first thing in the morning.

A short time later, after having spoken to the proprietor who now understood how lucrative it would be for him to become deaf to the activities in the room at the top of the stairs, Simon reentered the bedroom, carrying his valise. He moved quietly, taking care not to wake Caroline, returning to the hall several more times to carry in a variety of items: a large copper tub, which he placed near the fire; four steaming buckets of water; a tray of food; and two bottles. Once his tasks were complete, he locked the door and tossed the key on his palm for a moment.

Then he walked to the mirror hanging on the wall near the door and placed the key on top of the frame.

A precaution only. He intended to keep Caro too busy to think about leaving.

A smile slowly formed on his lips as he turned back to the bed, sweet expectation pervading his thoughts. She looked angelic with the covers pulled up over her ears, her tousled curls spread on the pillow, the flush of sleep pinking her cheeks.

He'd have to apologize, of course; he wasn't usually such a brute. Although, if he needed cause or excuse, Caro had been as difficult and opinionated as ever.

Not that she wasn't a delightful change from the overly willing women who normally shared his bed.

Picking up a bottle from the table, he moved to a chair near the fire. Dropping into it, he stretched out his legs and slid into a comfortable sprawl. Pulling the loosened cork from the bottle, he poured a long draft into his mouth and savored the taste of a very fine whiskey.

Life was good, he thought.

He was out of the storm, away from London, locked in with one of the most fascinating women he'd ever known.

And she hadn't had sex for a year.

He grinned. It almost made one believe in God.

Chapter
3

Enveloped by a rare contentment, Simon half-dozed by the fire, lassitude seeping into his pores. He hardly noticed the wind rattling the windows or the icy snow pelting the glass. Lost in reverie, the outside world seemed distant from the snug, cozy room. But as the fire burned low, the air cooled, rousing him. He shook himself awake, and came to his feet. After stoking the fire, he stripped off his trousers and moved to the bed. Lifting the covers, he slipped between the sheets and stretched out with a sigh.

He hadn't slept in days, his departure from London sudden, his journey north in the manner of French leave—accelerated. But he'd found more urgent reason to pause and that reason was sleeping peacefully beside him.

He smiled and closed his eyes.

"You!"

The breathy exclamation brought him awake with a start; he blinked against the dawn light.

"What do you think you're doing?"

That wasn't a question he could answer honestly when she was staring at him with such rancor. "There weren't any more rooms . . . with the storm and all," he added, hoping his tone was suitably apologetic, and then he offered her a smile that never failed to melt female hearts.

She scowled. "I'm supposed to believe that? And I know that smile, Simon. It's not going to work."

He didn't belabor the point about the rooms when they both knew he could buy the entire inn if he chose. "I'll be serious then. There actually weren't any single rooms and I thought— well, you had suggested that we, ah . . ." He ran his fingers through his hair in a disarmingly shy, boyish gesture, his eyes still half-lidded with sleep.

That damnable winsomeness was capable of charming the birds from the trees, she thought; it almost made her forget he was sleeping with every woman in the world. "Look, you're not fifteen," she muttered, her comment eliciting a blank look. "I mean—us . . . this room—well . . . whatever I might have said, I didn't mean it. You're going to have to leave."

"Not a chance."

She should take offense, but his voice was hushed and low, temptation in his gaze and even while she knew better, it seemed as though she'd never been away. But suddenly a door banged downstairs, breaking the spell and she remembered why she despised him. He'd wakened with a woman in his bed too many times—too many to count—and in her saner moments she didn't want to be added to that tally again. "If you won't leave, I will." Lifting the quilt, she began to roll out, squealed as the blood-chilling cold struck her and quickly rolled back.

"I'll stoke the fire." He began rising.

Torn between comfort and principle, she struggled with her conscience.

"That icy air can leave one speechless, can't it?" he murmured with a grin, turning back to tuck the quilt under her chin.

She glared at him.

"There are times when men and women aren't completely equal," he said with a touch of irony.

"I'd be a fool to argue with you, wouldn't I?"

"Perhaps we have areas of agreement after all," he replied, his gaze amused and with a wink, he rose from the bed. He walked across the room to the fireplace as though he were impervious to the cold. As though his breath wasn't visible. As though he wore more than his cambric undershorts.

He really was unconscionably gorgeous, she thought, taking in the splendor of his tall, rangy form. She could see the scars from the war, visible now in the rising light of dawn; they'd gone unnoticed in the darkness. He'd always discounted them as "nothing . . . a little shrapnel" when he'd almost died from loss of blood. They'd faded since she'd seen him last, although the scars still streaked his body. He was leaner than she remembered, breathtaking in his raw virility—his taut, hard musculature honed, no doubt, by his life of excess.

It wasn't at all fair when she hadn't had sex for so long, she thought, resentful in a totally illogical way that ignored the circumstances of their lives and society's disparate sexual standards. She shifted her hips faintly, as though she could repress the shimmering heat turning liquid between her thighs as she gazed at his damnable perfection. "You're irritating me," she said, apropos of nothing even remotely reasonable.

"You'll feel better when you warm up."

"Simon, listen to me. We have to be rational about this." Even as she spoke, her body was intent on defying reason, a molten heat beginning to melt through her veins.

"I am."

"I'm not talking about having tea here," she said, pettish and much too aroused for her peace of mind.

"I know what you're talking about. I'll have this fire going in no time."

How could he speak so calmly when her emotions were in tumult? Could he really be unaware of how irresistibly male he was squatting on his haunches, his powerful torso twisting and turning as he transferred logs from the wood box to the fire, his muscles rippling and contracting with each unhurried swing.

Licks of flame were beginning to leap from the coals, igniting the kindling. "There. We'll have a blaze going in no time," he said as though he were a eunuch, as though they were asexual strangers, as though the pulsing inside her hadn't accelerated at the thought he might be coming back. Rising to his feet, he brushed off his hands and turned to her. "Are you hungry?"

"Meaning what?" She spoke a trifle too breathlessly.

This wouldn't be the time to make any sudden moves, he understood. "I have food here . . . that's all."

"Please, Simon, for God's sake, don't talk to me about food or the weather or the state of the world in that calm voice when I'm ready to scream or hit you or bang my head against the wall."

She needed sex, he thought, but sensible of his audience, he said, "We'll talk about something else then. If it's not too late, I'd like to offer my abject apology for last night."

"Simon . . . everything's too late for us. And you don't know what abject means."

He smiled faintly. "Maybe I could learn."

"And maybe I could sprout wings and fly."

"Come, darling," he cajoled, undeterred by her sarcasm. "You have to admit, Lady Luck or fate or some jinn spirits had a hand in our meeting." He smiled. "This is a god-awful place to bump into each other."

She blew out a breath, her pagan antenna twitching fiercely at the mystical implications of so rare an occurrence. "Like ships passing in the night, you mean."

"In a blizzard, yet." His brows rose. "Think about it."

She pulled the covers over her head. "I don't want to think about it."

Her muffled words made him smile. "Would you like to think about it over breakfast? I do have food."

Flipping the covers back, she gave him a hard, flinty look. "Whatever works? Is that your strategy?"

"Jesus, Caro, I don't have a strategy. I wish like hell I did and then you wouldn't be scowling at me. You'd be smiling. I'd be smiling. The world would be sweet-scented and untainted by iniquity."

She wrinkled her nose. "Speaking of iniquity. Finding you in my bed isn't very subtle."

He gave her one of those tolerant looks that parents give to a child who's being unnecessarily obstinate. "We've slept together a thousand times."

"Don't remind me. How do you do it, by the way?"

"What?"

"Keep from having an erection?"

She'd noticed. A definite point for his side. "I try to think of something gruesome—like decaying cadavers." He glanced down. "But right now, it's colder than hell." He grinned. "Do you think I could come in and warm up?"

She nodded at his crotch. "Just to warm up. That's all."

He rolled his eyes as he walked toward the bed. "Talk about fifteen."

"Am I making too much of this?"

He shrugged. "You're asking the wrong person."

"Because a fuck is a fuck is a fuck."

"Sometimes." He lifted the quilt. "Not now."

"How charming."

"If I wanted to be charming," he said, sliding into bed, "I'd lie."

"Because that's what you do best."

Lying back on the pillow, he slid his hands under his head and glanced at her. "That's not what I do best."

She grimaced. "I'm not entirely sure I don't hate you."

"For this?"

"For everything."

He didn't ask what everything was. He knew. The specter of their parting had haunted every word they'd spoken since they met downstairs. "I'm sorry about that night. I was drunk. I thought it was you."

"Then you should have come after me and explained."

"I know." And if she hadn't called him every vile name on earth, he might have.

"But you didn't. You stayed with her all night."

"I'd been drinking for two days if that's any excuse. I probably fell asleep."

"You probably didn't. I know what you probably did."

"And you ran to Louvois," he said as bitterly as she.

"Do you blame me?"

He shut his eyes for a moment and then stared at the ceiling as he spoke, his voice constrained. "I don't want to fight about this. He's gone; she's gone. Five years are gone. I missed you. And that's God's own truth."

"Because it's useful to say that right now."

He turned his head and looked at her. "Because it's the truth."

It took her a very long time to respond.

"Very well, then."

His gaze narrowed. "What a condescending tone. Are you my mother?"

"I dearly hope not," she said in an altogether different tone, "considering my carnal interest in you."

His smile was suddenly sunshine bright. "Are you finally sure?"

She nodded.

It was his turn to pause. "Just to be absolutely certain there's no misunderstanding," he said, each word measured, "say five years from now or five minutes from now—you have to ask me."

"Don't be ridiculous." She edged away.

"I don't want any recriminations later about who did what to whom."

"I'm *not* asking."

"Jesus, Caro, you never had any problem asking before."

"That was different. You're *making* me say it."

He took a deep breath. "Fine. We'll both ask. Would that be better?"

Another long pause and then she nodded.

"Arranging the peace treaty with France was probably less onerous," he grumbled, sitting up and drawing an imaginary line between them on the bed. Holding out his hand so it rested directly above that designated halfway point, he tipped his head in her direction. "I would very much like to make love to you, Lady Caroline. If you approve of the arrangement, we could shake on it."

She held up one finger to test the temperature of the air.

"It's warm," he said.

"Your warm and my warm are different."

He grinned. "They never used to be."

"Very funny." But she rose to a seated position and held out her hand just short of his. "I find myself inclined to make love to you, Your Grace."

His laughter filled the room and then he grabbed her hand and shook it soundly. "I accept, although I don't believe I've ever been propositioned with less enthusiasm."

"I'm impelled by circumstances," she said with restraint.

He grinned. "Me too."

"You mean you're next to a woman with a heartbeat."

"Come, Caro," he murmured. "Stop sulking. We both want the same thing." His voice went soft. "And it has nothing to do with proximity," his brows rose faintly, "or at least for me it doesn't." He could send for one of the serving maids if he just wanted a woman. He'd received enough sly looks downstairs to know they were interested. "I consider myself the luckiest of men to have been driven off the road by this storm and to have found you."

If only his charm weren't legend; if only she could believe him. But suddenly she wanted to believe. Whether it was weariness that persuaded her or whether she'd been alone too long, she simply wanted to be held in someone's arms whether they cared or not. "Perhaps the storm was serendipitous for us both." She looked at the man who had once meant so much to her and gave in to her impulses and his allure. "I'm going to kiss you, now." A small smile played at the corners of her mouth. "Are you ready?"

"I've been ready from the moment I saw you in the parlor downstairs."

She had been too, if she cared to admit it. Which she didn't. "You're persistent. I'll give you that."

And you've become cautious, he wanted to say. "I had good reason," he said instead.

"Stop talking."

"Yes, ma'am."

A second later, she brushed his cheeks with her palms, a light, petting touch. "You're scratchy."

"Should I shave?"

A tiny frisson shimmered through her senses. She shook her head.

"I'll be careful, then," he whispered.

And they both remembered how he'd always shaved twice a day for her and why.

She drew him near, her hands warm, her breath delicate against his mouth and it took every shred of willpower he possessed to keep from pulling her into his arms. He waited for her lips to touch his, feeling as though a decade had rolled away and he was waiting, with bated breath like this, for Caro's first kiss.

Finally, her mouth grazed his in a velvety caress, the tiny flecks of gold in the green of her eyes so close he could count them. "Do you remember our first time?" he whispered, feeling as though he were going to burst.

Her heart lurched and letting her hands fall, she eased back as though putting distance between now and then.

Leaning over, his hands at his sides, he kissed her gently like he had that night because she'd been trembling then too. "It was my eighteenth birthday," he said, sitting upright again, not wishing to frighten her.

"It was stormy like this." Her voice was barely audible, her hands clenched in her lap. Every detail of that night was etched in her memory.

"And our parents never got out of London because of the snow."

She smiled because he had and she'd gained control of her susceptible emotions. She wasn't fifteen anymore; she'd learned how to guard her heart. "The cook had made you a cake," she said in a normal tone.

"But you were my best present."

You were the best everything, she wanted to say, but too many disappointments clouded their past. "Thank you," she said instead. "I regarded you as a wonderful present that night as well."

"You weren't wearing a nightgown though." He touched the top button near her collar and then ran his fingertip down the row, hesitating at the last where the button lay on the swell of her breast.

She drew in a sharp breath, his touch inciting an answering tremor in the heated core of her belly, treacherously reminding her of all she'd missed since leaving England.

"Our coats were covered with snow." His voice was rough but soft. "We'd just come in from the stables. Remember?"

She nodded her head and leaned into the slight pressure of his finger, wanting more, wanting everything he had, like she had that night so long ago.

The pad of his finger sank into her soft flesh, and she moaned, the imprint, however light, riveting to senses so long denied. Her body was aching with desire, opening of its own accord, immune to principle or caprice and after five long years and a night of wavering indecision, she could no longer wait.

"I want you now," she said, because she wasn't an innocent like she'd been that snowy night long ago and she wanted him for reasons that had nothing to do with romance. Or at least so she told herself. "Hurry," she charged. "I don't want to wait."

He generally took offense at females giving orders, but what he wanted was immune to scruple. She could insist on being master of the world and he wouldn't have cared. "Yes, ma'am. Right away ma'am."

But the difference between logic and male prerogative was evident in the brusqueness of his tone.

Her eyes widened for a moment.

"Actually, now is good," he added in an altogether different tone, an obliging tone he'd perfected in countless boudoirs on countless occasions when he'd seen women look at him like that. He was deftly unbuttoning her gown, another competence acquired over the years in boudoirs. And a moment later, he murmured, "Lift up your arms." When she did, and he'd tossed her nightgown aside, he thought—how could he have forgotten?

Her breasts were magnificent, opulent; she'd not changed while abroad . . . except perhaps—were her breasts larger? Her graceful pose with her hands crossed before her, her arms framing the mounded fullness of her breasts, called attention to them. Or perhaps the way she sat, almost as though she were presenting herself as some lush female ornament or plaything, emphasized their glory?

Suddenly gripped by a stabbing jealousy, he wondered how many men had gazed on her splendid, nude beauty? How often had she displayed herself with such natural grace?

"Hello there . . ." she whispered into the silence, and reaching out, she took Simon's hand and placed it on her breast.

Her courtesan's gesture did nothing to mitigate his resentments and mounting jealousy. He was about to say something rude when she guided his hand over the plump swell of her breast, the sensation exquisite, warm, his rough palm grazing her silken flesh, his erection particularly taking note. And he was instantly reminded of more important things.

She smiled, a familiar smile from his youth and he was able to relegate his umbrage to some lesser sphere, banish the last five years to some amorphous netherworld and smile back. "Sorry. You were in a hurry."

She didn't recognize such reticence; Simon had never been a man of reserve. "Let me," she said, no longer a passive young girl and reserve or not, she was too heated to care. Leaning over, she pulled away the blanket covering his legs and paused, the quilt still gripped between her fingers. "You're looking . . . spectacular," she purred. "At least what I can see."

He slipped out of his shorts with quick finesse.

Too quickly, she heatedly thought, knowing how familiar he was with occasions like this. But the allure of his rampant penis hard against his stomach curbed her displeasure. Dropping the quilt along with her qualms, she leaned back on her hands, and opened her thighs. "It's been a long time," she murmured.

His eyes narrowed. "I may not want to," he said, surly and resentful, wondering whom she'd entertained with that artful pose before.

"Don't be childish." If she could overlook his life of excess, certainly he had no reason to take issue with hers. "It's just a fuck," she said, deliberately provocative, letting her thighs fall open, offering him a tantalizing glimpse of paradise.

"Bitch."

"But fortunately for you, available right now," she replied, silkily.

"I suppose I should count my blessings," he murmured, his voice once again suave. Who better than he understood that sex was just sex.

"You should. I've learned a few things in five years."

"I'm intrigued. Should I put in my order?"

"I expect you're still well ahead of me in expertise. Why don't you surprise me instead."

Her voice was low, teasing, irritably coy, and five years of lurid possibilities flashed through his mind. He knew what she was like in bed; she'd been one of the best. And apparently, she'd been gaining additional experience abroad. It shouldn't matter, but it did.

She wanted a surprise. How convenient. Because he felt like giving her one.

A second later, she was flat on her back, her legs forced wide, his body braced above her—save for his erection that was nudging her throbbing labia. "Now then," he said with a wolfish smile. "Why don't you ask me politely?"

Her gaze beneath her half-lowered lashes was sultry, assured, confident in her allure. "I thought I *was* being polite."

"Maybe the word I was looking for," his voice lowered to a husky rasp, "was . . . submissive." At the spark of temper in her eyes, he felt a perverse satisfaction. "No ready quip?"

"I've never been submissive," she drawled. "You must be thinking of some other female."

"I have a feeling you might change your mind."

"Not likely."

"But I want you to." It was an ultimatum no matter the softness of his tone.

She glared at him. "Go fuck yourself."

"Did Louvois teach you that?"

"Yes, and any number of other things," she replied, oversweet and smiling. "If you're very nice to me, I might show you."

"If you're very," his smile was cheeky, "submissive, I might let you end your long celibacy."

"I'm not begging, Simon."

"Really." With devilish finesse, he guided the taut, engorged crown of his penis up her sleek, pulsing labia, and then very slowly, down again, the answering flush rising on her cheeks gratifying evidence of her response. "You're really wet, slippery wet . . . here—feel this." He circled her lubricated flesh with the rock hard tip of his erection, and smiled faintly at her stifled gasp.

"If you'd like me to go deeper . . ." he murmured, teasingly penetrating a inch or so, "I'd be happy to accommodate you."

The color on her cheeks had deepened, her thighs had gone rigid, and when he eased into the liquid heat of her vagina a fraction more, she shut her eyes and softly moaned.

"Would you like all of it?" He swung his hips in a supple, teasing motion, so every surface of her aching tissue felt the intoxicating friction and her panting changed to a plaintive whimper. "All you have to do is ask me nicely, and I'll ram this big cock into your tight little cunt. Do you remember how you used to scream when you were crammed full of cock?" At the memory his erection surged higher, driving in a small distance more, forcing her throbbing flesh to further yield, bringing her already trembling orgasm to the veritable brink.

"Damn you," she ground out, her voice barely audible, her palms pressed against the bed as though she could forcibly restrain the fevered tidal wave. But it had been too long and breathless with need, she couldn't stem the coming flood. Regardless, he'd barely penetrated her, with a suffocated little cry, her climax broke . . . too quickly, prematurely, the cursory orgasm so frustratingly inadequate, she wanted to hit someone. And conveniently . . .

"Jesus," Simon muttered, rubbing the red imprint of her hand from his cheek. "Don't blame me."

"Who else should I blame?" she exclaimed. But his erection was still tantalizingly poised and rigid at the very entrance to her vagina, making it difficult to be completely vexed.

"You *could* be a little more amenable . . ."

She knew what that meant. "I'm not playing games."

"As I recall . . . sometimes you do." Dipping his head, he drew one of her nipples into his mouth and moved his hips just enough to gain her attention.

She clutched at his shoulders, the exquisite pressure of his mouth, the compelling promise in his erection lodged against her vulva, effectively stifling her protest. She shouldn't be so willing and had she not been without sex so long, she might have been more blasé. As it was, within moments, she was melting with longing and suddenly it didn't matter who set the rules.

She was famished, the wild thrill rushing downward from her tingling nipple to her throbbing cleft, obliterating discord, fierce need effectively erasing contention. All she wanted was to feel him deep inside her. Arching upward, she lifted her hips to draw him in.

He pushed her back, his large hands splayed over her hips, holding her captive. "Ask for it," he whispered, spurred by an inchoate jealousy, and a quixotic sense of betrayal that wouldn't be assuaged.

She tried to jerk away.

His fingers bit into her flesh, jerking her back. "Ask," he muttered.

She hit him so hard he tasted blood.

"Fuck this," he growled, abruptly done with useless argument, intent on doing what he'd been wanting to do from the second he'd seen Caro downstairs. He plunged into her, driving in with such unbridled violence, he lifted her off the bed. Her scream exploded in the silence of the room. But he wasn't in the mood to apologize. Her cunt was too damnably wet, and hot and welcoming. It was so fucking drenched, any cock would do. Tightening his grip on her hips, he rammed in deeper in retaliation.

She whimpered this time, but not from pain.

If he heard, he gave no indication, swinging his hips back for another plunging downstroke, blaming her for the insatiable lust burning through his brain.

And then her arms twined around his shoulders and she pulled him closer, opened her thighs wider for him, absorbing the huge, long length of him with a gloating sigh. "I'd forgotten," she breathed. "I would have begged for *this* . . ."

He didn't want to hear that. It was the last thing he wanted to hear when he needed some inexplicable virtue from this women he wanted to fuck to death. Even he realized the brute illogic in his wishes and he breathed, "I'm sorry," in blanket atonement . . . for now, for the past, for the fierce violence of his lust.

"I've been waiting for you . . ." she sighed, warmed by rapturous bliss and fond memory, by scented lust.

His fingers loosened on her hips.

Their eyes met in unspoken détente.

She smiled and moved her hips because she could now—in a distinctive flowing undulation that caused them both to catch their breaths.

When she could speak again, she gently brushed his cheek with her fingertips. "I like being with you in storms . . ."

"I'll have to see that it keeps snowing," he murmured, guiding her hand to his mouth, lightly kissing her fingers. "Or barring that," he whispered, settling into a dextrous, practiced rhythm of thrust and withdrawal, "I'll find something else to keep you happy."

This time when she was about to come, he took care to gauge the exact measure of her need; he went still when she wished it and moved when she moved and held himself hard against her womb at the last as she uttered a high, keening primordial scream. And when her last gasp had died away and her rippling orgasm had subsided, he finally allowed himself his own climax, pouring onto her stomach with such explosive spasms he felt the shuddering ejaculations down to his toes.

He couldn't move when it was over, nor find breath enough to fill his lungs.

She couldn't have moved if she wished with his body braced above hers.

The fire crackled in the hearth, their labored breathing counterpoint to the light snapping sound. Even the whisper of snow on the windows was audible in the hush of the room.

Caro brushed a kiss over Simon's jaw. "Thank you," she whispered. "You don't know how much I needed that."

His head swung around. "Don't say that."

She measured his critical gaze for a moment and then softly exhaled. "Am I supposed to pretend I'm some innocent . . . or— what, Simon? Since when has the style of your bed partners changed?"

He didn't answer; he rolled away. "Screw you," he said, reaching for the sheet.

"If you want to say you were celibate the last five years, I will too."

He growled deep in his throat, an indistinct contemptuous sound, glared at her for a second and then began wiping himself dry.

"Is that a yes or no? Are we still playing games? I don't usually, but I can."

"Don't tell me what you usually do," he muttered. "I don't want to hear it."

"And I don't want you sulky and sullen like a prudish ascetic when we both know you're not."

He gave her a sullen look in answer.

Sitting up, she took a portion of the sheet for herself and began wiping her stomach.

The silence was oppressive.

Having swabbed away his semen, she crumpled up the soiled portion of sheet and sitting cross-legged on the bed, made a small moue. "Why can't we just enjoy our time together? Is that asking so much?"

Her voice held a small plaintive note, as did her gaze.

And he had to admit, he didn't know what he wanted—other than sex with her for the next million years. Not necessarily a realistic desire. "Forgive me." He smiled faintly. "You're right. I always had a partiality for carnal excess; why change now?"

She laughed. "Ah . . . the darling Simon we all know and love . . ."

He shrugged away his reservations and reaching out, trailed his finger across her thigh. "Friends?"

She nodded, liking the sound of the word, pleased to be with this man she'd missed more than she'd realized. "Very good friends," she murmured, glancing at his undiminished arousal, "from the look of things."

He rolled closer and touched her cheek. "I'd better shave before next time. I've scratched you."

She gave him an sportive look. "You mean there's more?"

"I've ordered a week of snow. Do you mind?"

"Despite that glorious orgasm, I'm looking at bedposts and doorknobs and beautiful erections like yours. I don't mind at all."

He grinned. "We always were a randy pair."

Her smile was affectionate. "I had a good teacher."

He shook his head. "Natural talent."

"And you would know."

"I guess we can't all be innocent like you," he murmured, a moody undertone to his voice.

"I'm not starting that fight again."

He softly exhaled. "Maybe I should buy this place and keep you in bed filled with cock." He grinned. "Mine, of course. Then you wouldn't have to look at doorknobs with longing."

She stretched luxuriously, her full, ripe breasts rising in the most delectable way. "The way I'm feeling right now," she murmured, letting her arms drop to her sides, "I might let you do that."

"God Almighty, Caro . . ." His voice was husky at the licentious thought. "Look what you're doing to me."

His erection had surged higher, the veins turgid, pulsing with blood, the large head swollen purple.

"I'll shave later," he whispered, reaching over, picking her up at the waist and swinging her up over his hips. He eased her down in a slow descent, his muscles flexing and then he guided her down his rock hard penis until she was firmly impaled. He was scarcely breathing, his senses skittish, inflamed, not sure he would survive this fortuitous reunion unless he could get a grip on his ravenous desires. Sheathed by her tight cunt, he could have come that second and the next one as well, and a dozen times after that. But in his new benign mood, he repressed his orgasmic urges, wanting to please the lady.

"I think I could come without moving," she whispered, her eyes half shut, her hands braced on his shoulders.

She was as feverish as he, their desperation predicated by their long separation, or by the heightened intimacy of the small bedchamber shrouded by the storm. Or perhaps their fevered senses had always been in sympathy.

Like now.

"You come first," he proposed, raising her, his hands light around her waist until she balanced on the tip of his erection.

Brushing his hands away with a smile, she sank back down with a luxurious sigh and slowly rotated her hips. "Ummm . . . don't move." She rocked lightly, feeling the rapture in every inflamed nerve in her body.

"Yes, ma'am," he whispered, thinking if this wasn't heaven, it was a very good approximation. Sliding the pad of one finger up her slippery cleft, he gently stroked her swollen clitoris in a lazy small circle. "You're running wet," he murmured, catching a droplet of pearly fluid on his fingertip. "Does that mean you like me?"

"I find you very pleasing, milord," she whispered, riding him in a slow, sensuous rhythm. "Very pleasing, indeed. If you keep me filled with cock, I'd be ever so grateful . . ."

Her gaze was angelic and playful and so filled with longing he seriously thought of coming in her and indeed keeping her in every sense of the word. But reckless emotion immediately gave way to the prudent habits of a lifetime. "I'm available, darling," he murmured. A facile, casual phrase implying neither past nor future, only the transient present.

And he made himself available for her as often as she wished that morning, both of them making up for lost time. Until, finally, hours later he rolled away. "Give me five minutes," he panted.

She was spread eagle on her back, every cell in her body languid from her most recent orgasm, and yet, she was ravenous still. "One, one thousand, two, one thousand . . ."

"If I could move, I'd put my hand over your mouth, you little witch. All right, three minutes, but you're going to have to do all the work."

She turned her head and smiled at him. "I'd forgotten how much fun you could be."

He chuckled and shut his eyes. "At least I'll die happy."

But short moments later, he glanced over at her because her counting had drifted off. She was sleeping.

He gently covered her, careful not to wake her, remembering how she could fall asleep in seconds while he would always lie awake, waiting for sleep. She'd been traveling longer than he though; she must be exhausted, although she looked rosy-cheeked in sleep, innocent as a babe, her unruly curls framing the beauty of her face. And for a poignant moment, he wished they were back at Monkshood on that stormy night so long ago. Before all the misunderstandings had come between them.

He sighed. Nothing was simple anymore, their youth far behind them. And Caro had left—not he, he reminded himself. Perhaps she'd been looking for greener pastures. She might be again. So there was no point in letting undue sentiment hold sway in this enchanting interlude from the storm.

She was starved for sex.

And he wasn't in any hurry to reach his destination.

The next few days should be memorable.

Brushing aside useless regret, he rose from the bed and started heating up the water.

He'd have a bath ready when she woke.

Chapter

4

It was one of the hardest decisions she'd ever made, Caroline thought, her gaze unfocused on the winter landscape outside the carriage windows. She could have stayed with Simon. On what basis, of course, was questionable, but he would have taken care of her—that she knew. But she wasn't ready to be taken care of . . . regardless the manner of it. Nor was she ready to fall into Simon's arms as though he had but to smile his devastating smile and she was lost. She'd gone through too much in the years of her marriage to ever completely trust a man again. Perhaps she'd simply grown up. Perhaps her notions of marriage had been impossibly idealistic. Or maybe being in a hot-tempered sulk and allowing herself to be talked into marrying hadn't been the most sensible thing she'd ever done. Whatever the reason, at the moment, she needed independence. After five years of marriage, she particularly wished to answer to no man.

Although the days with Simon had been the happiest she'd experienced for a very long time. He was as charming as ever, as loveable—not that loving him had ever been at issue. What had been at issue was his capacity to love or rather his capacity to love too well. He'd been rakehell wild. She smiled, recalling particular nuances of that wildness. He was willing to do anything, anywhere, anytime; they'd shocked the ton on more than one occasion.

Simon's wealth and title had insulated him from the worst of the disapproval while his heroism in the Peninsula War had put him firmly above reproach. Her blood was as blue, but she hadn't a penny, nor did her gender allow her the same degree of indiscretion. Her escapades had been viewed with a more critical eye. Not by her father of course; his love had been unconditional. But then he wasn't a particularly good judge of propriety considering he was gambling them to ruin. She sighed. At least she'd still had him with her five years ago . . . before his slim hold on sobriety and the enormity of his debt had driven him to suicide.

She shook away the sense of loss that always overcame her when she thought of her father's sad decline—a technique she'd perfected in order to survive. She thought instead of all the wonderful years they'd had together, of the good times, of the joy and laughter. She and her father had been the best of friends. Like she and Simon had been friends. Lovers too, as time had gone by. But always friends.

The days at Shipton had been sheer bliss and not for the amorous pleasure alone. She'd forgotten how pleasant it was to talk without fear of censure, to be treated as an equal—to laugh.

Henri had too much of the ancien régime in his blood to condone anything that smacked of female freedoms. With the restoration of the French monarchy, his world had returned to what he considered the order God intended and his autocratic tendencies had intensified. A shame she hadn't been aware of his reactionary sentiments before she married him and a greater shame the government hadn't yet restored his estates. She suddenly laughed. On the other hand, Lady Luck had definitely been on her side when the newly widowed Duchesse of Closont had revived her friendship with Henri. She had to thank the duchesse for their divorce as well. How convenient the duchesse's husband had had the good sense to invest in munitions during the war and then opportunely die.

Henri's leaving hadn't hurt, only the manner of it. He

shouldn't have taken everything. But he was gone and for that she was content. And despite her demur when Simon had offered to call Henri out, she hoped to have her vengeance someday. Which thought always lifted her spirits and for the next several miles, she contemplated various means of exacting retribution. Call her mean-spirited, but Henri owed her.

Simon was sourly contemplating similar vengeful thoughts as he stood at the window of their bedroom at the inn. His attempts to cajole or threaten the grooms and ostlers to divulge Caroline's direction had been unsuccessful. God knows what story she'd given them; they'd looked at him with disdain. And now duped and deceived, he was at an impasse. She could have dropped off the face of the earth for all he knew. Damn her. This was the second time she'd left him without so much as a word.

He swore, his breath frosting the window pane. It wasn't as though he'd dragooned her into staying. She'd obviously enjoyed herself, unless her orgasmic screams were pretense and he'd bet his estates they weren't—hell . . . they'd barely left the bed. He swore again, his expletives having to do with deceitful women and his own gullibility. He'd actually considered asking her to accompany him on his hunting holiday—like some idiot wet-behind-the-ears pup. And maybe he would have asked her more . . . maybe he would have asked her—his low growl interrupted the humiliating thought.

Damn! How could he have been so stupid?

Probably because women didn't run away from him, he sullenly thought. On the contrary—they were always in pursuit. Although he wasn't so vain or crass that he didn't understand Caroline had a life of her own. He wouldn't have asked her to make undue or drastic changes in whatever plans she might have.

She needn't have left like a bloody thief in the night!

He blew out a frustrated breath, staring unfocused at the busy street below, resentment and desire warring in his brain. Sighing, he contemplated his nonplussed situation. Then, despite himself, a smile slowly formed on his mouth. God, she was good. His smile broadened. Incredible actually. And he should know after fucking his way through a multitude of ladies here and abroad for a great many years.

His libertine propensities well honed, he turned from the window. Looking for Caroline was certainly worth a day or two of his time. And should he find her—no, *when* he found her, his frustration would be mitigated on *numerous* levels.

His smile this time was wicked.

It shouldn't be too difficult picking up her trail. He'd head south first, he thought, moving toward the door. Presumably she was on her way to London.

Chapter
5

While Simon was scouring the countryside south of Shipton, Caroline was traveling north as quickly as bad roads would allow. Her employers had expected her two days ago and she didn't dare lose this job. It wasn't as though there were dozens of governess positions that paid this well, nor were there many conveniently located at the proverbial ends of the earth. Her employers' proximity to the Scottish border appealed to her need for seclusion.

As she neared her destination, Netherton Castle came into view. Perched on the heights above a north branch of the River Tyne, its crenellated silhouette was visible from afar. One of the early border fortresses built by England to keep the northern marauders at bay, the fort had been added to and improved upon over the centuries, the latest Palladian wing pale against the sky. But the sprawling structure was still predominantly medieval: gray, massive, built for defense, its dark shadow casting the valley below in shade.

At close range, Caroline was awed by the immensity of history that had transpired inside and without its walls. She surveyed the great pile of granite with wonder as her carriage clattered over the drawbridge, rolled over the cobblestoned court, and came to rest before an enormous door crisscrossed with great iron bars designed to keep out an enemy. Stepping down from the carriage, she gazed at the family motto carved over the formidable door: HE SHALL RULE THEM WITH A ROD OF IRON.

Harsh, unwelcoming words.

Struck by a sudden chill, she wondered if she could really do this—become a governess . . . assume a subservient position . . . give up the freedoms she so dearly craved. Maybe she should take Simon's two hundred pounds and flee back to the Continent where no one knew her—where she could at least live an independent life, albeit in the demimonde. Taking herself to task a second later, she reminded herself there would be time enough to run should her employment prove untenable.

Taking a deep breath, she straightened her shoulders, moved toward the imposing door and reached for the knocker.

The Countess of Netherton was in a small sitting room, writing at a white and gilt desk when Caroline was shown in. She immediately smiled, rose to her feet and hurried forward, holding out her hand. "Do come in. May I call you Caroline? We're quite informal out here in the wilds. Thornton, have tea brought up." She took in Caroline's paleness. "You look chilled to the bone. The weather's been dreadful, hasn't it? Come," she drew Caroline forward. "Sit by the fire."

Within moments, Caroline was put at ease, her new employer so genuinely kind the tightness in her shoulders melted away. Tall and fair, Lady Carlisle was dressed in a scarlet wool gown without ornament, her hair, fashionably short and curled, her smile quite capable of renewing a cynic's faith in humanity. They spoke of the weather and the state of the roads, of the castle's history and antecedents, of children in a general way and in short order, Caroline was feeling as though her new position was going to prove agreeable.

Tea arrived as Lady Jane was describing her two children in the glowing phrases of a doting mother. "You'll meet the little darlings later," she said with a teasing smile. "Hugh and Joanna are out riding with their father. Since it warmed up slightly today, Ian agreed to take them to the village for sticky buns. It's not as though our cook can't bake sticky buns, but you know how much better they taste when you're away from home."

"I understand. My father and I would ride to our village for cream cakes," Caroline said. "The pleasure as a child is out of all proportion to the simple treat."

"Isn't it just . . . although Ian and the children enjoy each other's company most, I think."

"I know the feeling." Caroline went silent, her childhood made perfect by a father who adored her, his loss like a wound that wouldn't heal.

"You said in your letter, your parents are gone." Lady Jane's tone was sympathetic.

Caroline forced her thoughts to the present. "My mother died when I was very young so I don't remember her well." How often had she uttered that phrase; it never got easier. "My father has been gone five years now."

"I'm sorry. My parents too are no longer with me. I understand how difficult it can be."

Caroline smile was strained. "One must make do."

"Yes, of course." Jane leaned over to pat Caroline's hand. "The passage of time helps, I've found, and keeping busy is an additional antidote. Tell me of your life abroad," she added, diplomatically changing the subject. "Your letter mentioned you'd been living in France."

"I was married to a French émigré. He died a few months ago." Divorce was often perceived as scandalous. Caroline chose caution.

"My condolences. Do you have other family?"

Caroline shook her head, suddenly unable to speak as a great rush of loneliness washed over her.

"How awful for you. Perhaps I could give you some of my eight brothers and sisters—please, I beg of you, take them," Jane said with a grin. "They all live in the neighborhood and are constantly underfoot."

Jane's attempt at levity served its purpose and Caroline smiled. "I look forward to meeting them."

"You won't be so gracious once you do. My sisters love to give orders and my brothers speak of nothing but their hunting dogs and horses." She chuckled. "I'm afraid, it's an instance of the pot calling the kettle black—but nevertheless, they are a trial on occasion. I'm the youngest, you see."

Caroline lifted her brows. "And always in need of their advice, they no doubt presume."

"So they contend." Jane shrugged and smiled. "I have quite a different opinion, of course."

"It sounds as though you have a busy household. I look forward to the distractions."

"Good. Perhaps we can help ease your loneliness. As for your duties, you needn't be apprehensive. I don't expect my children to be serious students. Neither Ian nor I are bookish. Our interests are almost exclusively horses and hunting," she added. "The countryside is perfect for coursing . . . and very beautiful." Jane waved her hand in a deprecating gesture. "Not so much now as in the warmer months. Should you like to ride, we have a good stable. Feel free to take your pick of the mounts," she offered.

"Thank you. I do like to ride." Caroline almost said, I used to hunt with the Beaufort Hunt.

"We'll see that you're set up then. Do you have any requirements in terms of books and supplies for the schoolroom? I must say, your education is splendid—intimidating as a matter of fact; you speak six languages. How very impressive," Jane said with a casual politesse; most of the aristocracy had little interest in education. "Your recommendation by the Duchesse of Montclair was impressive as well."

"The duchesse was extremely kind. She's a distant relative of my poor departed husband." Caroline inwardly cringed at her fabrications, but she needed privacy and hermitage right now—somewhere far from London and the ton where she could take stock of her options. And additionally, since Shipton, somewhere Simon couldn't find her.

"I have a feeling we're going to muddle along famously," Jane observed, brightly. "Please, have more cakes and jam. You've hardly eaten a thing. Let me freshen up your tea," she declared, reaching for the teapot. "I can't wait until Ian and the children meet you. They're going to love you!"

Chapter

6

Several days later, in the early evening, a mud-spattered carriage arrived at Netherton Castle, and a tall, dark-haired man leaped down to the cobblestones and strode toward the same door that had intimidated Caroline on her arrival. He was glowering, his mouth was set in a grim line and if it had been possible for fire to actually spark in one's eyes, he would have incontestably illustrated that principle.

When Thornton greeted him in the cavernous entrance hall, the butler glanced at the man's muddy boots, but knew better than to make mention of the muck he was leaving on the oriental carpet.

His host, however, wasn't so politic when the visitor entered his drawing room.

"Good God, Simon, take off those filthy boots. Jane will have your head if you ruin her carpets."

A muted growl issued from Simon's pursed lips, but he sat, pulled off his boots and handed them to Thornton who received them with relief, grateful the muddy trail from the entrance hall up the grand staircase, down the corridor to the drawing room had come to an end.

"You look like you need a whiskey," the Earl of Netherton said.

Simon nodded and rose to his feet. "It's been a miserable few days."

"In what way, although from the look of you, I'm not sure I want to know. You look ready to do battle."

"Damned women," Simon muttered, moving toward his host. "They're the bane of my existence."

Well aware of his friend's reputation with the ladies, the earl's concern lessened. "It's nothing serious then." He handed Simon his whiskey. "I stand relieved. I thought I might have to serve as second to you in some duel." He turned to pour himself a drink.

"What makes you think it's not serious?"

Ian Carlisle glanced over his shoulder, his brows arched in surprise. "You mean to tell me, it might be?"

Simon didn't immediately answer. He tipped the whiskey down his throat, handed the glass back, said, "Fill it up," and blew out a breath so obviously of frustration, Ian's concern returned. "It could be serious," Simon murmured. "Under the right circumstances . . . Oh, hell, I don't know if it is or not . . . It doesn't matter anyway. I can't find her."

Ian turned with their drinks and surveyed his friend's less than impeccable attire. "You've been looking for some time apparently."

"For three days. She disappeared off the face of the earth."

"Anyone I know?"

"No. She was gone from London when you and Jane first came down." Ian and Simon had become friends at Waterloo. "Oh, bloody hell." Simon lifted the glass to his mouth. "Screw it. Tell me about the hunting."

Dismissing women was more the norm than the exception with Simon. Back on familiar ground, Ian waved them into chairs near the fire and proceeded to describe the state of his coverts, deer herds, and hunting pack. By the time Jane came back with the book she'd gone in search of, the men were deep in a discussion of the next day's hunt.

After welcoming Simon, Jane saw to it that he had a dinner tray brought to him from the kitchen. They'd already dined, but she and Ian joined Simon for coffee. By the time Simon had eaten his way through several servings of roast beef, a variety of vegetables, fresh bread and honey, his mood had lightened. Ian and Jane were always the best of company, far removed from the brittle gossip of the ton, less interested in the scandal of the day than the weather and the state of their crops. Their peaceful existence, sensible view of the world, their obvious happiness were all reasons he accepted their invitations when he felt a need to escape the profligacy of his life.

Pushing his plate away, Simon leaned back in his chair and surveyed his hosts with a faint smile. "I forget what contentment is until I come to Netherton." He half lifted his hand. "Thank you for reminding me there's a better life somewhere."

"You're always welcome, Simon," Jane pleasantly noted. "You needn't wait for an invitation."

"When the lure of the bright lights wane . . ." Ian intoned facetiously.

Simon shrugged. "I seem to be reaching that stage with greater frequency of late."

"You're not getting any younger," Ian waggishly reminded him.

Simon's dark brows rose. "Meaning?"

"Marriage, of course. You might find you like it."

Simon smiled. "Jane's already taken."

"You'll always have an excuse, won't you?" Her expression was sportive.

"Probably." Simon's gaze turned introspective for a moment, then he grimaced. "In any event, the young ladies on the marriage mart are all insipid. I'd be bored in a week."

"That long?" Ian drawled.

"I was being polite. I can scarce stand to talk to them."

Jane cast him an assessing glance. "What you need is a woman with backbone who can stand up to you."

"Maybe I do . . ." But she'd run away.

"You need a challenge."

He was hard-pressed to beat back the lust that spiked through his senses at the thought of Caroline's irrepressible ardor; that was challenge . . . just keeping up. "Wouldn't that be nice," he said half to himself.

"Simon has recently misplaced a woman who appealed to him," Ian explained, correctly interpreting Simon's murmur.

Jane's eyes widened. "Misplaced?"

"She ran away."

Astonished, Jane was hard-pressed to restrain a gasp. "She ran away from you?"

Simon smiled faintly. "Ironic, isn't it?"

She grinned. "Long-delayed justice, perhaps."

"Don't tease, darling. Simon's heart and/or ego has been bruised."

Jane tipped her head, her gaze searching. "Which is it, Simon?"

"It doesn't really matter," he said, softly. "She's gone."

"Who's for another drink?" Ian interposed, recognizing his friend's discomfort, turning a warning glance on his wife. "I for one, am."

And the conversation turned to less emotion-wrought topics.

Chapter

7

Despite overcast skies, Simon and the Carlisles left early the next morning for the hunting field. A great deal of the snow from the recent storm had melted with the rising temperatures and now a hint of rain was in the air. They tramped the countryside with the dogs and gamekeepers all morning, bagging a brace of grouse and one small roebuck for their efforts. At noon, servants met them in the field with baskets of food for lunch and as the sun conveniently came out from behind the clouds, they dined al fresco on a rise overlooking the valley.

The morning hunt had been invigorating, the brisk air and physical activity uplifting to mind and spirit. Simon felt refreshed and restored and he said as much to his hosts as they drank a fine claret and decided on the direction of their afternoon hunt.

"You should think about buying a hunting lodge in the neighborhood," Jane suggested. "Then you could escape the city whenever you wished."

Simon's estates were close to London, occasionally much too close when unwanted guests appeared on his doorstep. "The distance from London is a distinct asset," he murmured.

Ian offered him a look of understanding. "You wouldn't be bothered so often by Clive and Bertie."

"That in itself would be reason to buy. Did I tell you they came with a carriage full of—er . . . shall we say actresses when my sister was visiting last summer?"

"At least Adele is understanding about your bachelor ways." Simon's sister and Jane were friends.

"She wasn't, however, overly pleased. It was two in the morning and they woke her children."

"You might like to look at Kettleston Hall." Jane waved her hand westward. "The viscount is rumored to be selling now that his father is dead. It's his one property not entailed and he has gambling debts."

"Perhaps some other time." Simon leaned back on his hands. "I'm in the mood to do absolutely nothing at the moment."

"Would you prefer we go back to the house?"

"I didn't mean hunting. I just meant in terms of my life."

Jane shot him a critical glance. "You've been doing nothing in terms of your life for a very long time."

"Don't begin, Jane," her husband warned. He smiled at Simon. "Every woman feels the need to matchmake and interfere."

Simon winked at his hostess. "Matchmake all you want, Jane. I'm immune."

At dusk they returned to the castle, pleasantly weary after a day of tramping over hill and dale. "I'd say a whiskey's in order," Ian declared. "My study is outside Jane's housekeeping purview," he added, "so we may track in mud to our heart's content."

Turning back from ordering tea from Thornton, Jane smiled. "I allow him some small freedoms."

"Including a good supply of whiskey from the local stills," Ian declared. "You'll enjoy McDougal's, Simon. He swears by the springs up near Doon."

Very soon, the men and Jane were enjoying McDougal's whiskey, the warm glow of the fire, and a well-earned rest after a long day out on the moors. Simon was sprawled in a large wing-back chair, his long legs stretched out before him, his whiskey glass resting on his chest. Ian and Jane were seated side by side on a settee, Ian's arms around his wife's shoulder, both their booted feet resting on a worn leather hassock.

"I hope the children are coming down," Simon said, thinking Ian a very lucky fellow to have found someone as restful and genial as Jane. "I haven't seen them since spring."

"They should be here soon." Jane looked up at her husband from under the curve of his arm. "Tell Simon how much Hugh has grown this summer. Was it four or five inches?"

"Five," Ian said. "And Joanna still wants to marry you, Simon, when she grows up," he added with a grin. "She much admires the consequence of dukes."

Raising his glass to his mouth, Simon smiled. "There's reason to wait then."

"As if you need added reason to wait," Jane murmured, "when you've already waited . . . Ah, the children are here. Darlings, come in and make your bows."

Simon's whiskey sloshed over the rim of his glass as he turned to the door and Caroline gasped as a slender, young boy with tousled, strawberry blond hair, shouted, "Simon!" and ran forward.

The earl and countess exchanged glances.

"You know each other?" Jane inquired, surveying her red-faced governess, then Simon who looked pale beneath his tan.

"I met Lord Blair years ago," Caroline quickly replied, terrified Simon might say something outrageous. "We—ah . . . lived in the same parish."

Brushing the wetness from his wool shirt, Simon sat up and set his glass aside. "I knew Lady Caroline's father, the Earl of Doulton."

"An earl?" Jane's feet dropped to the floor, her eyes wide.

"If you'll please excuse me," Caroline whispered, her face bright pink. "I'll return for the children when you call."

"No, stay!" Joanna tugged on Caroline's hand. "Come have cakes with me!"

"Some other time, darling." Caroline tried frantically to disengage herself from the little girl's grasp.

Joanna's grip tightened, her mouth turned down in a pout. "But I want you to make those fairy towers with the cakes and tell me the story about the princess who looks just like me!"

"She thinks she's a princess," her brother scoffed, glancing at his mother who was still looking stunned.

Joanna's golden curls bobbed as she quickly swung around to confront her brother. "Am too a princess!"

"Are not."

"Am too!!" She turned back to Caroline. "Tell him, Caro; tell him about the tower and the dragon and how I was saved—"

"I'll explain later when you don't have company, darling." Having freed herself from her young charge's grasp, Caroline had begun to back away. "Go and drink your chocolate now. You know how you like chocolate with whipped cream clouds in it."

Joanna cast a quick glance at the tea table, making certain the whipped cream clouds were there. "Promise, you'll tell him later?"

"I promise."

Another swift glance and chocolate won over. Joanna skipped away.

Caroline ran from the room, and raced down the hall as though all the fiends of hell were in pursuit. She didn't care that her exit might have been precipitous; she didn't care that her new employers might wonder at her discourtesy. She couldn't possibly stay and face Simon.

She didn't dare.

"Did you bring Black Templar with you? Did you, did you?" Hugh was hopping from foot to foot before Simon, his excitement visible. "If you did, may I ride him? May I, may I?"

"He's here and you may ride him if your parents allow." Simon kept his voice calm with effort. His heart was beating like a drum; only sheer will kept him seated. Caroline was *here* in this very house—not in London . . . here!

"Me too, me too! I want to ride Black Temper too!" Joanna

screamed, always wanting what her brother wanted like little sisters everywhere.

Reaching out, Simon lifted her into his lap, looked at Ian for approval and at his nod, said, "You may both ride him tomorrow."

The children's squeals of delight were only equaled by Simon's delight at having found the object of his pursuit.

And so conveniently near.

He was hard-pressed to restrain his smile.

He'd never slept with someone else's governess before.

The children immediately claimed their mother's attention and for the next few moments she was busy helping them with their chocolates.

"What the hell was that all about?" Ian said under his breath.

Taking his cue from Caroline who apparently didn't want to acknowledge their acquaintance, Simon offered his friend a casual shrug. "She reminded me of someone for a second. My mistake."

"Whatever you say." But the earl had known Simon long enough not to be deceived.

"Is your governess new?" Simon asked, his tone deliberately mild.

"She arrived two days ago."

"From?"

"London, I believe. You'd have to ask Jane the particulars. She's rather stunning, isn't she?"

"Definitely stunning." Simon held his glass out for a refill. "A beauty of the first water."

"And you should know."

Simon's gaze snapped up, but Ian's wink was only cheeky, not knowing. "Don't you hold all the boudoir records?"

"Not really," Simon lied.

A few moments later, once the children were thoroughly engrossed in dunking their scones in their hot chocolate, Jane glanced at Simon with warning in her eyes. "Stay away from her,

Simon. It's difficult finding a governess who's willing to live so far from London. I don't want you seducing her. And don't look at me with such innocence. I saw your response when she walked in."

"I promise not to seduce her." It wasn't an intentional lie. He didn't expect any seduction would be necessary after their passionate reunion at Shipton.

"I'm not sure I like that tone of voice."

"What tone?"

"That casual libertine's tone you've employed far too many years for any proper lady's peace of mind."

"Is she proper?"

"That's not for you to question or even speculate on," Jane firmly noted. "But yes, she is. She's a widow."

"Ah, a widow . . ." Low, silken words, insinuation in every syllable.

"That's quite enough, Simon," Jane said, sharply. "I had a very hard time finding a qualified governess and I won't have you jeopardizing Miss Morrow or whomever she is—" Her brows quirked in uncertainty. "Caroline speaks six languages. Do you know how impossible it is to discover a woman with those credentials willing to live so far from London? I mean it, Simon. Stay away from her."

"Relax, Jane. The last thing I intend to do is seduce your governess. How did you find her?"

And while Jane explained the manner in which she'd acquired her new governess, he politely nodded his head at what he hoped was appropriate intervals. But he wasn't entirely sure because he wasn't really listening, his thoughts consumed with desire. All he could think of was seeing Caroline again.

Alone.

In bed.

Although, in his current mood, a bed wasn't a requirement.

Chapter

8

Have to get away, have to, have to, have to get away . . . Panic-stricken, her thoughts in chaos, Caroline rushed up the stairs, needing to put distance between herself and Simon, needing time to *think*. Dashing into her room, she slammed the door behind her and for the first time since her arrival looked to see if there was a key in the lock. She grimaced. None.

HOW COULD THIS BE HAPPENING?

In all of England—how could it be that Simon was not only in this backwater area of the country, but *downstairs! In this very house!* It wasn't just bad luck, it was incredibly bad luck—of which she'd had more than her share of late. Even a rank amateur wouldn't have bet on them meeting in this remote castle in the middle of nowhere! "Damn," and "double damn," and any number of other pithy observations on her misfortune escaped her lips as she slumped against the door in frustration.

Simon was sure to be trouble . . . enormous, persistent, unrelenting trouble—with everyone watching. She groaned, her position untenable with Simon in the house. He wasn't one to take his congé with good grace—or at all, which seriously impacted her options.

Much as she'd like to pretend some reasonable solution was available to her, it was impossible to even transiently delude herself that she had anything but limited choices. She could go or stay. That was it. No third or fifth or twentieth alternative existed. Biting on her bottom lip, she tried to assess the advantages and liabilities in going or staying without undue emotion, but she found herself trembling despite her best intentions. "Stop it," she said aloud, consciously stilling her fears and drawing herself up to her full height, she took a deep breath. Calmly now. Option one, first. Flight.

It was the dead of winter and already dark outside which seriously curtailed immediate flight. But even should she wait until daylight, she still had limited funds, no other employment, and the nearest coaching inn was miles away.

Well . . . that was easy.

Now how exactly would she manage the staying part? Presumably, she would have to keep Simon at bay. Impossible, of course. He wasn't a man of temperate impulses. On the other hand, she could simply capitulate, and if she knew him as well as she thought she did, she would be well taken care of. He was more than willing. Their time at Shipton had made that plain.

But if she allowed that, what would she have become?

Pushing away from the door, she walked to the window and pressed her forehead against the cool pane, as though the chill glass would soothe her confusion. There were women at all levels of society who were paramours. Women of rank, women of substance, intelligent women. And if she put herself under Simon's protection, she'd no longer have to deal with the precariousness of her life. She wouldn't have to worry about the price of a pair of stockings, or mend her outdated cloak for the tenth time, or wonder if she might offend her employer and be cast out into the cold.

It was tempting. She'd been struggling for so long.

But stark reality couldn't be so easily ignored and she better than most understood Simon's record on constancy . . . and faithfulness.

He was incapable of both.

She'd known that five years ago and knew it still and if she was looking for either quality in him, she was a fool.

It was a shame he was so loveable.

And more unfortunate still that he knew it and used it to his advantage.

Her brief moment of blissful fantasy dissolved before the painful truth and she turned from the window to face the harsh uncertainties of the real world.

Now . . . how best to deal with Simon's expected pursuit? Although she wasn't a novice at eluding men, Simon in such close proximity would prove a formidable challenge. Particularly, she thought, glancing at her door, in this keyless room. "Never show fear," her father had always said. "Remember your game face, darling . . . It's the first rule." Not that staring down Simon would prove useful for more than a second or two; he wasn't easily intimidated.

But suddenly another of her father's maxim's came to mind and she experienced a heartened moment of hope. "Only bet on a sure thing," he'd always said and of one thing she was sure— Simon would come for her. She'd bet her last shilling on that.

So if she played her cards right, she just might be able to put herself in a position of power. Moving to her small desk, she lit a candle, sat down, pulled out a sheet of paper and began writing.

When a servant came to fetch her sometime later, Caroline returned downstairs for the children in a new frame of mind. While not precisely calm, she was at least composed, her decisions clarified. Arriving at the door to the study, she paused for a moment, feeling as though she were about to step on stage.

Taking a deep breath, she raised her fist and knocked.

Simon hadn't known exactly how he would respond when next he saw Caroline, although numerous possibilities had passed through his mind. In the interest of good manners and his present company, however, his preferred choices had to be delayed for a more opportune occasion.

But he'd watched with keen attention as Jane had gone to the bellpull and rang for a servant. With raised consciousness, he'd listened to her instruct the servant to fetch Caroline, then silently chafed as he waited for her arrival. When the knock on the door finally sounded, he set his glass down so he wouldn't spill it this time and turned toward the door.

Caroline stepped into the room.

Simon blew out a breath he hadn't realized he'd been holding.

Ian frowned.

Jane sent Simon a warning look, then turned to Caroline. "The children have eaten so many sweets they may not want their supper," she noted, her tone constrained. "I'll be up later to tuck them into bed." She smiled at her children. "Now, go with Miss Morrow or is it Lady Caroline?" Jane lifted her brows in query.

"Miss Morrow is fine."

Jane nodded. "We'll talk in the morning."

The statement had an ominous sound, but Caroline gave no sign of her misgivings. "Very well, ma'am. Come, children." She studiously avoided Simon's gaze as she shepherded her charges from the room.

Once the door closed, the silence in the study was oppressive.

Jane stared at Simon with such gravity he felt a twinge of guilt. "I hope I don't have to remind you to behave."

"You needn't remind me."

"I should hope not," she said crisply.

Chapter
9

That evening, dinner seemed endless for Simon, course after course passing in a blur. He ate without tasting, drank without noticing, conversed without recalling a word. Finally, the last glass of port was drunk at table, the men joined Jane in the drawing room for tea, the clock eventually struck eleven, and praise God, his hosts suggested an early bedtime before the next day's hunt.

Simon immediately returned to his room where he paced and waited for the house to quiet. He couldn't be seen leaving his room, especially after being warned off by Jane. Impatient, chafing at the need for further delay, he made the circuit of his room countless times, the hands on the clock seeming to move so slowly he felt like hitting something. But at last, no sound could be heard and opening his door, he glanced up and down the corridor. Blessed silence. Stepping out into the hall, he softly shut the door, and quietly moved to the third-floor stairway where he paused, listening. Absolute quiet. He smiled. Even his duenna, Jane, was asleep. Taking the stairs at a run he came to a stop on the top landing. Several doors faced on the corridor. Two on his right, three on his left . . . the children, nanny, playroom and governess. Which was Caroline's?

* * *

She looked up as he came into her room. Setting aside the book she was reading, Caroline surveyed him with a cool glance. "What took so long?"

It wasn't welcome, it was sarcasm. "You were the last room on this floor; the nanny snores, the children are both asleep, even the cat is sleeping. Also, I'd promised Jane not to bother you," he said, shutting the door behind him. "So I had to wait until she was sleeping."

"A man of honor."

He stood with his back against the door. "I was particularly careful with my wording."

Even in the indistinct candlelight, she caught the flicker of amusement in his gaze and for a moment she couldn't decide if she was relieved or annoyed. The same old Simon. Had she expected someone different? Lifting a sheet of paper from the bedside table, she held it out. "Here."

His brows rose, but he didn't move. "What's that?"

"The rules of the game."

"Meaning?"

"Forgive me. Were you coming up here to propose?"

"What if I were?"

"I'd say you were being particularly careful with your wording again."

"I'd forgotten what a little bitch you can be."

"No, you hadn't. We both know each other too well. Read this." She extended the paper again.

This time he moved forward, plucked it from her fingers and sitting down on the bed, leaned toward the candle flame and began to read. His mouth twitched on occasion as did the muscle high over his cheekbone, but he made no comment as he perused the document, save for the air he blew out of his nostrils on reading the last line. "What makes you think I have to agree to any of this?"

"If you don't, I might decide to leave suddenly—say, when you're out hunting."

"You're bluffing."

"You don't know if I am or not."

A small silence ensued.

"You're dancing a damned fine line, here," he observed, tipping his head toward the sheet of paper before slowly surveying her. "You don't look the part in that buttoned-up nun's nightgown . . . the ladies who make demands such as yours are generally—"

"I suggest you don't finish that statement," she said with exquisite softness.

He shut his mouth.

She smiled. "You *can* be sensible."

He glared at her for a moment before his frown eased. The line between propriety and desire was a fine line for him as well. While he wanted her for all the obvious reasons, there were additional reasons that he chose not to acknowledge. Particularly not after chasing up and down the countryside looking for her like some jilted, lovesick swain. Any tender emotions he might have felt had been extinguished by days of frustrating search. So, perhaps they were both on the same page—literally. He glanced down at her list. Although inamoratas generally couched their demands in more diplomatic language, this was distinctly Carolinesque in its bluntness. "Very well," he said, looking up, holding her gaze. "I agree to your rules."

Her look of triumph was quickly shuttered, but he'd seen it. "You may not win every round, pet. Keep that in mind."

"This isn't about winning or losing, Simon. It's about me keeping my position and you recognizing my need for it."

"You may not need it for long at these prices." Setting the paper on the bedside table, he drew out some bills from the inside pocket of his dinner jacket. "I believe you said five hundred pounds."

"It's a business arrangement. Not an unfamiliar one for you, I'm sure."

"Your price is high."

"The easier for you to decline, I thought."

"Did you really?"

"What?"

"Think I'd decline."

"In all honesty, I was hoping you might." She softly sighed. "It would make everything so much easier. You understand that, don't you?"

"I understand I'm going to be jumping through considerable hoops." His brows rose. "It must have taken you some time just to write down all those conditions."

"They're necessary. I don't want you compromising me."

"In public, you mean," he drawled, his gaze openly carnal.

"Of course in public. If sex with you was compromising, I would have long since been in jeopardy, now wouldn't I? Really, darling, such ingenuousness. Have you been amusing yourself with virgins of late?"

"I've never had a taste for virgins."

"I'm gratified to hear it."

"With one exception, of course," he said, softly. "Long, long ago. And that particular instance still remains one of my fondest memories."

Her blush was evident even in the dim light. "Kindly refrain from journeying down memory lane. You and I have come too far." She lifted her hand in a small sweeping gesture. "As you see."

"Very well . . . then we'd better get to it," he said briskly, rising to his feet. "Since you've stipulated I must leave by half-past one."

"I need my rest. I have two children to teach."

He kicked off his shoes. "And one client to please."

She refused to be baited. Her smile couldn't have been improved upon by the actress, Sarah Kemble, herself. "Perhaps if I don't please you, you may not return, and I'll no longer have to deal with your impudence."

His narrowed gaze held hers as he slid off his dinner jacket and waistcoat. "Rest assured, darling, you always please me. Now, kindly take off your nightgown. We don't have much time."

When she didn't move, he half smiled. "If we're going to play by these rules, you'll have to do your part."

"I don't *have* to do anything except leave tomorrow when you go hunting. You're the one who wants something. You're the one who's disturbing my sleep and life. I'm perfectly content to pretend I barely know you. In fact, I would prefer it. So, don't give me orders."

"Or," he said, softly, "I could take you away, now, this minute, anywhere I chose, so perhaps I can give orders after all."

"I'll scream." She smiled. "Checkmate."

"Maybe I don't care if you scream. Maybe I don't care what Ian and Jane think. By the time they can get out of bed, I'll have you downstairs and into my carriage."

"It's not harnessed."

"How do you know?" He smiled. "Checkmate."

A brittle silence fell.

"Now take off your nightgown." He slid his suspenders down his arms.

"What if I don't want to?"

"I gave you five hundred pounds. You have to."

She scowled. "You're not making this very easy."

"Whoa." He held up his hands. "Who's not making this easy?"

"You don't understand."

"You're right about that," he said, grimly.

"Life isn't always about you having what you want when you want it."

"You seem to be having your way more than I."

She snorted. "If that were the case, you would be back downstairs in your bedroom and I would be peacefully sleeping."

"So you have no interest in making love?"

His voice was velvety and low, his dark gaze heated and what she wanted was always equivocal when Simon was close. "I can't afford to lose this job," she said, her voice trembling slightly at the last.

"You don't *need* a job. I'll take care of you."

"For how long? You see how practical I've become."

"If you need money, I'll give it to you."

She glared at him. "Of course I need money. What a stupid thing to say. Do you think I'd be a governess if I had money?"

He blew out a breath. "Jesus, Caro, tell me what you want me to do."

"I want you to leave me alone."

He was silent.

"Did you hear me?" Challenge in each syllable.

He shook his head. "I can't."

"Of course you can."

He shook his head again. "No, I can't." Although the reasons he couldn't weren't entirely clear. Or maybe they *were* clear, but he refused to acknowledge them. Or maybe wanting and having were two different things, although the wanting part wasn't open to discussion right now. He began unbuttoning the collar button on his evening shirt.

"Simon, don't!"

"I'm willing to accede to your rules, but that's all I'm willing to do. I'm not leaving. So scream if you wish."

"And if I do?"

"I'll take you away, right now, this minute."

"I hate you," she whispered.

"No, you don't."

"Then I should."

"Don't. I'll live with your ridiculous rules. That makes you triumphant."

"Damn you, Simon!"

He smiled. "Is that a yes?"

"Only to the most obtuse."

"I doubt you're obtuse either. Make up your mind." He glanced at the clock. "If we're staying here, there's not much time left."

He'd take her away if she refused; he'd made that plain. "No comments in public, now?"

"I'll be completely circumspect."

"You won't be staying long, will you?"

"Probably not," he lied. His curfew tonight was less than two hours away and he didn't want to waste it in further conversation.

"Very well."

He laughed. "Your enthusiasm is gratifying."

She glanced at his obvious erection. "It doesn't seem to have affected your interest."

"We've missed you."

"I suspect you say that to all your women."

"Are you mine, then?"

She took note of the time. "For an hour and a half I am."

"I'm flattered," he said as casually. "Would you like me to undress you?"

"In these kind of arrangements, don't the ladies usually undress themselves?"

"Are you asking me or telling me?" he asked with a hard look, his hands arrested on one gold cuff link.

"Good God, Simon. I didn't sleep my way across Europe, so kindly stop acting like a jealous husband."

His eyes narrowed further as he set the cuff link on the bedside table. "Did your husband have *reason* to be jealous?"

"Are we questioning degrees of intemperance here? Because I don't think you of all people have the right. And I doubt, in these circumstances, you grill the ladies you're about to sleep with on their virtue."

"I've never exactly thought of you in those terms." He slid the second cuff link free, set it aside and tugged his shirt out of his trousers.

"Then don't start. But if you'd rather, I wouldn't mind saying good night and best wishes for your future. Truthfully, I'd prefer that."

"No." His voice was unrelenting and partly muffled as he pulled his shirt over his head. He tossed it aside.

"Yes, Captain."

He went still, his gaze shuttered. "I haven't heard that for a long time."

"Your scars stand out in the candlelight." His nude torso was burnished by the flickering light, his virility impossible to ignore.

"They're almost gone," he said, brusquely.

They weren't, nor would they ever be, she thought, remembering how she'd helped care for him when he came back from Waterloo, nearly dead.

He didn't remember the misery of those days, he recalled instead the bewitching game they'd played as he'd recuperated. His sigh was part memory, part regret. "What the hell went wrong?" he murmured.

She didn't need clarification. She shrugged. "Too many things to count." She looked past him for a moment, at a loss to even begin to define when the ruin had begun. Then her gaze returned to his and she suddenly smiled. "Do you want to play because I don't want to remember the disasters."

He inhaled softly, the disasters having come in stages he didn't want to think about either. He nodded. "You choose which one."

"The one where you knock on the door."

His mouth turned up slightly at the corners. "Your favorite."

"You asked," she said, not quite able to read his tone. "Would you rather do yours?"

He shook his head. "I like that one too."

She tipped her head faintly, her gaze on his trousers. "I can tell."

He chuckled. "They were all my favorites. What the hell happened to us?"

She could have told him the truth—that aside from any number of adjunct disagreements he hadn't been ready to think of marriage . . . not really, although they'd talked about it since they were young. "I felt like traveling," she said, lightly instead, rising from the bed and moving toward him. "But right now, Captain, I can't let you in," she murmured. "It's very late, and I'm alone in the house."

The words were like a line from a song, forever etched in his memory and he answered as he had so many times before, "Forgive me, my lady. But I have my orders to bivouac here."

She clutched the front of her nightgown, holding it tightly at her neck. "Surely . . . there . . . must be . . . some mistake."

The hesitation in her voice was exactly the same, innocent, winsomely appealing and he felt the same surge of desire he'd always felt when he heard it. "I'm afraid there's no mistake. The campaign has moved this way and we're in pursuit . . ." His voice trailed off.

She didn't find it difficult to mimic apprehension; he was gazing at her with naked lust. "I . . . don't know . . . what to say."

"Forgive me. But my orders are plain."

"If you insist on coming in . . . you must stay . . . in the parlor."

"Of course. You needn't fear, my lady. You're completely safe."

"Thank you." A faint smiled played about her mouth and she nodded at his partial nudity. "You're ahead of me." She waved her hand in a small circle as though moving them along. "Would you like to dry your coat by the fire?" Her voice had reverted to her actress intonation.

"If I may . . ."

She turned and made a pretense of placing his coat by an imaginary fire, her breath in her throat.

He came up behind her like he had so many times before; she could feel the heat of his body, the hard length of his arousal pressed into her buttocks. As she shivered at the sudden flaring heat, his erection moved and swelled against her.

"I've been on campaign for weeks," he whispered, lifting her hair from the back of her neck, the coolness a signal memory from the past. "I haven't seen a woman for so long . . ."

She stiffened in anticipation.

And then he bent his head and touched his mouth to the nape of her neck.

So light a kiss shouldn't have made her so frantic, so covetous and eager. It hadn't always. Not to this staggering degree. Please, please . . . *now*, she wanted to say. I can't wait another second.

But he whispered, "I'm sorry, my lady. I shouldn't have done that."

And for a flashing moment she wasn't sure what was now and what was then. But he'd stepped back, like he was supposed to and she turned to him. "I don't know if I can do this," she breathed, her agitation plain.

He took her hand and rubbed it across the front of his trousers, so she could feel the breadth and length of his desire. "You have to," he said, not caring if this was fantasy or reality, knowing why he was here.

She jerked her hand away.

He didn't move, although he'd quickly scanned the room. "You can't go anywhere," he whispered. "I won't let you."

Inundated by carnal longing, she drew in a sharp breath. "Because you're—the captain." She'd almost said My captain, but caught herself just in time.

He'd heard the minute pause, took note of the altered wording, resolved to change it back again now that he'd found her. But he uttered the expected words in order not to frighten her. "You needn't worry, my lady. No one will know."

"Your troopers will know."

"Not unless I invite them in. Would you like me to?"

"No . . . no—no."

He saw the uncertainty in her eyes, heard it in her breathy reply. "Are you sure? They won't touch you."

"You said *you* wouldn't touch me."

"I haven't yet." His voice turned silken. "Not really."

Her skittish gaze glanced downward to the bulge in his crotch and her voice when she spoke, was almost inaudible. "There's more?"

"Invite me in and I'll show you."

"You *are* in."

"In here," he murmured, touching her mons, slipping his fingers downward, forcing the soft linen of her gown into the moistness of her vulva. "Lift your gown," he ordered. "I can't feel you." His dark eyes held hers. "And I want to."

"No . . . no—I couldn't . . . I can't—my family would disown me. I'm betrothed to the local curate."

His gaze was half-lidded; his fingers buried in her cleft were damp from her wetness. "I won't tell the curate. He'll never know." She shook her head. "He'll know. Truly, he will."

He stroked her gently, the fabric of her nightgown slippery under his fingers. "I'll be gentle," he whispered. "You could have lost your virginity riding." He brushed her mouth lightly with his. "You ride don't you?"

She quickly nodded, her thighs pressed tightly around his hand, her breath coming in short little pants.

"Lift your gown, my lady . . . for me."

Temptation in the wilderness or in a small English hamlet or in a governess's room under the eaves. Unable to resist, she closed her fingers on the fabric of her gown, bunched the skirt in her hands, and slowly lifted it.

"That's a good girl," Simon whispered, stroking the smoothness of her exposed belly. Sliding his hand downward, he nudged her thighs apart and slipped in one finger palm deep. "Ummm . . . you're a very good girl. Have you let your curate feel you all wet and juicy like this—have you?"

She shook her head, not meeting his gaze.

"So I'm the first man to touch this?" He stroked her liquid flesh. "I think you could take more than one finger, couldn't you?" he whispered, probing her slick passage.

She should say no to such cool self-possession; she shouldn't be so shameless in her need—so insatiable. And if she weren't aching to feel him deep inside her, she would.

He touched her cheek. "Answer me."

His dark, seductive gaze further incited the scandalous throbbing between her legs. He was too beautiful. That was the problem. She craved him for his beauty alone. "Yes, yes, . . . yes," she said, her voice sounding as though it were someone else's. Someone ignominiously in rut; someone who would have lain with him anywhere.

And when his second finger eased inside, she whimpered and squirmed, the penetration quickening her senses, adding urgency to her carnal longing.

"Am I hurting you?"

The sound of his voice drifted through her seething hysteria, but she couldn't find the breath to speak.

Her overwrought passions were answer enough; he forced his fingers deeper. At her breathy sigh, he felt her muscles contract, felt the slick lubricant of desire flow more profusely. She was ready for sex, more than ready and without asking permission, he added a third finger. Slowly exerting pressure, he penetrated deeper, stretching the verges of her vulva until his third finger was fully submerged.

She moaned, shuddered, uncontrollable desire vibrating through her body.

He looked up. "Relax, darling..." And when she did, he jammed in a fourth finger.

She gasped, delirium washing over her in heated waves. "I don't want to play anymore," she panted, reaching out, stroking his erection. "I want this."

"Unbutton my trousers and you can have it."

Even through her fevered need, his unruffled calm was grating. Her hand stilled. "It doesn't matter to you?"

"I didn't say that." His smile was wolfish, his fingers moving inside her with deft subtlety. "Indulge me."

Grabbing his wrist, she arrested his compelling massage. "Since when do you need to be indulged?"

He unclasped her hand from his wrist and withdrew his fingers. "Since I'm paying you five hundred pounds a night," he said, wiping his fingers on her nightgown.

She slapped his hand away. "Take your money back and leave."

His gaze met hers. "We shouldn't have started this," he said, gruffly, his own feelings impossibly disordered. "But I'm not leaving. I'm going to make love to you. Me, Simon—no games," his voice deepened, "whether you want it or not, although I think you do."

She frowned.

"You know I'm right."

She didn't answer for a very long time. "I don't want to feel what I'm feeling," she said, ill-tempered and sulky. "Breathless with need, practically crazed."

"I know." His emotions in turmoil, he understood.

"I don't think you do. I think this is another night with another woman in a long list of similar nights for you."

"No," he said, thinking of the days he'd spent looking for her, of the years she'd been abroad without him—with other men. "You're wrong. This isn't the same."

There was another long pause. She sighed, grimaced, finally spoke. "You still have to observe—"

"Your rules? Agreed."

She gazed at him with patent discontent. "I'm still not sure why you're here or why I'm allowing this." She blew air through her teeth. *"Merde.* Maybe I'm thinking too much."

His smile was tight. "Maybe we both are." Untrammeled behavior wasn't unusual in his life; this irrepressible craving was. "Why don't we both stop analyzing?" he murmured. "I'm going to undress you because I want to, not for any other reason, and you're going to let me." Taking her hand, he began to draw her to the bed.

"Carpe diem," she said, under her breath.

"I suppose," he muttered. "Probably," he added. His dark brows drew into a faint frown, and he forcibly tamped down the discontent that always came with too much speculation on Caro's past. Having reached the bed, he turned to her, unbuttoned her nightgown in silence, pulled it over her head and pointed at the bed.

There was a certain irony in his reluctant seduction that made her smile. "I suppose since you're paying me, I have to do what I'm told."

"It would be a welcome change," he grumbled.

"Oh, dear, was I supposed to be docile and amenable?" she purred, throwing him a look over her shoulder as she climbed into her narrow bed.

He snorted. "That I'd like to see." Stripping off his trousers and undershorts in the same businesslike manner, he left them where they fell.

"I know what I'd like to see," she murmured.

He swung back at the seductive whisper.

And his thick upthrust penis swayed in provocative allure. "Ummm . . . you're going to hurt me with that great big—"

"Cock with your name on it," he murmured, moving toward the bed.

She opened her arms.

And he felt a kind of joy he only felt with Caro.

A second later, the bed squeaked under his weight and a second after that they were joined and the creaking was so loud, Caro went stiff in his arms.

"Stop!" she hissed. "We're going to wake—" Her words ended in a low moan as Simon held himself perfectly still within her, or almost still; the pulsing of his penis against her vaginal walls, against her clitoris, the faintest of sensations at the very mouth of her womb were unbearably intense.

"Don't move," he whispered, his mouth resting against her ear. "And you can't make a sound," he added, the faintest whimsey in his tone. "Can you do that?"

She nodded, delirium coursing through her body—willing to do anything to keep him inside her.

"Good girl." His voice was warm against her ear as he slid his hand over her mons and upward just to where the dip of her stomach began. He flexed his hips minutely, forcing himself fractionally deeper at the same time that he put pressure on a small sensitive area under his fingertips.

She gasped, went rigid at the shocking pleasure and felt an orgasm begin in a headlong, monstrous rush of rapture. She began to scream and he covered her mouth with his. "No," he said against her teeth. "Understand?"

She nodded or she thought she nodded, overpowered by the staggering pleasure.

He kept her in thrall to stupefying orgasmic pleasure, bringing her to climax over and over again until she nearly fainted from excess. And then he took his pleasure with his little governess courtesan, climaxing quietly in hot, deep, hammering, internalized waves that seemed to rise up from the very center of his body to explode on her stomach.

But neither was sated, their sexual hunger perhaps exaggerated by the days at Shipton, their senses attuned to a new level of carnal need. And they explored the limits of sensation that night, on the floor, on the chair, against the wall—anywhere but on the noisy bed. Until with morning coming, Caro whispered nervously, "You have to go."

He almost said, Screw your rules and the Carlisles, and everything that had to do with the curtailment of his pleasure. But he didn't, because she was looking at him with a gravity even he recognized as deeply earnest. "I'll be back tonight." He didn't ask; it was a statement of fact.

And like some lovesick maid, she murmured, "I'll be waiting . . ."

"It's going to be a helluva long day," he grumbled, but he carried her to her small bed, tucked her in and gently kissed her.

And when he was dressed, he stood beside the bed for a moment, his smile affectionate. "I'm really glad I found you."

He didn't look like a disreputable rake or a celebrated duke or the man who fueled most of the lascivious gossip in the ton. He looked eighteen again, his cheeks flushed, the same smile on his face as the young boy she'd fallen in love with so many years ago.

"Take your money," she said, nodding at the bills on the table. "I don't want it."

He hesitated.

"Take it or you can't come back."

He grabbed the bills and shoved them in his jacket pocket. "Thank you . . . for—" he tipped his head "everything."

"I should thank you." She smiled. "As usual. Now go, before I say something I'll regret."

He took a breath as though to speak, then grinned instead and turned away. At the door, he swung back and blew her a kiss. Like he always had a lifetime ago.

Then he was gone.

At the soft click of the latch, she fought back sudden tears welling in her eyes. She refused to cry about the past. What was done was done, and all the tears in creation wouldn't change a single second. She and Simon wouldn't be naive and young again, although the word naive and Simon perhaps had never been a match. But she at least would never be naive again. Nor would tears bring back her father or her former life. Or wash away the misery of her marriage.

And more pertinently, she'd be a fool if she waxed nostalgic about her relationship with Simon. It was sex—no more, no less. Although, certainly . . . the very, very best of sex, she mused, a half-smile playing on her lips. She might fault Simon for any number of sins, but she couldn't fault him for his talents in bed. He was unrivaled.

She smiled. She probably shouldn't have mentioned that to Henri. Although, under the circumstances—what with the light-skirt in her parlor that afternoon—he richly deserved it.

Chapter

10

At the faint knock, Caroline dragged herself up from the depths of sleep. Taking note of the pale dawn light, she came fully awake, and a small knot of alarm formed in the pit of her stomach. Why was she being wakened so early? Her teaching duties didn't begin until nine.

"Come in," she called out, struggling into a seated position, trying to shake the cobwebs from her brain.

A young servant girl appeared on the threshold. "The mistress wants to see you right quick . . . afore she goes off ahuntin'. It be all right fer you to come in yourn nightrobe, she said. She be waitin' for you in her bedroom."

Caroline's alarm intensified as the servant relayed her instructions. Surely some crisis was on hand. "Thank you, Betsy. Tell Lady Jane I'll be right down." Tossing aside her blankets, she rose from the bed and walked to the small armoire that held her wardrobe. She put on her worn robe with reservations. Hopefully, she'd meet no one in the corridors.

Running a brush through her hair, she tied it with a ribbon at the nape of her neck, slipped her feet into a pair of slippers and reminded herself she'd dealt with crisis before. Compared to losing her family and home, surely this was manageable.

But apprehension followed her as she moved through the corridors to Lady Jane's bedroom. Had her rendezvous with Simon been discovered?

It required steel nerves to knock on Lady Jane's door, to enter when she was invited in, to present an appearance of calm.

"Come sit, Caroline." Jane waved to a chair opposite her at a small table. "And my apologies for waking you so early. But I wanted to speak with you before I left for the hunt. Have some tea." She began pouring a second cup. "The scones are warm."

Such banality vanquished Caroline's fear. She moved to the table with lighter spirits.

"Now, then," Jane said, as Caroline took her seat, "first things first." She handed her the plate of scones. "It's Lord Blair."

Caroline almost dropped the plate, and had not Jane immediately said, "I've warned him to stay away from you," she might have had a mess on her hands. Instead, relieved, she said, "Thank you, ma'am," took a scone and carefully set the plate down.

"That's another thing . . . There's no need for such formality. Simon mentioned the difficulties of your father's—er . . . passing at dinner last night. Please, call me Jane, and if I might, I'll call you Caroline."

"Yes, of course, I'd like that."

"Good. Perfect. That's all settled then."

But her eyes wouldn't quite meet Caroline's gaze.

Girding herself for something unpleasant, Caroline said, "Is there more?"

"It's rather delicate . . . I mean—it's probably none of my business, that is . . . you may have already heard of—" She stopped, her face flushed in embarrassment.

"Please be plain," Caroline remarked. "I'd prefer it." If she was going to hear bad news, she'd rather not be kept in suspense.

"I'm afraid, it's about Lord Blair. And the reason I hesitate is because you may think me interfering in your life and being uncharitable about the duke who is a very dear friend. But regardless," the countess picked up her teacup and then nervously set it down again, "I must speak my mind. You see, although you both are from the same parish, you may not be fully aware of the duke's libertine propensities. I wanted to be sure you were advised of them." Her expression was grave. "He can be quite charming . . . indeed enormously charming. I wouldn't wish you hurt should he turn his attention on you. I have, of course, warned him to mind his manners in my household, but I'm afraid he's very used to doing as he pleases. So . . ." She fluttered her hands. "I feel very foolish. But I thought you should be cautioned."

"Thank you. I shall take care."

Jane exhaled. "Then my duty is done. Lord Blair has left more women with broken hearts than any man alive. I'm afraid for all his charm he is quite without true feelings of affection for our gender. His relations with women are in the main purely, er—"

"Physical?"

"Indeed. In fact, he left his latest inamorata vastly stricken when he rode north to visit us. My sister wrote me. All of London is abuzz with the scandal. It seems Lady Blessington informed Lord Blair she was with child and it was his. Lord Blair, who was in bed with her at the time, rose from her bed, bid her good night and left town."

That was why he was riding north in a storm. "He seems completely lacking in feeling," Caroline replied, her mouth set in a grim line.

"I'm afraid he assumes no responsibility for anything but his pleasure. In a way, it's very sad. Lord Blair has much to offer should he care to make the effort." Jane offered Caroline a rueful smile. "You must think me a false friend to speak of him so, but other than his dealings with women, Simon's the best of men."

"I understand." More than you think, Caroline reflected, having experienced Simon's selfish pursuit of pleasure firsthand. "I thank you for the warning. As a widow, I've learned to be wary of charming men. It was kind of you to be concerned."

"I felt it my duty and now we needn't discuss such rubbish

again." Jane picked up her teacup and smiled. "I much prefer talking about my children and horses and dogs. You don't hunt, I suppose."

"I haven't for a long time."

"Would you care to join us," she grinned, "now that you're suitably warned?"

Caroline glanced at the freezing drizzle on the window. "No thank you. The warmth of the schoolroom holds more appeal."

Jane laughed. "Ian and I are quite mad, aren't we? But we so love the outdoors. It's impossible to describe our feelings to the uninitiated."

"Nor should you have to if you're content."

"We are. I feel quite fortunate. Now then," the countess straightened the napkin in her lap, "I'm done with my lecture. You're excused. Tell the children I'll see them at tea."

As Caroline traveled the corridors and mounted the stairs to the nursery floor, all she could think of was how she would word her question concerning Lady Blessington when next she saw Simon. *Damn his odious black soul.*

Chapter

11

Caroline found it difficult to concentrate on teaching French verbs with Simon's latest iniquity bombarding her consciousness. The children noticed. "I already did *aller*, twice, Caro," Hugh said, gazing at Caroline intently. "Aren't you listening?"

"Me too," Joanna interposed. "I did it too. Are you sick?"

"No, darling. I was thinking about something else. Forgive me."

But after losing her train of thought twice more during the children's French recitation, she decided her pupils could spend the rest of the morning working on their drawings for their Twelfth Night costumes. She would only be required to make appropriate comments of praise from time to time. But even that proved too much.

"You must be sick, Caro!" Joanna exclaimed when she inadvertently referred to the little girl's angel costume as her fairy costume. "There's no fairies at Christmas!"

"Your eyes look funny," Hugh offered. "Maybe you are sick."

Caroline took note of his hopeful expression. "I suppose it wouldn't matter if we took a day off from the schoolroom."

"Mama says too much reading leaves wrinkles," Joanna declared. Hugh nodded his agreement. "And Papa won't care."

"It's not a very nice day to be outside," Caroline observed.

"Is too! My pony likes the rain!" Joanna had already jumped to her feet.

"Charlie will take us out," Hugh said. "We could bring you back cakes from the village."

How could she refuse such generosity? "I'd like that," Caroline said.

A moment later, the children had run off to get dressed for the cold outside and she was left to wonder when cheerful, outgoing little boys changed into self-centered, dangerous men.

Although, it was pointless to take umbrage at Simon's profligacies or waste a minute of her time on indignation. Regardless of her wishes, he would live his life as he wished; he always had.

Rising from behind her desk, she returned to her room and stood motionless for a moment, troubled, disconcerted, faced with hours of unoccupied time. What she needed was activity and distraction from her thoughts . . . or better yet, another life, she facetiously mused. Barring that unlikely possibility, perhaps today would be a good day to take out the manuscript she hadn't looked at since leaving France. The novel she'd been writing intermittently for two years was her flight from reality. And if ever she needed deliverance and escape, certainly today qualified.

While Caroline was poring over her much edited pages and laughing from time to time at the foibles of her characters, the conversation during luncheon in the hunting field had taken a wayward turn.

"Since Lady Caroline is an acquaintance of sorts, why don't we have her join us for dinner tonight?" Simon was saying. "As a gesture of friendship. You said she'd recently lost her husband."

Ian looked skeptical. "Your gestures of friendship toward women generally take a different tack, don't they?"

"I'd rather not have her join us," Jane said.

"Why?" Simon inquired, taking note of Jane's clipped tone.

"As a matter of fact, I've—ah—warned Caroline against you, if you must know. She may prefer not dining with us."

Caro hadn't mentioned it last night. "When did you warn her

off?" He asked out of curiosity only; Jane had every right to caution her governess.

"I spoke with her early this morning. You've left more than your share of scandal in London of late. I thought she should know."

Simon's gaze turned cool. "You told her *that?*"

"No . . . no, not precisely," Jane lied, his displeasure causing her to retreat. "I simply said you could be dangerously charming."

He surveyed the flush on her cheeks and wondered how much she'd actually disclosed. He'd find out soon enough, he suspected. If she knew, Caro wasn't likely to ignore the Lady Blessington scandal. "I hope you also mentioned I can be extremely well mannered," he remarked, his urbanity restored. There was time enough before he saw Caroline again to consider his explanation.

"Yes, of course. I told her you were the best of men in a great many ways."

"Ah." He recognized the omissions; he also recognized he had his hostess on the defensive. "If I promise to be a perfect gentleman at dinner, will you allow Lady Caroline to join us? We *are* both from the same locale and it seems discourteous to keep her upstairs with the servants."

Jane sighed. "Gentleman or not, you'll turn her head and I'll be left with a lovesick governess."

Or worse, Ian thought. "Jane tells me Caroline's interested in seclusion. It was one of the reasons she'd chosen Yorkshire. She may not wish to dine with us."

"Can it hurt to ask her?" Simon persisted. "I'll be gone in a day or so anyway. I've decided to buy Kettleston Hall."

Ian's gaze sharpened. "When did you reach that decision?"

"This morning. I sent Viscount Manley a note and received an immediate reply. You were right about his need for money, apparently. He readily agreed to my offer."

"But you haven't seen the estate."

"You said it was an excellent property. I'll take your word for it. Which direction is it from here?"

Ian pointed. "You can see the house from our tower. It's scarcely a mile cross country, although it's farther by road. Would you like to walk over?"

Simon shook his head. "That's not necessary. My requirements for a hunting lodge are flexible." Proximity to Netherton Castle the first consideration. "Now, is there something I can do to change your mind about having Lady Caroline for dinner?"

Jane frowned. "You won't be deterred, will you?"

"It's a harmless dinner."

"Humph. Don't look at me with those guileless eyes. Such determination makes me question your motives."

"I have no motives." About dinner at least, he could say without perjuring himself. "It's simply four people dining together."

When he said it like that, Jane didn't have much choice unless she wished to look exceedingly foolish. "Very well, but you must absolutely promise not to captivate my governess . . . or try to do anything," she blushed, "seductive."

Simon nodded. "I will keep my remarks strictly impersonal . . . the weather, the state of the roads, the success of our hunting—nothing I wouldn't say to your children."

Jane and Ian exchanged dubious glances.

"Lady Caroline used to hunt with the Beaufort Hunt. As I understand, she's a bruising rider."

Jane's eyes lit up. "She never said a word."

"That world, perhaps, is quite distant for her now."

"Ian, you must find her a good mount," Jane quickly declared. "She might enjoy the jumps near Hungerford."

"Yes, dear." Ian shot Simon a censorious look and met one of imperturbable calm. "But if Caroline decides to leave because of you," he said, holding Simon's gaze, "I swear, I'll call you out. And don't think I won't."

Simon grinned. "No need for that. I'll be on my best behavior, tonight. Wait and see."

O'BRIEN, MAGGIE

Pickup By: 6/30/2015

Again and again

4910683

Please check out hold

at the self checkout station

Thank you

*

*

Chapter
12

I t looked as though Simon's best behavior would be unnecessary because Caroline refused Jane's invitation. If the Carlisles
had wished her company at dinner, they could have invited her
anytime before Simon arrived.

They hadn't.

Simon was behind this invitation.

And the last person she wished to see right now was the father
of Lady Blessington's child.

Shortly after refusing Jane's invitation, Caroline responded to
a knock on her door and found Simon's valet outside. "It's a pleasure to see you again, my lady." He held out an envelope.

"And you as well, Bruno." When had he arrived? She smiled at
the man who had been taking care of Simon for as long as she
could remember. "Although Simon wasted your time sending
you up here."

"You know the master, my lady," he replied, tactfully. "I have
orders to wait for your answer."

"One moment." Shutting her door, she opened the envelope
and pulled out a card that was embossed with Simon's ducal crest.
COWARD, he'd boldly scrawled. I WON'T BITE.

Damn him. She'd refused the dinner invitation because of his
unsavory, profligate life, not out of cowardice. Taking the card to

her writing table, she sat down and wrote on its back: *You are the coward in not facing your responsibilities!* She underlined *responsibilities* twice, slid the card back into the envelope, and returned it to Bruno. "Tell Simon, he's wrong."

"Yes, my lady. I told him if you said no, you meant no."

"Exactly right, Bruno. He's had his way too often."

"Yes, my lady." Although he'd known Lady Caroline from the cradle and she and his master were well matched when it came to willfulness.

"I wish no more correspondence from him. Make that plain."

"I'll tell him, my lady. And Bessie would want me to give you her greetings. She waits for your letters."

"Thank you, Bruno. Tell Bessie I miss her." Bruno's wife had been like a mother to her. "If all goes well, perhaps I'll have time to come and visit next summer."

"We'd like that, ma'am." He knew better than to say Simon would like it too. "If'n you ever need something . . . you make sure you let us know."

"Thank you, Bruno. I'm doing well at the moment."

"The Carlisles seem right nice."

"Yes, yes, they are. You see that Simon understands."

"Yes, ma'am." And with a bow, he walked away.

Caroline was back at work on her manuscript when she heard the heavy tread of footsteps moving swiftly in her direction. She quickly piled her pages together and began to slide them in the table drawer when her door opened with such force, it crashed into the wall.

She squealed, and dropped the manuscript.

Simon held up the card with her message. "What the hell does this mean?" Striding across the scattered manuscript pages, he tossed the card on the table.

"Shut the door," she hissed. "Do you want the entire nursery staff listening?"

"You think they don't know?"

"They'd better not know," she snapped, and glaring at him, she jumped to her feet and ran to the door. Jerking the knob out of the shattered plaster, she closed the door, and turned back, quivering with rage. "Say whatever you came up here to say and then get the hell out!"

"No one calls me coward."

"But you're allowed to do so to me?"

"Mine was in jest."

"Mine wasn't."

His eyes narrowed to slits. "If you were a man, I'd call you out and kill you."

"But then men are exceedingly stupid."

"Really," he surveyed her room with a derisive glance, "and women aren't?"

"I'm here because my father chose to drink himself to death— not exactly a model of wisdom . . . and my husband was enticed by avarice."

"Rather than your beauty."

"That's *your* speciality isn't it—beautiful women. Although, I hear you've left one such beauty in London somewhat the worse for your company."

"Why don't you just come out and say it," he growled. "Jane told you, didn't she?"

"Very well." Her gaze was chill. "I heard you left Lady Blessington with your child in her belly. Is that blunt enough?"

"Have I ever come in you?" he inquired, his voice acrid with restraint. "Have I?" he said again when she didn't answer.

"Well?" he muttered as the silence lengthened.

"No."

"And why is that do you suppose?" Smooth as silk.

"Don't take that tone with me," she bristled. "I'm not ten years old and you're not without guilt!"

"Lady Blessington isn't ten years old either; she understands where babies come from. In this instance, her child comes compliments of her stable boy. She'd prefer the child be of ducal blood, of course," he said, an edge to his voice. "A common enough desire, I've found. Which is why I'm extremely cautious." His smile didn't quite reach his eyes. "I'll accept your apology."

"Why should I believe you?" she countered. "And even if I did, Lady Blessington is only one small portion of my frustration with you."

"You didn't seem frustrated last night."

His soft drawl was unmitigated arrogance. "Neither did you," she retorted, as capable of arrogance when it came to her sexual talents as he.

A cheeky smile tugged at the corners of his mouth. "You *are* damned good."

"I know." That should wipe away his smile.

It did. "What the hell does that mean?"

"You know very well what it means. Do you think you're the only person who likes a little variety in their bed?"

"How much variety?"

"I don't see how it's any of your business, do you?" she purred.

A muscle along his jaw twitched. "No."

"Good. Then you won't take offense when I tell you that I've decided to look farther afield . . . in terms of bed partners."

One brow quirked in derision. "The stableboy at the castle, perhaps?"

"Acquit me of Lady Blessington's tastes, present company excepted, of course. It's no one you know."

"What if I told you, I wasn't ready to relinquish your company yet."

"I'd say it's eighteen twenty-one and women are no longer chattel."

"A shame the queen didn't know that before she died."

Touché, she thought, although she wouldn't give him the satisfaction. "I live under less restrictions than a queen. Protocol hardly applies to me."

"And yet you insist I not compromise you."

"Damn it, Simon, stop! I don't want to argue endlessly with you. You have spent years dallying with whom you please. Kindly give me the same options. You don't own me. You have no familial rights if such still exist. We're friends, no more."

He knew when to retreat. He had considerable experience with appeasing women. "You're right," he said, pleasantly. "I shouldn't have been so insistent. You have every right to live your life as you please. If it's friends you want to be, then it's friends we'll be."

His sudden volte face gave her pause and she scrutinized his face for a moment. His gaze was open, his smile warm. "Thank you, Simon. I appreciate your understanding." But at some inexplicable level, she felt deflated. Didn't he care anymore? Could he walk away without a backward glance?

"Since we're simply friends, why not come down for dinner? I'd enjoy your company. Not that I don't like discussing Ian and Jane's favorite topics of hunting and riding, but I'd welcome a breath of fresh air in terms of conversation. We could debate, say, France's restored monarchy and its reactionary policies."

She smiled. "Don't get me on *that* subject."

"Particularly when your dear, departed husband is so sadly missed," he noted, mockingly.

"If he were indeed departed, the world would be a better place," she replied without a hint of irony.

"I suppose this isn't the time to ask why you married him?"

"Not unless you wish me to ask you what you found so fascinating about Lady Blessington. I've always found Daphne incredibly dull."

He raised his hands. "You decide on the topics of conversation tonight at dinner. I'll take my cue from you."

Wouldn't it be nice if he would? she thought with a touch of wistfulness. "Did I say I'd dine with you?"

He grinned. "I thought I heard you say you would."

"What if I don't have anything to wear?"

He almost exhaled in relief at her apparent acquiescence.

"Whatever you wear, will be perfect, I'm sure." I'll buy out London for you, he wished to say. And Paris too. "What you have on now will do nicely," he said instead.

She laughed. "You *do* know how to charm."

"I'm way behind you, darling, in terms of charm." And if he dared, he'd walk across the room, pull her into his arms and kiss her soundly.

The look in his eyes warmed her heart. She should take offense at his outrageous seduction. She should say, Don't think I don't know what you're doing. But she didn't. "Go, now," she said. "I have to dress."

"Champagne in the Tudor drawing room first."

"When?"

"Come early. I'll be there."

His smile was heart-stoppingly sweet. Not dangerous or seductive, nor cynical and knowing. When the door closed on him, she felt a joy quite out of proportion to the simple conversation.

How could it hurt to enjoy an evening of company downstairs? And regardless of Simon's cavalier manner with women, apparently this time, he wasn't to blame.

So, now . . . what in her much reduced wardrobe would be appropriate to wear?

Chapter 13

When Simon returned to his rooms, his good spirits were evident. "She said no at first. You were right. But—"

"She changed her mind," Bruno said, looking up from polishing Simon's hunting boots.

"Just barely. So have bathwater brought up posthaste. I want to be waiting for her in the drawing room when she arrives. She's skittish."

His valet glanced at the clock. "It's two hours until dinner."

"I can tell time." Simon began stripping off his jacket.

"Yes, sir, bathwater right away, sir."

Simon entered the Tudor drawing room less than a half hour later, quickly searched the interior and smiled. Good. He'd arrived first. He didn't wish to take any chances Caro might change her mind should she enter an empty room.

Jane had said drinks at eight. That would give him time to talk to Caroline without interruption. God only knew if she was serious about variety in her bed. But if she was, he'd have to change her mind. Gently, of course. She didn't take orders.

He drank three quick brandies while waiting. If he'd been introspective, he might have taken note of his unease. But over the years, he'd become adept at ignoring introspection. A wise choice for a man of intemperance.

As the door opened and Caroline walked in, he came to his feet with a smile. "I've started without you. Come sit by the fire. Would you like brandy or champagne?"

"Brandy, please."

Of course, she preferred brandy. He recalled that fact with inordinate pleasure, as though he'd discovered a long lost memento. "You look wonderful." She'd plaited her hair and drawn it into a coronet atop her head, her shoulders were bare, her décolletage breathtaking. She wore a small cameo brooch that looked vaguely familiar at the neckline of her gown. Her gown, while dated, was expensive. Someone had had money enough to buy her that. His smile tightened at the thought.

"Is something wrong?" She moved across the room toward him.

"No, no . . . I was admiring your gown." And the graceful sway of her hips.

"It's a castoff from a friend in Brussels. Outmoded, I'm afraid. But I love the Genoa velvet." She brushed her fingertips over the rippling azure fabric.

"It's lovely." His temper instantly dissipated. "Your friend has excellent taste."

"Yes. She, like I, once lived in a much different world. She died shortly before I left."

"I'm sorry. I really am, Caro—about everything. You should have written me. I would have helped. I'd still like to."

"Don't start, Simon." Sitting down on the chair he'd pulled out for her, she smiled up at him. "Like you, I value my independence. You understand, certainly more than most . . . about independence. Now," she added briskly, "the past is the past. Weren't we going to talk politics?"

"We'll talk about whatever you like." He moved toward the liquor table.

"I adore you when you're amenable."

"Aren't I always?"

"Yes, of course."

He looked up from opening a decanter. "Now who's being amenable?"

"I don't want to argue tonight. I just want to enjoy my brandy and the pleasure of your company."

Picking up the two glasses he'd poured, he crossed the small distance between them. "I'm not sure what to say when you're so obliging."

"I have my moments, darling." She put her hand out for her drink. "Surely you remember."

Her complaisance was unnerving or pleasing, depending on how mistrusting he wished to be. But her moments as she so bewitchingly put it, were indeed memorable. He placed the brandy in her hand and smiled. "To fond memory," he said.

She lifted her glass. "And to freedom."

He raised his glass. "Freedom," he said, softly, suddenly not sure looking at her whether his freedom mattered as much as he once thought. But fear of entanglements was stronger than transient emotion and when he spoke a second later, his voice was neutral. "You've been inculcated with revolutionary principles while abroad," he remarked, taking a seat opposite her. "Liberté, égalité, fraternité."

"All of which Napoleon disregarded in his climb to power. You must admit, though, they're noble virtues." She grinned. "Not that you're likely to agree. As one of the premier dukes in England, you have tradition to maintain now, don't you, Your Grace?"

"I'm not sure I'm particularly traditional. Have you become a radical since you left England?"

"My former husband would say so, although, in his estimation, anyone who doesn't agree in absolute monarchy falls into that category."

"You disagreed on politics?"

"Among other things. I haven't had enough to drink yet to discuss that particular hell."

"Jesus, Caro," he said, leaning forward. "You should have written to me."

"And said what? Climb out of the current bed you're in and come and save me? You couldn't save me, Simon. You can't save yourself."

He relaxed against his chair back once again. "I'm not touching any conversation about beds with a ten-foot pole."

Her brows arched into perfect half circles. "Good decision."

Quickly reviewing a number of subjects in his mind, he chose the least controversial. "Tell me where you were living when you accepted the position at Netherton Castle."

Her gaze was mocking. "Do you really care?"

"Yes," he replied, graciously. "Where you in Brussels? How did you know the Carlisles were looking for someone?" Tell me everything about your life since you left me, he wanted to say. "Tell me about your friend."

Caroline drained her brandy and held her glass out. "Yes, I was in Brussels," she replied, watching him walk to the liquor table, thinking there wasn't a man alive so handsome. "I bought a copy of the *London Times* and searched the ads for governesses. As you know, aristocratic ladies fallen on hard times have two choices; they can be governesses or companions. And the thought of fetching shawls and medicines for an elderly lady would have brought me screaming to Bedlam in a month."

He glanced over at her, wondering what degree of fate had brought them together again. "Did you apply anywhere else?" When she hesitated, he said, "Apparently you did."

"I sent my resume to a mill owner from Manchester." She grimaced. "He replied with much too personal questions."

Returning with their drinks, Simon handed hers over. "Tell me his name."

"You needn't call him out. My letter in response to his questions was quite sufficient, I guarantee. I also sent his letter of inappropriate questions to his wife."

His brows flickered. "Remind me to stay off your grudge list."

She smiled. "Too late."

"Perhaps I can make amends in some way," he murmured softly.

"Perhaps after a dozen more brandies you might," she murmured back with a grin.

He laughed. "Have I died and gone to heaven?"

"Are you speaking of my little heaven on the third floor or something more conventional?"

After quickly glancing at the clock and the door, his gaze swung back to her. "Perhaps we could re-create a degree of heaven here, if you wish."

"You, apparently, do not understand the meaning of the word discretion."

Ignoring her sarcasm, he smiled. "There's time."

"Later," she said.

His lashes lowered faintly. "When later?"

"When I see whether you embarrass me at dinner."

He grinned."Not likely, darling, if I have good reason to behave."

"I'm not your darling—or anyone's darling," she said, pronouncing the words with clarity. "Thankfully, I'm discharged from such obligations."

She spoke with such conviction he wondered what had happened to her in her marriage. But she was also in such convivial good spirits he wasn't about to inquire. "To emancipation, then," he said, lifting his glass. "It becomes you."

She winked at him over the rim of his glass. "Yes it does."

Now that he'd purchased Kettleston Hall, he would have time aplenty to become better acquainted with her particular style of emancipation. Although, as a matter of prudence, he decided against mentioning the fact that he was about to become a neighbor.

At the appointed hour, when Ian and Jane arrived, Caroline and Simon were laughing together.

"You changed your mind," Jane said to Caroline.

"I hope you don't mind."

"Not at all. I'll see that another place is set." She walked to the bellpull.

Taking note of the half empty decanter, Ian understood the

partial reason for their companions' high spirits. Although, with or without liquor, Simon would have been pleased that Caroline had joined them. This afternoon, he'd been absolutely determined to have her invited, and after fighting alongside Simon at Waterloo, Ian had recognized Simon in his resolute mode.

He and Jane had disagreed on whether Caroline would appear. She owed him a guinea.

Chapter
14

Simon's conversation at dinner would have passed muster with the most conservative prelate. Caroline was pleased. Ian was shocked. Jane, who knew Simon less well, began to think all the gossip about the duke might have been overstated. He was a pattern card of good manners.

He never raised his voice. He had a well-considered opinion on any topic of conversation, although his tact in allowing others their say was really quite extraordinary. Jane even began wondering if her sister might have been wrong in her latest tidbit of gossip from London. Simon's every action was unequivocally gallant.

She hadn't realized he was so committed to his tenants. Apparently, he'd rebuilt entire villages on his properties, equipping them with schools and hospitals as well. He also served on the village council and supported a parish church that was renowned for its charity. Before long, Jane began to view her single-minded devotion to the hunt as a wholly inadequate use of her time. Perhaps she should show more concern for their tenants. But when she made mention of her unease, Simon immediately assuaged her guilt. He not only hunted with three of the premier hunts in England, he noted, he often traveled abroad to hunt as well. So he fully understood, her love of the chase.

Comforted and consoled, she was soon smiling once again.

Knowing the reason for Simon's obliging politesse, Caroline observed his performance with a more jaundiced eye. But regardless his motivation, she couldn't fault him for his cultivated charm. Dinner was delightful, the conversation, suavely directed by Simon, offered everyone an opportunity to express their views.

All in all, the evening couldn't have been more convivial.

After dinner, while the men drank port, the ladies retired to the drawing room for tea and Jane was fulsome in her praises of Simon. "I feel awful," she added, after characterizing Simon's virtues at length, "for slandering Simon so this morning. Since you knew of him in the past, you must have thought me quite mad."

"Not at all. Simon's charm and grace, are, as you mentioned this morning, enormous. That's not to say, he doesn't have a foible or two."

Jane offered Caroline a conspiratorial smile. "As do all men."

"Undoubtedly. But I want to thank you for inviting me tonight," Caroline remarked, preferring not to discuss men's foibles should the subject of husbands and *her* dead husband come up. "I enjoyed myself immensely."

"Please, dine with us whenever you wish. I apologize for my tardiness in extending the invitation."

"There's no need to apologize. A governess isn't a member of the family, after all. The children are very bright, by the way. You must come and sit in the schoolroom sometime and listen to their recitations."

"I will, of course. Tell me more of your friend in Brussels. She seemed so fascinating."

Understanding Jane had little interest in her children's schooling, Caroline immediately complied. "Did I tell you about her visit to the sultan's harem in Constantinople?"

"Ohhhh . . . how very exciting!"

Caroline went on to describe in detail Flora's various excursions into the harem.

"My word," Jane said, breathless with wonder as Caroline finished. "Even her name is exotic . . . and her life: Constantinople, the tragedy of her husband's death, the harem, palace coups." She sighed. "It makes the provincial moors of Yorkshire seem tame in contrast."

"Your life would have held considerable charm for Flora. She often spoke of growing up at her grandmother's estate in the French countryside."

"She died so young," Jane murmured.

"She'd been in fragile health for some time. And the circumstances that brought her to Brussels took their toll."

"Her husband's brutal family in Portugal you mean."

"Yes. When they refused her refuge, she was forced to make her own way in the world. Nevertheless, she was never disheartened. She sustained her belief in silver linings till the end."

"Who did?" Simon asked, coming into the room carrying a decanter.

"Flora."

"Ah, your friend from Brussels. We thought you ladies might like some port."

"It's the reserve stock." Ian followed Simon into the drawing room. "And damned good."

His red face gave evidence of his imbibing. Simon, in contrast, looked sober.

A short time later as Jane and Ian were debating which glasses best suited the reserve port, Simon took the opportunity to pour some of the liquor into a glass for Caroline. Walking over, he handed it to her with a smile. "They could be talking about the next coming and I wouldn't care."

"You're showing well," she said, lightly, gazing up at him.

"I've good reason to."

She grinned. "Are you counting the minutes?"

"The seconds, darling . . ."

A shiver raced up her spine at his heated look. "Simon, please . . . don't," she whispered.

"They're busy. I could kiss you and they wouldn't notice."

As he began to lean forward, she pressed back against the chair. "Don't you dare!"

Her breasts swelled above the décolletage of her gown as her spine went rigid, and Simon clenched his fists against the impulse to reach out and stroke the mounded flesh. "It's been a long evening," he murmured. "Right now, I'm just about ready to dare anything."

Skittish, fevered, she sharply inhaled and her nipples strained against the silk of her gown. "Please, Simon . . ."

She meant to abjure, but it sounded as though she were asking and her enticing nipples were close enough to touch. Lust spiked through his senses; he quickly stepped back. "Let me know if you like the port," he said in a conversational tone, every syllable taut with constraint.

Then he walked away before he lost control.

As Ian became more inebriated, he expounded on a great variety of subjects with a decreasing clarity of thought.

Simon barely spoke. Restless, edgy, he watched the clock, his hosts, and waited.

Caroline was waiting too, although she would have preferred feeling less needy. Desperately wanting sex with Simon placed her on a very long list of females. An annoyingly long list. And while Ian droned on and on, she attempted to regain her sanity—or at least, some measure of control over the desire burning through her body.

To little purpose, apparently, because when Simon surreptitiously winked at her in the midst of one of Ian's long, meandering monologues, every carnal nerve in her body leaped in response.

Finally, as Ian began describing his new hunting dog for the third time, Jane said, "Ian, that's enough. Come now, before the servants have to carry you to bed."

"Can walk jus' fine," he retorted, rising from his chair and promptly pitching forward.

Lunging to his feet, Simon caught him before he hit the floor.

"I'll call for help," Jane said, calmly, as though this occurrence wasn't new. "Can you hold him upright a few moments more, Simon?"

"Why don't I carry him upstairs?" Simon offered. Anything to put an end to this torturous evening.

"Nonsense. Ian for heaven's sake, sit or stand."

Brushing Simon away, Ian fell back into his chair.

Jane smiled. "He does so like his port."

Caroline and Simon responded in some desultory fashion to Jane's comments while they waited, although neither could have recalled the conversation with their minds otherwise occupied.

And after what seemed a very long time to two people on the verge of carnal combustion, three servants entered the room to carry Ian away. By this time, he was softly snoring, a casualty to Portugal's best port.

Following her husband, Jane turned to wave from the doorway. "I'll see you both in the morning."

And a second later, Caroline and Simon were alone.

Chapter

15

They came to their feet.

"Finally," Simon said.

"May I attack you now?"

He opened his arms.

She ran to him and he held her close.

"It was torture," he whispered.

"Absolute torment." She gazed up at him. "I want you up-stairs. I want you upstairs, *now*."

"I may not want to wait."

"You have to."

"Because?"

"I'm the boss."

"Are you now?" he said in a velvety breath.

"Now and always."

He grinned. "You're obviously drunk."

She shook her head, her breasts moved against him with a de-lectable friction and he suddenly didn't care who was what to whom. Sweeping her up into his arms, he gazed at her through half-lowered lashes. "If you want to go upstairs, we'll go up-stairs."

"You have to be quiet."

He was already moving toward the door. "I'm always quiet. You're the screamer."

"I'm sorry. I'll try to be better."

"Now I *know* you're drunk."

Not wishing to have their tryst curtailed, she was discreetly silent on the passage up two flights of stairs to the third floor. As was Simon who wasn't about to jeopardize their time together. As he moved cautiously down the nursery floor corridor, he listened for any unusual sounds. Everyone should be sleeping at this time of night.

The moment he entered her room, Caro rained a flurry of kisses on his face. "Finally," she whispered. "Now put me down, because I'm in a vast, vast hurry."

The instant he set her on her feet, she reached for his trouser buttons. "Wait a second—the door," he murmured, holding her at arm's length, trying to shut the door while she struggled to reach him.

Held back with Simon's stiff-armed grip, she wiggled her fingers just short of their goal. "Hurry, darling, hurry . . . no one will come in."

He glanced back from pulling a chair under the latch. "You seemed more concerned last night."

"But no one came in, so there," she replied. "Just undo the bare minimum, darling—really, the absolute minimum—hurry."

She was clearly willing to say anything in her current mood, but one of them at least had to be rational. Only when the door was secured did he relinquish his grip on her shoulder. "So, now, do you want something?" he teased, turning back with a grin.

"As if you don't," she said, pettishly. "Now, hurry," she added, waving him after her, kicking off her slippers as she moved toward the bed. "We'll sleep on the floor."

"I wasn't planning on sleeping."

"Well, that's fortunate, because you won't be." Pulling the quilt from the bed, she spread it on the floor and began taking down her braids.

"Are you giving orders tonight?"

"I thought I would for a change." Under his interested gaze, she loosened her hair with a few combing sweeps of her fingers and lifting her skirts and petticoats, lay down on the quilt. Raising her hips enough to shove a remnant of azure velvet out of her way, she drew up her legs, opened her thighs and offered Simon a sultry smile. "Come, Your Grace, I won't make you to do anything you haven't done before."

"I think I like your shyness best," he murmured, sardonically, taking in her wanton pose with a connoisseur's appreciation.

"Just so long as you like it at close range, Your Grace, I would be grateful."

"How grateful?"

"As grateful as you wish, naturally," she purred. "But do hurry, darling, or I may come without you."

He immediately complied because it had been an extremely long evening for him as well and Caro was very apt to do what she said. Swiftly unbuttoning his trousers, he knelt between her outspread legs and moved into her welcoming embrace and body, fully clothed.

She rose to meet him, and he sank into her heated warmth, her sleek, tractable tissue closing around him with gratifying tightness.

They fit with unerring accord, as though they had together contrived the prototype for sexual splendor. And he more than she understood the rarity of that ravishing bliss. Gorged full as she was, Caro was more intent on the immediacy of sensation than on theory. "Don't move, don't move . . . don't move," she breathed.

But he did, a soul-stirring measure more and with a small cry, she climaxed.

He raced to follow her, on the same wild, impetuous ride as she after the tedious hours of waiting.

When their breakneck orgasms were over, she looked up, her expression fretful. "That was too fast."

He chuckled. "Then you should let me slow the pace."

She wrinkled her nose. "I don't like that either when I—"

"Want what you want." He smiled. "I know. We'll have to work on that." Kissing her gently, he rolled away. "I warn you though," he said with a roguish grin, "it could take hours of fucking to get it just right."

"You do know how to charm a lady," she purred.

His grin was pure impudence. "Some ladies are easier to charm than others."

Her smile was as cheeky as his. "Lucky for you."

"Indeed," he breathed, considering himself the luckiest of men.

"Now take your clothes off," she ordered.

"You *are* drunk," he murmured, pulling his handkerchief out of his pocket and quickly wiping himself dry.

"I don't think a man who drinks a bottle before dinner should be questioning anyone's sobriety."

"You're right." He reached for a towel from her washstand.

"Did I tell you I was the boss tonight?"

"I believe you did." He dropped the towel on her stomach.

She smiled. "Good, because I want sex again."

He grinned. "You're not going to remember anything tomorrow, are you?"

She rubbed the towel over her stomach and sat up. "What was your name again?"

"Fucking tart." But his voice was teasing.

"Your favorite kind of female if I recall." And seemingly oblivious of his assessing gaze, she began rolling one garter and stocking down her leg.

She *was* drunk and for the briefest moment, he took issue. Not with her present inebriation, but with what may have been past instances when she'd been similarly hell-bent on having sex. Placing his hand on hers, he curtailed her undressing. "Do you know where you are?" he asked, softly.

"Do you mean whom I'm with?"

His grip tightened over her hand. "That's what I mean."

"I adore you when you're jealous, Simon Blair of Monkshood. Satisfied?"

He released his hold.

And she continued rolling down her stocking as though they'd been discussing the weather. She stripped off both her stockings and her petticoat under Simon's critical gaze. Then, raising her arms, she said, "Be a dear and lift off my gown. It comes off rather easily." She had to say, "Please," a moment later because Simon hadn't moved. "You're the only man I've ever slept with," she added in a sportive tone.

"Fuck you," he muttered, but he finally complied, pulling her gown over her head as directed.

"There now," she said, cheerfully, a moment later, seated beside him, nude and lush as a hothouse orchid. "I think it's your turn to undress."

"You're going to be insatiable tonight, aren't you?"

"It rather seems that way. Would you like some help?" And without waiting for an answer, she tumbled him back, straddled his hips and reached for his erection. "Speaking of insatiable," she murmured, stroking the length of his aroused penis.

A second later, he was buried deep inside her and she was moving her hips in a delectable rhythm while she pulled his cravat loose. She took pleasure in playing the teasing sorceress for a time, undressing him slowly as she rode him, flaunting her voluptuous body, not letting him touch her, moving up and down on him with tantalizing deliberation.

He obliged her although he was taut with the effort, fiercely aroused and not sure how long he could play the subservient role. She made the mistake of saying, "I never let men touch me," as she slid his trousers and undershorts down his thighs. That plural noun seriously provoked him, his jealousy very near the surface and instead of obliging her this time, he took her lavish breasts in his hands and gently compressed the pliant flesh.

"You aren't allowed," she said, her voice coolly imperious.

"Now if only you could stop me," he murmured, raising the pale mounds of her breasts upward as he kicked off the last of his clothes.

"I insist."

He kept lifting.

"Simon! Stop!"

He didn't and she was forced up on her knees until she was resting on the very tip of his erection. "You're going to let *this* man touch you, aren't you darling?" His voice was whisper soft.

Her breasts were jutting out like great ostentatious globes, her spine arched against the pressure of his fingers. "Yes, yes."

"And if you're very good," he whispered, lifting his hands a fraction higher so she whimpered at almost losing contact with his penis, "I'll let you come again."

"I'll be good." She was utterly still, the tip of his erection barely grazing her vulva. She bit her lip. "Really, I will."

A wave of jealousy so intense he felt its heat, washed over him. How many other men had brought her to this state? "Fucking slut," he growled, his fingers closing cruelly on her flesh.

Her cry was one of desperation, not pain and she tried to move downward on his erection.

He should have pushed her away.

If they weren't so well matched in lust, he would have.

"Please," she whispered, her gaze half-lidded, smoldering.

And he rolled her under him with quicksilver agility, plunged to the very depth of her body and rode her with a ferocity and brute force that he couldn't have controlled for God himself.

She met him, thrust for thrust, her wildness matching his and he offered up a small prayer to all the spirits that had brought him to Netherton Castle and reunited him with this flame-hot, glorious woman.

No one played at amour as well as Caro.

Or was so greedy.

Or ravenous.

She could set the pace as well as he and keep up with his most outrageous sport.

He hadn't realized how much he'd missed her, how much he wanted what she gave him.

How alike they were.

Chapter

16

As the sun rose, he held her close, not wanting to leave, frustrated at the thought of having to pretend they were nominal strangers when they met downstairs.

It was exasperating they couldn't be together—doubly so to a man who had commanded the world to his whims for most of his life. There wasn't a reason in creation why Caro had to be a governess. Good God, he could pay for a hundred governesses—a thousand. Not that he was interested in her for her governess abilities, he reflected, heated memory spiking through his mind. Nor was he interested in playing a milksop role before Ian and Jane for the indefinite future. He couldn't stay at Netherton Castle forever. He didn't want to. He wanted Caro beside him like this when he woke in the morning. He particularly wanted her warming his bed at night. The obvious solution leaped to mind. "Come live with me," he said.

She came out of her doze with a start and stared at him in the dawn light. "Live with you?"

He nodded. "Precisely."

"Why?"

"Why? Because we get along famously, that's why."

"If I were to live with you," she said a trifle too softly, "what would that make me?"

"I didn't mean it like that, Caro."

Her gaze turned cool. "I've not yet sunk to the level of whore."

"I meant nothing of the kind. I'll buy you a house of your own. You can be independent. Isn't that what you want? And we wouldn't have to sneak around like fugitives."

She sat up and moved away. "My independence would be your reward for sexual favors? Don't look at me like that. Of course it would. I don't have the funds to support a house even if I let you buy one for me."

"You're making this much too complicated," he grumbled.

"You needn't buy me anything, Simon. I don't want you to buy me anything. I can make my own living."

"With the stated price for your favors, no doubt you can." The resentment in his tone matched hers.

"That list and those conditions were meant to discourage you."

His gaze turned cynical. "You obviously don't understand men."

"Or men of your ilk, who insist on having their way."

"I don't see you obliging me, so obviously I don't always get what I want."

"A shame. Or perhaps a lesson in humility."

"So you're saying no to me?"

"Is that a shock? Having a woman refuse you? I suppose women are standing in line to be your mistress," she said with icy sarcasm.

"Damn you, Caro. It's not about being my mistress." In fact, he'd always scrupulously avoided making such an offer to a woman.

"Good. Then I'll say no thank you to your kind offer and you'll politely go back to London."

"What if I don't want to?"

"That's not my concern." She began to rise from their makeshift bed. "If you'll excuse me, I have to get dressed for my workday."

"Not just yet," he murmured, grasping her wrist.

"Release me." Her voice was chill.

"You want me to leave?"

She struggled against his grip. "I distinctly want you to leave."

"And you're not interested in my offer?"

"If I ever decide to become a whore, I'll let you know. I don't at the moment."

"But you might?" he lazily drawled.

She was rigid, her gaze filled with rage. "Perhaps when hell freezes over, but I wouldn't guarantee it even then."

"In that case, why don't we call this a farewell fuck?" He jerked her back.

"If you dare, I'll scream."

"Scream away."

He meant it; he didn't care. "Since when do you force women?" she spat.

"I never do."

"Arrogant bastard."

He shook his head. "I just know how to pick the right women—you know, the ones who like to fuck. Now, spread your legs, darling. Both of us know you're hot little cunt is always ready for more."

She scrambled to get away, but he grabbed her as she rose to her knees and hauled her back, his grip on her waist brutal. "Now what do we have here?" he murmured, his gaze on her lush, pink bottom. Balanced on her hands and knees, she was conveniently open to him and he drew her closer despite her struggles to break free. "Down, sweetheart," he whispered, sliding his palm down her spine. "I'm not quite finished with you. Five hundred pounds should certainly buy a last fuck in the morning." With one hand splayed across the base of her spine and the other gripping her waist, he ignored her resistance and hauled her back until she was poised in all her bounteous beauty, wet and ready for his prick.

His erection was stiff against his stomach. Moving his hand from her waist, he guided his penis to her exposed vulva and plunged in.

If he heard her gasp, he gave no indication; he was already drawing back for the next powerful downstroke. Holding her hips in a harsh grip, he drove in over and over again, convulsed with rage, his breathing soon becoming rough and shallow as though he'd run ten miles. But it was untrammeled fury that brought him panting, that made him want to humble her and he took out his frustration in a brutal pounding assault, as though sheer force would mitigate his anger.

He could have come a dozen times, but he curbed the impulse, wanting retaliation more—craving vengeance for her refusal, needing to make her submit at least in this crude physical act, if no other way.

But then he heard it, as though his ears were attuned to her passions—that soft whimpering sound she made just before she climaxed.

Damn her; damn her burning hot cunt; did nothing blunt her insatiable hunger? In case she hadn't noticed, this wasn't a benevolent sex act meant for her enjoyment. Withdrawing quickly, he released his orgasm, spurting hot come on her back while she trembled and sobbed, unfulfilled.

The second he was finished, he rose from the floor without a backward glance and quickly dressed. He was swift and proficient; he'd left in a hurry once or twice before.

Pulling some bills from his pocket, he tossed them on the table. "You were worth every shilling," he said, silkily. "And I should know."

Grabbing up the bills, she threw them at him. "I hope you burn in hell or better yet, have Daphne as a millstone around your neck the rest of your life!"

He stared at her briefly, ignoring the bills at his feet. "Wake up to the realities of the world, darling. There is no hell and Daphne doesn't stand a prayer of getting what she wants," a wicked smile flashed across his face, "unless it's her stable boy. Now, if you should ever tire of instructing children, let me know. We could probably work something out."

He ducked as she threw a candlestick at him, the brass holder striking the door with such force it chipped the wood. "Temper, darling," he murmured. "You don't want to lose this job."

"Get the hell out before I forget how much I need this job," she hissed, the sound of servants moving around the house becoming more audible.

He bowed faintly, looking disheveled and irritatingly handsome in his rearranged evening rig. "If you're ever in London, look me up."

"If I'm ever in London, I'll take every precaution to avoid you."

"That's not very friendly."

"But then you're not really interested in a woman's friendship, are you?"

He hesitated, and his mouth formed in a grim line for a moment. "Let's say, I thought I was." He reached for the doorknob and faintly tipped his head. "But then we all make mistakes."

The knock on the door echoed through the room.

Caroline's pulse rate soared.

"It's only a servant at his hour," Simon remarked, unconcerned. Opening the door, he offered the maid holding Caroline's breakfast tray a pleasant good morning and strolled from the room.

Flushing with embarrassment, Caroline wished she could disappear into the floor. Since that wasn't a viable option, she covered her nakedness with the quilt and tried to be invisible.

"Oh, miss," Betsy sighed, turning back after watching Simon stroll away. "You be so lucky. All us girls been hoping the fine lord would look our way, we were. Oh, my, he's ever so splendid."

So much for her concern about appearances. Now if only she could be as cavalier as Betsy, Caroline thought. But perhaps the maid had the right perspective after all. *Enjoy the fine lord and then get on with your life.* With luck and a very bad memory, perhaps she could do just that.

Chapter
17

Leaving his hosts a note of apology for his early, precipitous departure, Simon was soon on his way back to London. Slumped in the corner of his coach, his greatcoat pulled up around his ears, he drank from his flask and cursed women in general and one woman in particular for making his life a holy hell.

Bruno feigned deafness as any good valet would. But he'd not seen his master in such a black mood since the last time Lady Caroline had disrupted his life. A shame they couldn't come to some agreement, but with two such stubborn personalities, perhaps any hope for harmony was a dream. On the other hand, at least, Lady Caroline was back in England without a husband.

He and Bessie would have to put their heads together.

The ruling classes occasionally needed a helping hand to manage their lives.

Responding to Simon's curt order to open another bottle, Bruno set aside his musing, although he wondered what would give out first on their southward journey–the duke's capacity for drink or the supply of brandy. Since they had orders to stop for nothing but post changes, the bottles in the coach would have to do. At least the trip home would be swift.

* * *

Caroline survived that first morning by sheer will, refusing to think of Simon, concentrating on the children's lessons as though they were the most important mission in her life. She focused all her attention on their studies, explaining all the constellations visible in the northern skies, tracing with them Alexander the Great's campaign to India, and when they began getting edgy, she played word games with them in all the languages they were learning, offering bonbons as prizes.

She ate more than her share of bonbons too, but after the nastiness with Simon this morning—which was inevitable, of course, he couldn't stay forever—she needed solace . . . ten large bonbons of solace as it turned out.

When she brought the children down for tea late that afternoon, neither Ian nor Jane made mention of their departed guest. Scrupulously avoiding the subject, they offered Caroline tea as though she were a member of the family, and spoke instead of the coming holiday season. They discussed the numerous guests and family members they were expecting, and outlined the tentative schedule of activities that would take place at the house, in the village, and at the parish church. Caroline was invited to each and every one of the events. "Please, think of yourself as part of the family," Jane offered, her tone so sympathetic, Caroline blushed at the implication.

"Thank you. I will," Caroline replied, wishing she could have avoided having tea with her employers, wishing desperately to escape to her room and never talk to another soul.

And perhaps cry for a month.

Although, she quickly jettisoned that irrational thought. She wasn't about to cry over Simon. Not again. She'd already cried enough tears for him to last a lifetime.

It had been sensible not to allow herself to care.

He hadn't changed one whit.

On his return to London, Simon resumed his bachelor life with a vengeance. But what had been pleasure in the past, no longer pleased and what had formerly amused him, struck him now with ennui. He went through actresses and courtesans, society ladies and serving wenches by the score, changing his bed partners so often, the women became a blur on his retinas. He even thought about paying Daphne a visit just to break the monotony—and inquire how her romance with her stable boy was doing. But he couldn't bring himself to care enough to make the effort.

After a fortnight in London in which he did nothing but drink himself into oblivion in the company of different women night after night, he called for his coach in the wee hours one morning. Bruno was wakened and given five minutes to pack a bag for the duke. He was off to Dover—alone. He had no wish to take Bruno from his family over Christmas.

As Simon climbed into his coach, he was hoping a change of scene would clear his head and obliterate the persistent images of a hot-blooded, auburn-haired beauty who preferred her independence to his company. Dropping onto the carriage seat, he rapped on the ceiling and reached for his flask. As the coach lurched forward, and began picking up speed, he gazed out the window at the street lamps flashing by, lifted the flask to his mouth and emptied half of it down his throat.

Damn her to hell. Didn't she know independence was much overrated? Didn't she understand independence for women didn't actually exist? It was a fucking unobtainable vision, for Christ's sake. Some nominal freedoms existed for bluestocking women he supposed. But only if they had money and only because no man would have them. *Damn it,* neither instance applied to Caro. Her father had much to answer for, though, in terms of her unorthodox notions. He'd raised her like a man.

At least in Paris, women knew how to act like women. Not that he hadn't had his share of feminine wiles in London. He grimaced at the thought, suddenly unsure whether he cared to reenter that jaded sphere.

Then again, if he were truly looking for diversion, maybe he could pay a call on Louvois.

*   *   *

The crossing was horrendous, the December winds at gale force, the waves so high the captain of Simon's yacht was certain they were going to take on water and sink to the bottom of the Channel. With mast-high waves washing over the decks and the yacht pitching and yawing, Simon took over the wheel and fought to keep the vessel afloat.

Half-drunk, lashed by the wind and rain, he tied himself to the wheel and battled the storm out of sheer rancor, pitting his fury against the elements. After weeks of an unyielding, elusive bitterness, at last he had a recognized enemy to conquer, a foe against which he could launch his silent rage. He welcomed the pitiless cold and violent seas, the harsh winds that took his breath away. At least he was feeling something after weeks of mind-numbing nothingness.

At least he remembered what it felt like to be alive.

Late that afternoon, they limped into Calais, the mainsail in shreds, the sprits and mizzens barely holding them on course. On docking, the crew fell to their knees and kissed the ground. As it turned out, their gratitude was well founded. Simon's yacht was the only vessel that had made the crossing without loss of life. The packet had gone down with all hands, six other vessels had crew members washed overboard, and a Dutch merchantman had been run aground just south of the harbor and his vessel was being broken to bits by the heavy surf.

Simon accepted the congratulations of the local seamen with a bland neutrality those viewing it ascribed to English phlegmatism. They didn't realize it hadn't mattered to him whether he lived or died. They didn't understand how joyless was his mood.

After making arrangements for his crew in his absence and after a last discussion with his captain, the duke boarded his coach that had been lashed to the deck, offloaded, and set off for Paris.

Not up to the usual holidays with his mother and sister's family, he planned on spending Christmas in the French capital.

Chapter

18

Guests began arriving at Netherton Castle a fortnight before Christmas. All of Jane's family came; Ian's parents as well. Even his brother stationed in India had arrived in time for the holidays. Then as Twelfth Night approached, the parties were enlarged to include the neighboring nobility and gentry. Wassail cups were raised; a yule log was dragged in from the forest and placed in the great hall fireplace; mummers performed for the guests; carolers caroled; plays were staged by the guests, the amateur actors taking to the boards with good cheer and high spirits compliments of the fine local whiskey.

Fortunately, Caroline was in charge of shepherding Hugh, Joanna, and their numerous cousins through most of the festivities, allowing her little time to interact with the visiting adults. With the children animated and energized by the multitude of gala events, they kept Caroline busy from morning till night.

In a way, she was grateful. She had little time to dwell on any unhappy thoughts. In the days since Simon had left, she'd had sufficient opportunity to come to terms with what might have been. But no matter how she rationalized—what he'd offered her was unacceptable.

As if she weren't already touched with melancholy over her ill-starred relationship with Simon, she dearly missed having a family this time of year. Even in the midst of the cheerful company at the castle she felt alone, although, the busy schedule and great number of activities were a welcome distraction. Her opportunities to fall into moping were limited.

Furthermore, on her rare evenings of freedom, she'd begun working on her manuscript again, often writing late into the night. The heroine of the story seemed to be facing the obstacles in her life with a new determination these days, the imaginary world of fiction perhaps mirroring Caroline's self-reliant spirit.

As soon as possible in the new year, she intended to send her manuscript off to London. If other indigent ladies could augment their income with great success, might not she? England had several female authors who had made tidy fortunes in the endeavor. It gave her hope. Or it gave her reason to hope.

Regaining her estate on a governess's salary was unthinkable.

But with literary success, even such castles-in-the-air were possible.

On the fourth night of the Twelfth Night, shortly before dinner, Caroline received a summons from the countess.

When Caroline entered Jane's boudoir, she found her mistress seated before her dressing table, her maids in attendance. One was arranging the countess's hair, the other fussing with the sleeves of her gown. Gesturing Caroline forward, Jane dismissed the maids and turned from the mirror with a frown.

Employers' frowns had taken on a new unwanted status in Caroline's hierarchy of values. She forced herself to smile.

"I have a favor to ask," Jane said. "My mother's cousin, Viscount Fortescue has just arrived quite unexpectedly." Her frown deepened. "He neither hunts nor shoots," a small grimace was added to her afflicted expression, "so I was hoping you'd be kind enough to converse with him at dinner and save me the trouble. He's been an undersecretary or something at some embassy or other," she waved a dismissive hand, "and frankly—is . . . well . . . too educated," she declared, a critical note in her voice.

"I would be ever so grateful if you would take him off my hands for the evening."

"Tonight?" Caroline murmured, glancing at the clock.

"Isn't it just like a man to arrive so late?" The fact that he was uninteresting to the countess was left unsaid. "But I *would* appreciate it so if you would help me out."

Caroline was in no position to refuse. "Yes, of course."

"What a darling you are. Kitty, Claire, come back in," the countess called, turning back to her mirror. "You can't imagine how I dreaded having to ask questions about"—she leaned forward and adjusted her earring—"I don't even recall what embassy he was in. And you speak all those many languages. There you are, Kitty. Fix this curl on my forehead will you? Thank you, Caroline. I'm sure you two will be vastly compatible." She waved her off. "Here, Kitty, this curl. Don't you think it should be just a bit higher?"

Compatible or not, more important, no longer a problem to the countess, Caroline thought, walking back to her room. It had taken a full measure of reserve to politely respond to Jane's request cum command. She wasn't by nature, deferential, although in her new station in life she was forced to accept a degree of humility. And also, apparently, converse with guests regarded by her employer as dismally too enlightened.

No doubt, the man would be elderly if he was Jane's mother's cousin, possibly dull—she unfortunately knew diplomats of that ilk—and he *may* take issue with having a déclassé governess beside him at dinner.

Reaching her room, she stood in the doorway for a moment repining her fate. She could have spent the evening in her room, taking her heroine to the Parisian opera, a scene she was delighting in writing.

Moving to her armoire, she drew out her azure velvet gown with a small sigh.

The evening was going to be tedious.

* * *

When Caroline was introduced to the viscount, she was pleasantly surprised.

Viscount Fortescue, for his part, was enchanted.

It turned out, he'd been undersecretary in Constaninople and knew Flora's husband well.

It also turned out he was thirty-two, unmarried and boyishly handsome. Not magnificent like Simon. But fair and fine-featured, with deep blue eyes and a smile so sincere, Caroline didn't wonder that he was successful as a diplomat.

They shared stories of Constantinople over dinner while the table at large talked of dogs and deer, grouse, and salmon fishing. Later over tea in the drawing room, they discovered further interests: books, opera, cards . . . Will was first-rate at whist and like Caroline, he spoke several languages. Although he didn't care to hunt, he rode, and when he learned Caroline liked to ride as well, he insisted they go out the next morning.

Caroline hesitated. "I'm not sure . . . my duties . . ."

"Nonsense. Jane has enough staff to look after her children." With a tactful authority, he made his wishes known to his hostess. Turning back to Caroline, a moment later, he winked. "There now. It's taken care of. We ride tomorrow morning. I suspect, you could use a little holiday from the holidays."

Caroline laughed. "It has been rather busy."

"And different for you, I warrant," he said, softly.

She smiled. "Perhaps, a little."

"You should be the diplomat. I doubt you've spent your life chasing after little children."

"The children are sweet and the earl and countess are pleasant in the extreme." Her gaze was candid. "I'm not in a position to complain."

"I understand."

He looked at her with such kindness, she suddenly felt an overwhelming urge to cry. It must be the holidays, she thought, tamping down her twinge of sadness. "How early a riser are you?" she asked, quickly, steering the conversation to safer ground.

"You need but state a time, and I'll be ready."

"How amenable you are." Her tone was light and playful and suddenly she remembered another man who was amenable, but in an entirely different way.

"One learns in the diplomatic service, although tonight, obligation is not an issue." The viscount smiled. "I'm vastly smitten and more than willing."

Chapter

19

While Caroline was finding Will a welcome change from those at Netherton Castle whose passions were for hunting alone, Simon was being ushered into the Parisian home of the Comte and Comtesse Louvois.

"I promise we won't stay long, darling," the Princesse de Mornay murmured, smiling up at him and squeezing his arm. "I simply have to make an appearance."

In his usual intoxicated state—commonplace since leaving England—Simon barely listened.

"You know most everyone anyway," she added. "We won't stay for dinner." Releasing his arm, she unclasped her ermine cape and let a servant lift it from her shoulders.

Simon handed his hat and cape to a flunky and with the automatic politesse that operated no matter the level of alcohol in his blood, he turned to the princesse and offered her his arm.

The reception room they entered was filled with guests, be-jeweled, well-dressed, their bloodlines representing the oldest families in France. Since the restoration, the ancien régime had returned to the exclusivity they preferred, which meant the more interesting salons were no longer held in the Faubourg St. Germain. The best attended parties were elsewhere, the criteria for admittance not bloodlines but quick wit. Simon hadn't been to the Faubourg St. Germain since he'd come to Paris.

Inebriated or not, he knew whose home he was in and a portion of his consciousness was alert to the presence of their host as he followed Estelle on her conversational circuit of the room.

Not that he knew what he'd do when he met Louvois again. Nor whether he even cared.

Estelle twined her fingers through Simon's as they left a group of matrons seated on the perimeter of the room who immediately were abuzz with comments on the Duke of Hargreave's charming address and good looks. "Just a few minutes more, darling, and we can leave. I have to make my bows to Althea and we're free to go." She surveyed the crowd. "I can't believe she's still dressing."

As if on cue, a voice behind them exclaimed, "Darling Estelle! I'm so pleased you could come."

When they turned, Simon came face to face with Louvois, and his new wife.

"What a lovely crush, Althea. But then your salons are always so delightful," the princesse declared. "Have you met the Duke of Hargreave? Simon, this is my aunt, the Comtesse Louvois. You men are acquainted, I believe."

"What a pleasure to meet you," the comtesse murmured, surveying Simon with a practiced gaze.

"The pleasure's mine, La Comtesse." Simon bowed gracefully over her hand.

Aunt and niece exchanged quick glances of approval over Simon's bowed head.

Louvois's gaze was chill.

"We aren't able to stay," Estelle explained. "We're expected at the theater." She smiled at her aunt. "Not that we'd be missed in this crowd."

"You can't stay? Then you must come for dinner soon." The comtesse gazed at Simon from under half-lowered lashes, open invitation in her eyes. "Will you be in Paris long?"

"I'm not sure." His smile was one of politesse; Louvoise's second wife wasn't his style.

"Simon's in his vagabond stage at the moment, aren't you, darling?" Estelle patted Simon's arm.

"Tired of English cunt, Hargreave?"

Shock and affront distorted the comtesse's countenance. "Henri! That's quite enough!"

"I heard *you* were the one tired of English cunt," Simon drawled, gratified Louvois had thrown down the gauntlet; his coming here tonight suddenly had reason.

"One reaches a certain level of boredom, I suppose."

"You left her destitute."

Even Louvois's wife who may not have understood the reason for the men's antagonism, understood the tenor of Simon's voice meant danger. "Henri, don't you dare make a scene here." The comtesse spoke with the authority of rank and personal wealth. "Take this elsewhere!"

"Simon, please . . ." Estelle tried to draw him away.

He shook off her hand. "Here or somewhere else, Louvois. I'm too drunk to give a damn."

Louvois turned and walked away.

"Don't wait for me," Simon said, ignoring Estelle's stricken expression.

The duke followed Louvois from the room. The men passed down the main staircase, then turned into a corridor leading to the back of the house. Reaching a door midway down the hallway, Louvois stopped and opened it.

Walking inside, he waited for Simon to enter.

A moment later, Simon stood facing him, the metallic click of the door latch loud in the silence of the room.

"You're a long way from home," Louvois murmured.

The duke glanced around the luxurious study. "You've done well for yourself."

"When the legislature passes the law to restore estates, I'll be doing even better."

The two men facing each other were both tall, handsome men,

but Louvois was older, his privileged life destroyed in his youth and it showed in the cynicism of his gaze.

Simon was immune to any subtleties of motive or desire, save his need for revenge. He rocked forward slightly on the balls of his feet. "Name your weapons, Louvois and we can be done with this."

The comte had no intention of fighting a duel with the head-strong young man. "You're too drunk."

"I'm never that drunk. Name your weapons."

"Come, Hargreave," Louvois murmured, a fastidious delicacy in his tone. "No woman is worth risking your life."

"Who says I'd be risking my life?"

"I, for one," the comte replied calmly.

Simon's gaze held the comte's for a moment. "I don't recall you fighting in the last war—on either side."

"Don't bother calling me a coward. I'm not going to fight you. Look around you. I'd be stupid to risk this."

"You shouldn't have married Caro if you didn't want her," Simon charged, his voice bitter. "You could have held out for someone rich."

"You shouldn't have slept with her maid, if you cared about her," Louvois countered, silkily. "And you wouldn't be here now."

"She told you about that?"

"She told me a great many things when she came to me that night."

"And you took advantage of the situation."

"I took advantage of your stupidity." The comte shrugged. "And perhaps, I lost all sense of proportion when the magnificent Lady Caroline talked about fleeing England."

"All sense of proportion meaning marriage."

Louvois smiled ruefully. "She wouldn't have me otherwise."

"But eventually someone better came along. Someone with money," Simon jibed.

Louvois sighed. "I don't know why I'm tempted to be benevolent—perhaps I still remember what it's like to be young and in love like you. But Caro had left me . . . in every sense of the word, long before Althea entered my life again."

"You still shouldn't have abandoned her without a penny."

"She had nothing when we married." Henri chose to overlook the fact that Caroline's expertise at cards had maintained them during their marriage.

"She's a governess now. Did you know that?"

"Am I supposed to feel guilty?"

"You could have spared her a small portion of your new wife's wealth."

"I wasn't so inclined." He wasn't about to expose the extent of his resentment at Caro's leaving. "Nor, frankly, would Althea have been so generous. She paid for the divorce—a considerable sum, as you know."

"You owe her, Louvois. I don't care who paid for what."

"I have no money of my own until my estates are restored."

"Jewelry, then."

"My wife's? Be reasonable."

"Something to go with azure velvet," Simon noted, as though Louvois hadn't spoken. "Knowing you, you'll think of some story for your wife."

"If I find something, will you leave?" The comte half-smiled. "I'm getting too old to deal with such volatile emotion. Come, have a drink with me while I decide what Althea isn't likely to miss."

"You refuse to duel?"

"Yes, I refuse. Is that clear enough?" He dropped into a chair. "The delectable Lady Caroline has deprived us both of our reason at one time or another. For God's sake, Hargreave, stop scowling and sit down. You have to admit, we have a great deal in common. Brandy?"

"She left us both, you mean."

Louvois's brows arched. "Among other things. Did she ever win against you at piquet with that *sunk* card trick?"

Simon swore softly.

Louvois laughed. "She's good, isn't she?" He held out a glass of brandy.

"She took all my money a few weeks ago with that," Simon remarked, and after a considered moment, he moved forward.

"You're in good company then. She's won against some of the best players on the Continent."

Taking the glass from Louvois, Simon sat down across from the man he'd viewed as an archenemy for years. "So, she left you too," he murmured, his former defined resentments shading into ambiguity.

"She has a mind of her own."

Simon snorted. "And a damnable temper."

Louvois smiled. "Undeterred by her rank of governess, I presume."

"She kicked me out."

Louvois raised his glass. "To common bonds."

Simon grimaced, but he lifted his glass.

"Hard for you to admit, isn't it?" The comte's tone held a hint of edginess. "Welcome to the club."

"There's probably more."

"Men like us? I suspect so."

Simon's expression turned sullen.

Louvois leaned over and added more brandy to Simon's glass.

Simon met his gaze. "Is your wife going to come looking for you?"

"Does it matter?"

"Not to me."

"Nor me, although Althea isn't apt to be concerned so long as we keep our disagreement away from her guests."

Simon lifted his glass and smiled faintly. "What disagreement?"

Several hours later, Simon rose to leave, considerably drunker and perhaps a modicum wiser about his role in all the events that had transpired five years ago. "I'll give Caro your regards."

Louvois looked up from his lounging pose, his expression amused. "Do yourself a favor. Marry her."

"Do you miss her?"

"Not as much as you." The comte gave a nod to his surroundings. "I've sufficient compensation for my bruised ego. By the way, she once told me you were unrivaled in bed." He grinned. "Maybe that's why I didn't leave her anything."

Simon didn't speak for a time. "We've known each other all our lives," he finally said.

"I suggest you hie yourself to Yorkshire."

Simon drew in a breath and slowly exhaled. "I suppose maybe I should."

"Do you still want some jewelry?"

Simon waved away the offer and began moving toward the door. "I'll buy some in London."

"Caro used to admire rubies."

Simon stopped at the door and reached for the latch. "She used to own rubies."

"Ah. That explains it."

"I didn't ever think I'd be saying thank you to you, but . . . I guess I am." He blew out a breath. "Thank you."

"I didn't ever think I'd be saying I hope you two are happy, but," Louvois smiled, "I hope you are. *Au revoir.*"

The door shut on Simon a moment later and Louvois leaned his head back against the soft green leather of his chair and sighed.

He envied the young cub.

Chapter

20

Viscount Fortescue was intent on paying suit to Caroline and to that end he convinced the Carlisles that their children could do without a governess for the remainder of Twelfth Night. He took Caroline riding each day, bought her presents in the village—little, appropriate gifts from a suitor: beautiful leather-bound books, a hand-knit scarf, a pretty little lappet of fur to wear under her red cape, a necklace of garnets. He sent her short poems he'd written and read to her one night from a travel journal for which she'd expressed an interest.

Caroline was grateful for his attention, for the holiday he'd procured for her, for all his lovely gifts. But she was unable to return his affection and in as gentle a fashion as possible, she informed him of her feelings.

"I'm a patient man, darling," he replied.

She didn't have the heart to tell him she wasn't looking for patience. And what she wanted, she couldn't have. Or *whom* to be precise. Although she was a fool to pine for someone as selfish and faithless as Simon.

Nevertheless, she'd not been able to resolve her emotional dilemma in the weeks that had passed since she'd last seen him. Or more aptly, last screamed at him.

Wasn't it odd, she thought walking up the last flight of stairs to the third floor after another evening with Will, that she didn't have the good sense to love someone as gentle and kind as the viscount? He would inherit his father's title someday. He offered her undying love and affection, along with a compatibility of interests that was almost eerie. And he would be faithful unto death.

Why couldn't she respond like a rational human being?

Why did she yearn for a rogue and a rake who had broken her heart?

As though nature was conspiring in Simon's impassioned mission, the Channel crossing was perfect. Light waves, a steady wind, and not a storm cloud in the sky hastened his journey home. The moment they docked in Dover, he jumped ashore. Too impatient to wait for his coach to be offloaded, he hired the fleetest mount in town and made for London.

The instant he arrived at Hargreave House, he called for his secretary. Within the hour, the entry hall was filled with tradesmen, solicitors, various men of the cloth and the most fashionable modiste in the city, all waiting for their audience with the duke.

His wishes were unequivocal and to the point when he met with them, each personage given their instructions and dismissed. He was traveling north the following afternoon. He expected all his purchases and orders to be fulfilled and in his coach by then.

He didn't relish traveling for three days in the company of the minister he required, but his secretary, Gore, suggested a young cousin of his he felt would be inoffensive. A younger son of a younger son, it wasn't as though the man had chosen the church as his profession for love of the Lord.

"My cousin likes to race most of all, Your Grace, but can't afford the bloodstock."

"Capital. Have the grooms ready Templar and Castor. We'll ride ahead and have the coach follow. He's not churchy, now. You said he wasn't."

"Not in the least, sir."

"He *is* able to read the correct marriage service though? He knows that much, does he?"

"I'm sure he does." But Gore made a mental note to mark the appropriate pages in the Anglican liturgy just in case. Cousin Aubrey hadn't seen the inside of a church since he'd been granted the stipend for the honorary bishopric of Coultrip four years ago.

"Good." Simon nodded. "Excellent." He glanced out the study window at the twilight sky. "It's still early, isn't it?"

"Nearly six, sir. Would you like the chef to speak to you about dinner?"

Simon cast his eyes about the room, tapped his fingers on his desktop. He suddenly smiled. "Why not."

The chef was so alarmed when he received his summons, his knees went weak. Quickly sitting down, he wondered what disaster had precipitated his being called upstairs. He'd never personally spoken with the duke. On the rare occasions when a dinner was given at Hargreave House, the dowager duchess or Lady Adele gave him his instructions.

Mounting the stairs to the main floor, he was certain he was about to be sacked and trembling, he entered the duke's study.

Simon looked up and smiled. "Good evening—er—"

"Fenellon, sir," Gore interposed.

"Ah, yes, Fenellon. May I compliment you on your fine work."

"Thank you, thank you, Your Grace." The chef's hands were tightly clasped in an attempt to repress his agitation.

"Gore tells me you might make some suggestions for dinner tonight."

Fenellon almost fainted on the spot. It was already six o'clock. "For . . . how many . . . guests, Your Grace?" he whispered.

"Just myself. Don't take alarm." The man's face was chalk white. "Anything will do."

The duke never ate at home. Never. Fenellon had no idea what he liked. Meat, fish, game? Did he eat salads, ices, vegetables? How important was presentation? And the wine list? He had no notion what the duke preferred.

"Maybe a sandwich," Simon suggested, kindly. The man appeared distrait.

"A sandwich!" The chef's face turned from white to red in an instant. "Impossible, Your Grace! A sandwich! It would be a disgrace to my kitchen!"

Moving to the chef's side, Gore spoke quietly to him as he guided him from the study.

Returning to the study a few moments later, Simon's secretary rendered clear the chef's sudden explosion. "I believe you startled Fenellon, sir. But rest assured, we'll find you something you like for dinner."

"It's not a concern. I could go out." Simon leaned back in his chair, rested his head against the tufted leather. "On the other hand, I have no interest in going out."

"Very good, sir. Should I have Manchester bring you a brandy?"

Simon sat up. "Yes, please, and have the lights turned on." He glanced at the clock. "Good Lord, it's only quarter past six."

"Would you like to look at your mail, sir?"

Simon surveyed his secretary with an amused gaze. "If I wanted to look at my mail, I wouldn't need you, now would I?"

"No, sir—er, yes, sir." Gore began backing out of the room. "I'll call Manchester."

The duke felt as though he were a boy waiting for class to end, the hands of the clock moving as slowly as they did when he was a young student. It took four-and-three-quarters minutes for Manchester to arrive with his brandy and nine-and-a-half very long minutes before Gore came back with a tentative menu for dinner. A minute more to glance over it and give his approval.

And then twenty-one long hours stretched before him.

He had his coach ordered for half past three.

Sipping on his brandy, he mentally reviewed the required items for his journey to Yorkshire: a ring—promised by noon; a marriage license, ditto; a wedding gown—even under intense

pressure, not until three; numerous pieces of jewelry from various jewelers, ten sharp; all the papers from his solicitors, first
thing in the morning. If he didn't need that damnable wedding
gown, he could leave London by noon. He frowned. Sighed.
Poured himself another drink.

Women liked fripperies like gowns, though.

He'd wait until three.

But it wasn't going to be easy.

Chapter
21

It was the last night of the holiday festivities and whether she was weary from the frantic pace of the last fortnight or touched with the amorphous melancholy that had plagued her of late, Caroline found herself fighting back tears.

The party had retired to the great hall after dinner to enjoy hot punch and the last night of the yule log. Hundreds of candles decorated the chamber, the scent of pine boughs was fragrant in the air, the sound of laughter accompanying a rowdy game of charades resonated through the room.

And Caroline felt like crying.

Pleading a sudden headache, she excused herself and left the room. Running down the corridor until she was well away from the great hall and any guest that might wander out, she leaned back against the wall, her hands against the linen fold paneling. Drawing in great gulps of air she swallowed hard, trying to quell the building pressure of tears.

She tried to tell herself it was senseless to cry; she was so much more fortunate than most. The problems she faced were trivial compared to those without the basic necessities of life. She was well treated; her employers were kind. Her teaching duties were far from difficult; her small bedroom was cozy and warm. She should be grateful for what she had. As she tallied all the positive virtues of her life, she found herself able to swallow her tears and breathe a little easier.

But just as she was feeling more composed, she saw Will coming toward her and she experienced an unsettling rush of emotion. He was always so kind and gentle, offering her the comforts of a life she'd almost forgotten existed, reminding her perhaps of all that she'd lost. Stirring emotions she wasn't sure she wished recalled.

As he reached her, he took note of her distress, her attempt at a smile pitiful. "Tell me what's wrong, darling," he murmured, gathering her into his arms. "Let me help."

Swallowing hard, she tried to reaffirm the goodness and satisfactions in her life—the man embracing her part of that good fortune and as she rested in the circle of his arms, it seemed as though she was more in control of her emotions, calmer. A bland platitude about gratitude was looping through her mind, soothing in its implications.

"You're not alone, darling," Will murmured. "I'll always be here if you need me—for anything at all."

With a hiccupy sob, she burst into tears—because she *was* alone no matter how she rationalized.

Drawing her nearer, he held her close, implicitly offering her his strength and understanding, his affection and she clung to him and cried as though her heart were breaking.

"Let me take care of you, darling and you'll never have to cry again," he murmured, gently stroking her back. "I'll keep you safe always and ever," he whispered, brushing away her tears with the back of his hand. "Just give me the chance."

Lifting her face to his, she gave him a shaky smile. What would it be like if she simply gave in and said yes to all he offered? she wondered. Would her melancholy vanish? Would she come to love him? Would she indeed find happiness?

"I can't stand to see you so sad," he whispered, as if knowing her thoughts. "Let me make you happy . . ." He dipped his head, his eyes, blue as the skies even in lamplight, were only inches away. "Let me love you," he breathed. And he kissed her for the first time, a gentle, tentative kiss.

Inexplicably, she kissed him back. Overwhelmed and lonely, no longer certain she wished to brave the world alone, she allowed herself the comfort of his affection. But almost as quickly as she'd given in to impulse, she regretted her unguarded response. Kindness didn't equate to love in her romantic soul and no matter how well-meaning the viscount, she could never care for him the way he cared for her. Even confronting the utter disarray of her emotions, of that she was sure. She tried to pull away. "Will—no, please . . . don't."

A sudden gust of cold air swept down the corridor, swirling her skirt about her ankles, the heavy front door slammed and a voice she knew said with fraudulent obsequiousness, "Do forgive us. Have we interrupted something?"

She jumped.

Without relinquishing his hold, Will turned toward the two men approaching them, the distance between them narrowing swiftly.

"Will, please." Caroline tried to ease away. "I should go."

As though the viscount sensed some connection between the tall, dark-haired man striding toward them and the woman he loved, he shook his head and tightened his embrace.

"Will, you *must* let me go."

Although she spoke quietly, her words carried in the silence.

"You heard the lady," Simon murmured, having come to a stop a few feet away.

"This is none of your affair," Will countered, challenge in his voice, his stance, in the taut dip of his drawn brows.

"Ahem. If I may intrude . . ."

Will's gaze shifted to the man who had come up beside Simon, his cleric's collar clearly visible at close range.

"Perhaps we could discuss this like gentlemen," Aubrey Galworthy suggested, his placid expression like his voice, forbearing and mild.

Will hesitated a moment more before he let his arms fall to his sides, his reluctance obvious.

Quickly stepping away, Caroline nervously straightened the neckline of her gown, tugging up the décolletage against Simon's piercing gaze.

Simon had last seen that azure velvet gown sliding down Caro's hips into a silken puddle on the floor of her bedroom. He beat back the provocative memory with effort.

Caroline dipped her head in polite withdrawal. "If you'll excuse me, gentlemen, I'll rejoin the other guests."

"Stay."

Her chin came up at Simon's curt order. "I beg your pardon," she said, sharply.

Aubrey coughed delicately. "Your Grace, if you please, allow me to intercede." At Simon's nod, he added, "Lady Caroline, I believe Lord Blair wishes to speak with you on a matter of some moment."

"You may tell Lord Blair, I have no wish to speak to him." She turned to go.

Simon moved with quicksilver grace and blocked her path. "Surely, you can spare a moment of your time, Lady Caroline. Bishop Galworthy will attend our meeting. You'll be treated with the utmost respect."

Every word was unctuous and suave, his polite smile beyond reproach. Caroline gazed at him with distrust. "Why should I bother?"

Simon met her distrust with so guileless an expression he would have passed muster on judgment day. "We've ridden hard from London to see you." He bowed faintly. "We'd appreciate your indulgence."

The cleric moved to Simon's side. "There's no need for concern, my lady."

Why did Simon have a bishop in tow? If nothing else, her curiosity was piqued.

"You needn't talk to him, Caro," Will interposed, a dogmatic note to his voice. "If this man's attentions are unwanted, I'm here to protect you."

And there was the devil's own dilemma—whether unwanted was indeed the case. The travelers had brought with them the fresh fragrance of the outdoors as well as that of wet wool, Simon's cape beaded with the winter mist. His mud-spattered boots were leaving small rivulets on the stone flags, his black hair was sleek and wet, pulled behind his ears to keep the unruly waves in place. He looked tired, a trace of stubble shadowing his jaw. He *had* ridden hard. But he was as beautiful as ever, dark and towering, his audacious gaze heated, tempting her with its boldness. "Thank you, Will. I appreciate your concern," she acknowledged politely. "But the duke is a friend from my childhood."

She had no idea why she'd referred to Simon in such a way; she had less idea why he tempted her when a man of substance and heart was at her side. But then, perhaps she'd not been raised to honor conventional goodness so much as foolhardy adventure. And the most rash and reckless man she knew had ridden all this way to talk to her. "Why don't we use the Tuscany parlor," she suggested, turning to Simon.

"Caroline, I must protest," Will exclaimed. "Let me accompany you at least."

"This won't take long, Will," she placated. "Wait for me in the study. I'll be there directly."

Simon repressed a smile, the word, *directly*, inappropriate under the circumstances. She perhaps would be gone a trifle longer than she suspected since he'd come north with but a single aim. But since it wasn't productive at the moment to make a scene, he bowed to the man he didn't know and didn't care to know and offered his arm to Caroline.

Waving away his escort, she moved toward the small nearby room, the contents of which a Carlisle earl had brought back a century ago from an Italian journey.

Simon was in good humor, his mission going much better than he'd anticipated. He'd considered the possibility he might have to abduct Caro from the midst of a crowd of holiday guests. The privacy of the parlor had much to commend it. Although he mustn't forget her sullen-eyed beau who was currently staring a hole in his back. He mustn't lose sight of the fact that Will may or may not wait in the study as directed.

On the other hand, Caro might accept his proposal with delight, fall into his arms, they could announce their marriage plans to everyone at the castle and then ride off to a future of scented rosebuds and silvery moonlight.

Wishful thinking.

With the bishop as witness, Simon escorted Caroline to a chair in the Tuscany parlor and then explained with utmost courtesy what exactly had brought him to Netherton Castle. His proposal, he thought, was all that was required—gallant, refined, couched in politesse. He couldn't quite bring himself to go down on one knee, but in all other things, he was the model of civility.

"Are you stark, raving MAD?" Caroline cried, unheedful of his extremely civil tone, not to mention the gravity of his proposal. Jumping to her feet, practically snapping with outrage, she stared him in the eye like some small terrier about to take a bite out of his hide. "What the hell makes you think you can barge in here with a priest and a marriage license and a wedding gown—"

"And a ring, I almost forgot." Pulling a small velvet packet from his pocket, he upended it and a ring set with a huge ruby fell into his palm.

"This isn't humorous, Simon!" She jerked her head toward Aubrey. "Does he have to be here?"

His grin was playful. "I might need protection."

"Everything's a joke with you, isn't it?," she exploded. "For your information, I don't find this amusing! Nor do I intend to marry your lying, cheating, heartless, disreputable, I-don't-care-if-you-can-buy-half-of-England bloody ass!" Spinning around, she made for the door.

This time it was Simon who jerked his head toward Aubrey before stalking after Caroline. "Don't leave just yet." His voice was mild, but his fingers were biting into her flesh as he lifted her off her feet. "Let's discuss our differences," he murmured, his deferential tone as spurious as his bland smile. He set her down directly before him, her back pressed hard against his body, his arm around her waist, vise-tight. "Shut your fucking mouth," he whispered in her ear. "Wait for us outside, Aubrey," he said in a conversational tone to the man hesitating at the door. "This shouldn't take long. We'll be ready to leave soon."

The bishop paused a moment more, but the duke had paid him enough to buy a modest race stable—in advance.

The duke had been generous for a reason and he waited now for his paid retainer to make the right decision.

A moment later, the door shut on the bishop.

Once they were alone, Simon released his hold, although he took the precaution of stepping between Caroline and the door.

"*We* will not be ready to leave soon," she hissed, standing rigid before him. "You're not going to order me about like one of your underlings. How much did you pay him," she spat, "to look the other way?"

"Enough," he said, grimly, his temper barely leashed.

Glancing at the door, she smiled tightly. "Apparently. But I'm not for sale, Simon and you're not going to be able to come up here with your accoutrements of marriage and buy me like some fucking cow! Good God, Simon, do you think you can command me to marry you like you command everyone within your earthly realm?"

"I asked you to marry me," he said, clipped and terse. "Something I don't make a practice of doing," he growled. "Something I was planning to avoid for another decade at least."

"Good. Then we're both in agreement. I'll wish you good journey."

He put his hands up and the muscle over his cheekbone began twitching. "Just a damned minute. As I recall, in our last conversation, you berated me for asking you to join me in an arrangement you perceived as irregular. I thought you *wanted* me to propose marriage. Fucking make up your mind."

She glared at him. "I should be gratified, I suppose, that a fine lord like you deigns to marry me. I should be kissing your toes, shouldn't I, for having made such a great and mighty sacrifice when you could have say—Daphne—or are you still fucking Arabella who dances better than she reads? Or maybe Chloe is still available; I've been out of touch. So marry one of them; don't do me any bloody favors. I don't need you!"

"I'm not deigning to do anything," he said, grimly. "I'm not making any sacrifices, other than wasting my time arguing with you. Do you know how many days I've been on the road to get to this outland? And it's colder than hell this time of year."

"As cold as your proposal?" she sneered. "I was under the impression a marriage proposal might actually mention the word love."

His gaze didn't quite meet hers for a moment and then he said in a tautly constrained voice, "Would it help if I used the word love?"

"Help?" Her voice rose to a breathy shriek. "What would help, is if you even knew what the hell the word *meant!*"

"I know what it means," he replied as calmly as his volatile emotions would allow.

"Tell me," she said, very, very softly.

The bishop must have been listening at the door, because the sound of his breathing was suddenly audible in the absolute silence of the room.

"Exactly." And for a moment she hated him and his flagrant indifference. "Now why would I want to be married to a man who doesn't know what love is? Or what marriage involves. In case you weren't aware, it's not all about fucking."

"I suppose you'd know that better than I," he charged, a sudden edge to his voice.

"Yes, I would," she said, crisply. "Which reminds me of another reason to refuse you. Your record of infidelity is a notable deterrent even should I be willing to overlook your lack of romantic feeling. Also, you don't like the opera and you drink too much. I doubt you're sober now."

Actually, he was well on his way because he'd emptied his

flask about two hours back—added reason, perhaps, why she was getting on his nerves. "Are you done?"

She shrugged. "For the moment."

"And name me a man who likes the opera," he muttered.

"Will does."

"I might have known. I suppose he writes poetry and tells you he loves you too," he added, gruffly, already knowing the answer. "Are you thinking of marrying him?"

She wouldn't give him the satisfaction of the truth. "I've thought about it," she said instead.

"And?" He was watching her closely.

"And, nothing." Her brows flickered. "It's none of your concern."

"What if I were to make it my concern?" His voice was a low rumble.

"It would have no bearing on my decision." Which may not have been the truth a scant half hour ago when she was racked with loneliness and indecision. Simon's continuing insensitivity to all but his selfish desires outraged her.

"So you're actually thinking about marrying him?"

She gazed at him with scorn. "This is pointless. We've never agreed on anything."

"Perhaps on one or two things," he murmured, silkily.

"I hardly think sex is a basis for marriage."

"But particularly fine sex might at least make it tempting."

"On that predictable and might I add, disagreeable note, I'll take my leave." She turned to go, struck with what had become very wide discrepancies in their lives. And if anyone understood that sex wasn't enough in a marriage, she did, she thought, moving toward the door. Perhaps it was fortuitous that Simon had appeared tonight of all nights when she'd been overcome with melancholy.

His frustrating inclination to assert his authority and his utter disregard for all but his selfish pleasures had destroyed any trace of her former sadness. She felt like causing him bodily harm.

Before she reached the door, he overtook her and scooped her up into his arms. "Did I mention the bishop will marry us at Kettleston Hall?"

Her eyes flared wide. "This is an enlightened age, you bastard. You can't abduct me!"

"A shame I didn't read the same page in the etiquette manual."

"Damn you, I won't allow this!"

"Nor will I allow you to warm darling Will's bed," he said, curtly.

"You're bloody crazed! I'll warm whomever's bed I please!"

"We'll discuss your amusements at a later date, but I don't think I'll be inclined to allow you any sexual freedoms. Once we're married, you'll be mine in every sense of the word, in the eyes of God and the courts." His mouth set in a grim line. "You'll be my property."

She slapped him so hard she felt the jarring blow all the way down her spine, but he only grunted, not altering his stride by so much as a centimeter as he moved to the door.

"Damn you, Simon! Put me down!" She opened her mouth to scream, only to find her cry stifled as his mouth came down on hers with a forbidding harshness. He'd suffered her rancor with a rare tolerance that had finally reached breaking point. He'd offered her his name, title, wealth, and if not his heart, as near to that as he was able. *Damn her perverse opposition.* It was about time she recognized he was done playing games.

Reaching the door, he leaned into it, forcing her against the solid oak, the pressure of his body exacting compliance, his mouth ravaging hers, the plunging invasion of his tongue making it plain who was master and who was not and exactly what he intended to do to her. The violence left her breathless. But far worse, his brute force stirred familiar echoes of desire she didn't wish to feel, quickened and excited her, pulsed through her senses, made her wet with longing.

She was panting softly when he finally lifted his head. "Now do as you're told," he muttered. "And if it matters," he added, gruff and low, "I can say I love you."

"So, you can say it when you want sex," she mocked.

"And you can stop breaking my balls when you want sex," he returned, his voice velvet soft. "Or was that someone else I heard panting."

"Very well. You're right and I'm wrong. But you needn't go to such outrageous lengths as marriage to have sex." Her brows rose faintly and the corners of her mouth tilted upward in a seductive smile. "Put me down, lock the door and we'll have sex under this mural of a Tuscany sky in summer." If she could keep him here, eventually Will would come looking for her and she wouldn't be spirited away as though she were living in some long ago age.

"Sorry. I'd prefer my own home." Simon grinned. "But it was a good try."

Suddenly arching her back, she kicked out violently and started pummeling him, trying to break free. Ignoring her struggles, he just gripped her more firmly, opened the door and walked out into the corridor without so much as a glance for possible observers.

"Follow me," he said brusquely, nodding at Aubrey between Caroline's flailing blows.

Then he broke into a run.

He knew she was going to scream.

He also knew it wouldn't matter because he'd be out the door before anyone could stop him. He was running full out as Caroline's cry erupted. He'd almost reached the entrance hall before she drew in another breath and while the servants on duty looked startled as she screamed for help, none dared stop a noble of such eminence as the Duke of Hargreave. Although, even eminence aside, his fierce expression and formidable size would have deterred any interference.

The party in the great hall continued apace, the holiday revelers blithely unaware that Netherton Castle's governess was being abducted. While Will, dutiful and obliging, waited patiently in the study.

In anticipation of a possible hasty exit, Simon had left Templar with a groom in the courtyard. Quickly mounting, he settled Caroline on his lap with only minor difficulty considering she was fiercely contesting her removal with sharp blows to his head. Wrapping his cape around her, he pinned her arms to her sides as he put spurs to his powerful black. Tucking in the folds of the cape to protect her from the cold with one hand, he guided his mount through the passage leading to the castle gateway. He didn't wait for the bishop; Aubrey was capable of keeping up.

He nodded to the guards at the gate, but took the precaution of holding Caroline's face hard against his shoulder, muffling her cries. He didn't want to risk one of them not recognizing him in the darkness and using their weapon, although it looked as though they'd imbibed their share of holiday punch as they waved him out. But the moment they clattered across the draw-bridge, Simon whipped his horse and released his hold on Caro's head.

Let her scream. Templar had stretched out into a pounding gallop, his huge strides lengthening, picking up speed.

And no one was going to follow them on Twelfth Night.

Chapter

22

The ride to Kettleston Hall was brief and surprisingly silent. Once they'd left the castle, Caroline decided it was pointless to scream; it would be like baying at the moon. And her throat actually hurt from shrieking at the top of her lungs—as if it had done her any good, she sullenly noted. For which Simon was entirely to blame. As he was for this entire, ridiculous, senseless, outrageously outdated abduction. Why he couldn't act like a normal, well-behaved man was beyond her. Although with Simon that might be asking entirely too much. In any case, she alone was going to be in charge of her liberation and to that purpose, as she lay mute in Simon's arms, she systematically surveyed her . . . relatively limited options as it turned out.

Since Simon had what he wanted, it mattered little to him whether Caroline talked or not. But he *was* grateful she'd stopped screaming. Ignoring Caroline's outcries had stretched the limits of his patience. Taking advantage of her protesting lull, he reviewed the schedule of events planned for Kettleston Hall. Hopefully, all his directions had been received and since they were riding double, Aubrey should soon overtake them. Once they reached the house, he'd remind Aubrey again to keep the ceremony brief. Caroline was unpredictable. Like now. He glanced down, wondering if she'd fallen asleep.

She looked at him from under her lashes. "I'm planning your demise."

And then, of course, in other ways, she was completely predictable.

He hoped he wouldn't have to truss her for the ceremony.

Even having to travel by the roads, the journey to Kettleston Hall wasn't long. On reaching the drive, Simon saw the fresh coach tracks and smiled. Good. Everything had arrived from London.

Tapers were burning beside the front door, the house was alight. He took note of the facade for the first time as they rode up the drive, pleased to see his purchase had clean lines. Some regional architects were eclectic in their tendencies, thinking more was better. The simple four-square brick house, flanked by graceful wings had a pleasing purity of design. He surveyed the three stories, the windows on every floor glowing with candlelight and wondered which of the windows were those of the master suite.

He'd sent orders ahead to prepare the rooms.

And the chapel.

He glanced down at Caro and smiled. Her eyes were shut now. She was pouting. But then he knew how to alter that pout. He'd learned how years ago.

Grooms came running up as they approached the entrance, familiar faces from his home in London. He'd sent a small contingent of servants north.

Dismounting with Caro in his arms, he surreptitiously glanced at her, hoping she wouldn't make a scene. Although, scene or not, he would marry her. He'd not once changed his mind on that score since he'd left Louvois's house in Paris. And while he may not know what love was, raw desire he knew. His craving for her had consumed his thoughts, destroyed his peace of mind, and had withstood a serious attempt to drink it into oblivion.

So, he'd traveled three days over hellish roads.

And curbed his tongue at Netherton Castle.

In order to marry a woman who said she didn't want him.

In a way, he was glad Caro was so far from London.

He would have been ridiculed mercilessly by his friends had his nuptials taken place there.

While the betting books at the clubs would have been filled with predictions on the birth date of their first child—and all the gossipy females would have been counting on their fingers. They still might. He grimaced, the issue of birth dates bringing a contentious matter to mind.

The front door opened and a butler came hurrying out, curtailing Simon's disconcerting thoughts.

As the elderly man approached them, his expression took on a note of concern. "Is the lady ill, my lord?"

Simon had been wondering as much himself, both Caroline's silence and compliance unusual. "She's fatigued," he said, hoping Caroline wouldn't say something outrageous.

"I *am* tired," Caroline remarked. While she had no scruples about venting her spleen on Simon, she didn't wish to embarrass the old butler.

"Why don't we get you inside where it's warm?" Simon offered, moving toward the door. "By the way, I'm Hargreave," Simon added, turning to the butler who was keeping pace.

"So we assumed, my lord. I'm Eaton, Your Grace, and this is my wife, Mrs. Hopper," he added, beckoning to a woman who was hanging back at the entrance. "She's been housekeeper to Viscount Manley for some twenty-odd years."

Stopping just short of the door, Simon smiled at the plump woman bobbing a curtsy. "I'm hoping you can serve me as well. I presume the staff is still all in place."

"Yes, sir." The undercurrent of trepidation disappeared from Eaton's voice.

"Good. Excellent. Well, then." Simon smiled again, the relief on his butler's and housekeeper's faces revealing. He should have had Gore assure them of their positions long ago, he reflected with a small twinge of guilt.

"Yes, sir, this way, sir. Everything that you wished for has been done. If you'll follow me."

Caroline felt de trop and overlooked, like part of the baggage. If she resisted, she would only make an awkward situation more awkward. The servants didn't know them. Apparently, Simon had never been here before. Nor were they likely to help her; she too had seen their expressions of relief when Simon had told them they could stay on. No doubt they'd spent a lifetime on the estate.

And if anyone understood the uncertainty of employment, she surely did.

But was she required to marry their master because she didn't wish to put them in a position that might endanger their livelihoods? Or more realistically, would anything she did have any bearing on Simon's attitude toward his staff or their marriage?

The answer, of course, was unpalatable.

And nonplussed, she wondered what her next move might be.

"Will you behave?" Simon whispered as they crossed the threshold.

"Do I have a choice?" she whispered back.

"Good girl." He set her on her feet as though it had been his intention from the start.

"We'll see about that," she said under her breath. "I'm hungry," she announced, in a carrying voice.

Simon cast her a suspicious look, but only met a bland smile.

"What would you like, my dear?" His voice was smooth as silk, but his gaze was wary.

"Cake," she said. "And tea to start with."

Her implication that there might be some mysterious more to follow, added to Simon's unease. "We'll have tea in my apartments." Perhaps a defendable position wouldn't be out of order. "And brandy for myself."

"Yes, sir, this way." Bowing to Simon and Caroline, the butler led them to the stairway.

The rooms in the master's apartment were large, a fire lit in each chamber, the furniture new and fashionable—perhaps one of the reasons besides gambling that Viscount Manley had decimated his fortune. Eaton showed them through the suite, shut all the drapes and with a courteous bow, left them to go and fetch Caroline's tea.

Walking to where Caroline stood in the middle of the sitting room, his cape so long on her it dragged on the floor, Simon unwrapped the layers of black wool and lifted it from her shoulders. Then he lightly touched her cheek with the back of one finger. "You look tired."

"After twelve nights of parties, I have a right to be." It was a deliberate remark, meant to provoke.

He tossed his cape on a chair before replying, needing the moment of delay to curb his temper. "Perhaps I won't be as demanding as your opera-loving beau." His eyes had turned cool. "Does he like to fuck all night?"

She realized she'd made a mistake when he looked at her like that. "I wouldn't know," she said, aware retreat was called for. "He only kissed me once."

"You expect me to believe that? Maybe when you were thirteen or fourteen I might." His drawl was pronounced. "But we both know you were a precocious little girl after that, don't we?"

"Not as precocious as you," she snapped, taking exception to his remark when it had been he who had prompted her precociousness. "Was it your nanny or governess? I forget."

"Both." He smiled. "Which makes me doubly suspicious of governesses." Reaching out, he gently stroked her throat. "I'm going to have to keep my eye on you after we're married." His long fingers slowly circled her neck. "Knowing you as well as I do," he added in a whisper before releasing his light hold. He plucked at the azure velvet of her sleeve. "I brought you something to replace this," he said in a normal tone of voice, as though he'd not just given her warning. "I hope you like your wedding gown."

"And I hope you have some plan other than coercing me into marriage," she replied tartly, having been his playmate for so many childhood years, she was the last person he could intimidate.

A hint of a smile played across his mouth. "Sorry. That's my only plan."

"You're completely, bloody mad, of course. I don't suppose you've once considered how grossly unfair this dragooning of yours is? Not just to me, but think how it will look to the outside world."

He didn't care about fairness although there was no graceful way to say that. "Come, Caro, is it so awful?" he asked instead, his tone cajoling, since he understood her objections even if he chose to overlook them. "You can have your freedom. You know I'm not an ogre. I missed you, that's all." The degree and scope of that deprivation indeterminate and highly problematic.

"And what of your freedom? Tell me about that." Her words were barbed.

He searched for a mollifying answer, not sure the truth would serve. But in the end he chose candor. "I'll try to be faithful. Will you settle for that?"

"Why do I have to settle for anything?" she asked bitterly.

Because he had all the power, he wished to say. "Because I found I was miserable without you and I'd rather not lie and say I'll be faithful forever. But I'll really try."

"That's not good enough."

His brows rose. "Do you think you have a choice?"

"Do you think you can lock me up forever?"

He grimaced. "Jesus, Caro. You're asking a lot. No men I know are faithful."

"Then you should marry someone like their wives who are willing to sell their souls and honor for a wedding ring and a title! I'm not for sale!"

He abruptly turned and walked away, passing from the sitting room through the dressing room into the bedroom where he dropped into a sprawl on the bed. Staring up into the pleated silk of the canopy, he debated how best to reconcile his wishes and hers and whether he even wanted to compromise on so ridiculous a point. Men of his class were rarely faithful; he actually didn't know any who were.

But the word, *rarely*, refused to be dislodged from his brain and he was forced to confront the uncompromising reality that some men *were* faithful. He'd heard of men who loved their wives to distraction, although those husbands had not been the standards of conduct among his friends. Could he deal with the possibility that he might become such an anomaly?

And how much did it matter if he were?

He heard her footfall and waited, still not certain what he'd choose to do. Although marry her, he would. With or without force.

She came to a stop in the bedroom doorway; he could hear her breathing. Her perfume drifted into his nostrils, but he still didn't move, his gaze unfocused on the canopy overhead.

"Whoever wins two out of three hands has their way? What do you think of that?" She was feeling lucky with that piquant flush of excitement she'd known since childhood. She was going to win.

He turned his head and looked at her. She was smiling and she wasn't objecting to the marriage anymore, only the manner of it.

"My cards," he said.

"A new deck," she countered.

He sat up and grinned. "Done."

"Now I don't know if I should," she murmured, leaning against the door frame and looking at him askance. "You're too eager."

He threw his legs over the side of the bed and sprang to the floor. "Can I help it if I feel lucky?"

"Lucky meaning you won't have to be faithful?"

"No, lucky I won't have to argue with you about this anymore," he said, moving toward her, smiling.

A knock on the door of the sitting room infiltrated into the bedroom.

He winked. "Your cake, my duchess-to-be."

"Maybe by the time I eat, I'll think of some way out of this marriage, or perhaps your luck might change."

"Or yours." He already had all the luck he needed; she was here and smiling. The rest could be resolved.

*   *   *

Sitting across from her at a table set before the fire, he drank a brandy while she ate her cake and sipped her tea. The firelight gilded her hair and he wished above all things to unpin her curls and bury his face in their scented softness. Her bare shoulders and arms, burnished by the glow of the fire tempted him. Would she take issue were he to reach out and slide his hand down her slender arm? She suddenly smiled at him as though giving him leave, and a curious warmth enveloped him. And if there was such a thing as contentment, he was content.

"Don't you want any?" she asked again, offering him a forkful of a gooey chocolate confection that obviously had found favor with her. She was eating her third piece.

"Maybe later," he replied, politely as he had on the previous occasions she'd offered him some.

"Do you think you have a chef here?" she asked through a mouthful of cake. "This is quite, quite marvelous."

He shrugged. "We'll have to ask."

"Why *did* you buy this place?"

"So I could be near you."

"How sweet."

Sweetness, perhaps, wasn't the precise word to describe his motivation, but he wasn't about to ruin her cheerful mood with the base truth. He smiled. "Thank you. We try."

She made a small moue. "I don't know why I can't stay angry with you."

"Why would you want to?"

"Out of principle, of course. You have some very annoying habits."

He wasn't about to touch that very dicey subject and in an effort to distract her, he said, "Would you like to see if your ring fits?"

"That was very thoughtful of you . . . the ruby, I mean." Was the chocolate unduly influencing her mood? She was finding it impossible to be cross with him. Although when he was lounging across from her like he was, looking ever so accessible, and astonishingly handsome and dissolute in a completely unassuming and enticing way, it was difficult to resist. Although for her peace of mind, she preferred the chocolate theory.

"I knew rubies were your favorites." He slowly slid up into a seated position, set down his drink and rose to his feet. "Shut your eyes . . ."

She didn't.

Waggling his finger, he smiled faintly. "If you want your Christmas presents, you have to shut your eyes. Don't you remember?"

Tears sprang to her eyes. Her father had always said that and then Simon had. She quickly shut her eyes, but Simon had seen the telltale wetness.

"Now you have to tell me you like your presents whether you do or not or I'll cry," he teased, moving to the armoire.

She laughed, which he'd intended. "I haven't had any presents for years." A small excitement trembled in her voice.

And *he* almost cried.

He'd dictated his instructions to Gore who had written them down and sent them north with the coachman. Caro's presents were supposed to be in the armoire. Which one was the question. He pulled open the armoire door in the sitting room and surveyed several shelves of wrapped packages and Caro's wedding gown hanging from a satin-covered hanger. He'd have to give both Gore and Eaton a raise.

He still had the ring in his waistcoat pocket, but he'd selected other pieces of jewelry to compliment it and his bride's beauty. Lifting several jewelers' boxes from the shelves, he carried them back to the table and set them down. "Open your eyes, although I know you were looking." His mouth quirked in a lazy grin.

She looked up at him, feigning innocence. "I didn't see anything. Really."

"I'll have to feed you chocolate more often," he drawled, charmed by her mummery.

She winked. "Maybe I'll let you."

All her animosity was gone, her playful smile wrenchingly familiar and he felt as though he were eighteen again and neither he nor Caro had a care in the world. "I think maybe I should get down on one knee and do this properly," he murmured, suddenly unafraid of how he felt or how she would respond or whether he might be walking off the end of the earth into nothingness. Dropping down on one knee, he took the small velvet wrapped package from his waistcoat pocket, pulled out the ring and reached for her hand. "Darling Caro, would you do me the honor of becoming my wife? I find, unaccountably," he said with a boyish smile, "I'm crazed with love for you."

"Or perhaps only crazed," she murmured, their eyes on a level, hers sparkling with laughter. "And I think it must be contagious, for I find myself crazy in love with you."

He slipped the large square-cut ruby on her finger, a quick sure gesture, as though sealing the bargain. "You know what everyone will say."

"That Hargreave has escaped Daphne's lure?"

"Bitch," he said with a chuckle. "No, everyone will say they deserve each other."

"Will that be a compliment?"

"Probably not," he replied, matter-of-factly as he came to his feet. "But I would view it as such. You make me happy. It's as simple as that."

She gazed up at him, her expression contemplative. "It may not be so simple. We are frequently at daggers drawn."

"Then I shall have to constantly ply you with chocolate and presents," he teased. "And if you want romantic words darling," he added, his voice suddenly sober, "write me a list. I'll learn them for you."

Not sure Simon was serious, particularly when it came to romance, Caroline opted for a neutral response. "How very kind," she said, as one might to an offer of a dance.

"I can be infinitely kind." His voice was like velvet as he took his chair opposite her and his eyes held hers for a lingering moment. "Wait and see."

Whether it was the chocolate or his close proximity, she was fast losing her sense of restraint. "I do hope I don't have to wait long," she murmured, thinking if he looked at her like that much longer, she wasn't going to wait at all.

A fact he was well aware of, having had his share of females throwing themselves at him since he'd reached adolescence. But he wasn't about to delay his marriage, no matter how eager Caro might be. "Open these." Leaning over, he pushed the presents toward her. "Then I'll help you with your wedding gown," he took a deep breath, "or then again, maybe I won't. We'll find a maid to help you, and quickly, I'm thinking." He shifted in his chair, his erection rising. He waved a hand at the packages. "Hurry."

She loved that his impatience matched hers or perhaps he was always impatient for sex and with that thought in mind, she recalled their wager. "The cards," she said.

"After the wedding."

"Before," she said, firmly, thinking she might yet regain her sanity if she had time.

"We'll cut for it." He glanced about, then pulled open a small drawer in the table. "Ah ha." He held up a pack of cards. "Manley was always ready for a game, apparently. High card?"

She nodded.

He shuffled, the cards a soft blur in his hands and then he placed the pack on the table, straightened the edges and cut. He held up a portion of the deck, the four of clubs facing out.

She felt confident. Her odds were good with that low a number. Reaching over, she slid a small stack of cards off the pile and held it up. A three of hearts.

His smile was beatific. "After," he said. "Now, open your presents," he added because he wished to avoid any further argument. "Two of them go with your ring."

She opened her mouth to speak, but he held out a package. "See if it fits."

It was a very tiny package. If it was clothes, she was in trouble. When she ripped off the paper, she found stunning ruby earrings that matched her ring. Large tear-shaped pendants were suspended from square cut rubies, the whole surrounded by brilliant diamonds. "Oh!" she breathed, awestruck.

"You had ruby earrings years ago."

"But not like this!" Hers had been modest, a gift from her grandmother.

"Here," he said, offering her another box.

And so it went, each item of jewelry more magnificent than the last until she had a queen's ransom in jewels spread out on the table before her.

"You were much too extravagant, Simon. I feel guilty."

"Nonsense. My duchess should have her own jewels. The Hargreave lot is an old-fashioned jumble. And I doubt you'd want to fight my mother for them."

"So Isabella hasn't relinquished control of the property?"

"Not if she can help it. She feels that she earned every hectare of land and every scrap of plate after living with my father for a quarter century."

"Is she still at Monkshood then?"

He shook his head. "I drove her out with my disreputable friends arriving day and night. But I fear she took the plate and jewels and anything else she fancied. The dowager house is crammed to the rafters. I hope you don't mind?"

"You saw what I had. A satchel, no more. I don't require much."

He smiled. "Only me."

"Exclusively if you please."

"I still have three hands of cards between me and the shackles of matrimony."

"Do I have that option as well?"

"I don't want to fight," he murmured.

"Ah."

"Don't say *ah* like that. You know what the world's like."

"I do. Once I've given you an heir, I'm free to take a lover."

He scowled, but he held his tongue. He wanted to be married before he took issue with that statement. Quickly coming to his feet, he said, "I'll have a maid help you dress." He put a hand to his cheek and rubbed his stubble. "I'll wash up and meet you in the chapel."

Biting her bottom lip, she looked at him dubiously. "Are you sure?"

He'd never been so sure in his life. "Yes," he said, but on some other level—one that didn't take into account insatiable sexual desire—his certainty was less intelligible. Aware his tone recorded that constraint, he quickly smiled. "I'm very sure. Don't keep me waiting too long."

Chapter

23

The small chapel was decorated with garlands and festoons of evergreen boughs and holly. Since the Viscount Manley had been unable to heat his conservatory, his flowering plants had succumbed to the cold, but in place of their color, the servants had lit great masses of candles—on Gore's suggestion and thanks to the generosity of the duke's bank draft. A wedding banquet, fit for a king had been prepared as well . . . on very short notice, the chef had bewailed. But with his reputation at stake, he'd come up to the mark with aplomb and the help of several bottles of the duke's brandy that had arrived to supplement the viscount's depleted cellar.

The chef was very drunk at the moment, but his sous chef—Viscount Manley had lived well beyond his means—was still able to function semicoherently. When he ceased to perform his duties, Mrs. Hopper would step in and take charge. Had she not for years, before the viscount had come into the title and begun to put on airs?

In the meantime, Mrs. Hopper and Eaton were hovering in the chapel wings, waiting for the ceremony to begin. The duke had specifically detailed the order of the events and Mrs. Hopper was to play the organ for the processional. The duke hadn't charged her personally, but he had sent directions to hire an organist, and she was better than the choir director at Ainsley who played for all the local occasions and charged too much for his rather mediocre skills.

She'd worn her best lavender silk for the occasion.

The duke arrived first, looking so handsome she found herself dazzled at an age when she should have been much beyond such foolishness. She stammered rather awkwardly, particularly when he complimented her on her gown. He was really astonishingly amiable for a man of such consequence. He thanked both her husband and her for all they'd done on such short notice. And with a bow—imagine a bow from a duke—he'd taken his leave and was now at the altar speaking to the parson he'd brought with him.

Suddenly a maid came running up and Mrs. Hopper knew it was time. While the maid spoke to the duke, she moved to the organ, seated herself and glanced back to the chapel entrance.

While the duke waited and Mrs. Hopper kept her eyes trained on the entrance, Caroline was standing utterly still midway down the corridor leading to the chapel, frightened to death.

Wasn't it the groom who was supposed to be indecisive and wavering? she reflected.

Wasn't the bride the one looking forward to the thrill of wedded bliss?

Didn't she care for Simon? Hadn't she always? All right, all right . . . Hadn't she loved him even when she didn't want to love him?

So what was the problem?

Why did it seem as though her feet were glued to the floor?

She touched the rubies at her ears and throat and wrist, smoothed her palms over her gown of priceless lace and cloth of gold. The veil itself would have kept her in funds for a decade. Why wasn't she mercenary enough to move forward for the prospect of her ducal wardrobe and jewelry alone?

*   *   *

Mrs. Hopper finally twisted around completely on the organ bench and sent her husband a searching glance. He only shrugged, as ignorant as she of the reason for the delay.

Not a patient man, very shortly, the duke strode back down the aisle, shoved open the chapel doors and disappeared into the hallway.

He found Caroline fixed in place, unable to move, racked with fear and doubt.

He bent low. "What's wrong?" He spoke very softly because she was ashen.

"I don't know."

"Are you ill?"

She shook her head.

"Does something hurt?"

She shook her head again.

"The gown is fine?"

A mute nod this time.

"Do you want to keep the rubies?"

Her eyes flared wide at the oddity of his question.

"Because I come with the rubies," he asserted, his smile roguish."

"Possession is nine-tenths of the law," she whispered.

"But I'm bigger than you."

She smiled at the familiar phrase, felt the tenseness drain from her body. He'd always been bigger and stronger and . . . curiously protective of the little girl who had tagged after him in all his boyhood games. Until suddenly, he became the one waiting for her—like now. "I suppose that's as good a reason as any to marry," she said softly.

Not any worse than your last one, he wanted to say, but he was in excellent humor and grinned instead. "Darling, admit, ours is a match made in heaven or perhaps more likely on some pagan Elysian Fields, knowing us. And if I'm bigger than you, you can scream louder than me, so we're even there." Taking her hand, he placed it on his forearm. "Everything's going to be fine, darling," he said, deliberately keeping his tone soothing. She still looked skittish. "Why don't we walk down the aisle together? Or I could carry you?"

She shook her head vigorously. "You'll wrinkle my gown."

He supposed this wasn't the time to mention her gown would be in a heap on the floor before long. "I wouldn't want to do that," he said, gently patting her hand. "Did I tell you Mrs. Hopper will be playing the organ?"

He spoke of ordinary things as they moved down the corridor to the chapel, wishing to distract her thoughts from whatever was alarming her. When they reached the chapel doors, he shoved them open without hesitating, and walked in before she had an opportunity to balk.

Catching sight of the duke and his bride, Mrs. Hopper spun around on the organ bench and struck the keys with a flourish. The powerful, full-toned chords burst forth, thundering through the small chapel, rising up into the soaring cupola in crashing waves, charming the nervous bride who found Mrs. Hopper's rustic fervor enchanting.

"The music's very nice," Caroline whispered, smiling up at Simon.

He looked mildly afflicted. "I'm sorry I didn't have time to bring in an orchestra."

"Does she sing?"

His brows rose briefly. "I certainly hope not."

They were almost to the altar where Aubrey, clothed in his bishop's robes, was looking dauntingly officious.

Caroline came to a stop, causing Simon a moment of panic. "Are you happy?" Her bottom lip quivered. "Tell me we're doing the right thing—that you're happy."

He gazed down on the woman he'd known all his life, the woman he thought he'd lost forever, the one with his rubies swinging from her ears. "I've never been happier," he simply said.

She drew in a deep breath, exhaled, offered him a tremulous smile and nodded. "I'm ready."

"Good," he said, jettisoning his facetious remark about the gallows for prudence's sake. He dipped his head toward Aubrey.

"We are gathered here . . ." the bishop began.

Aubrey kept rigorously to Simon's program, the ceremony so brief, Mrs. Hopper said afterward in the kitchen that if she didn't know that the parson was genuine, she might have thought the duke was trying to pull the wool over the lovely lady's eyes.

"But I saw the marriage license, I did, and the parson had Eaton and me sign as witnesses. So the duke married her right and tight, although you wouldn't have known it from that double quick pace of that marriage."

"Might there be a reason fer a right hasty ceremony?" one of the maids asked with a sly look. "Maybe the duke wants his first-born to be his heir, no questions asked."

"She don't look in the family way," another maid countered. "I helped her with her wedding gown and she be right slender in the belly."

"We'll see now, won't we?" a footman noted. "It don't take that long fer her to show if'n the duke's got a bun in the oven."

"For heaven's sake," Mrs. Hopper exclaimed. "Can't a young couple want to marry each other in a rush because of love?"

The murmured responses were noncommittal; no one was unwise enough to disagree with the housekeeper. But most of the staff were going to be more apt to count on their fingers than subscribe to Mrs. Hopper's romantic notions.

The noble class didn't as a rule marry for love.

Chapter

24

The bride and groom entered the dining room directly after the ceremony. The room was intimate, one of the lesser halls, Caroline noted with relief. A dozen footmen were standing at attention, the duke's livery familiar and she gave him high marks for organization.

Or perhaps, young Gore was to be complimented.

"Did Gore arrange all this?" she asked, lifting her hand to the liveried staff and sumptuously appointed table.

"You say that like you think I can't."

"I'm not sure you know how many servants you have."

"Good point." He smiled. "Although, now I have you to count them for me, don't I?"

She gave him a lowering look. "I haven't gotten any better at running a household."

For which she'd always had Bessie's cousin. "Fortunately, Bessie and Rose are at Monkshood."

"Rose!" Caroline spun around as much as her train would allow. "She's with you?" she asked, a flush of excitement coloring her cheeks.

"All your staff are with me."

Her eyes widened. "Why didn't you *tell* me? I would have married you in an instant."

"Precisely the reason I didn't." He gave her a roguish grin. "I wanted to be loved for myself."

"Not for your title or wealth or charm."

He winked. "Or my good looks."

"Arrogant man. I'll have you know, I married you for these rubies," she said, lightly, touching her earbobs with a fingertip.

He glanced sideways at the line of footmen. "I need slightly more privacy to tell you why I married you. *And,*" he said, listening to the sounds of activity coming from the entrance hall, "right now, I have to bid adieu to Aubrey."

"He's not joining us for dinner?"

Simon shook his head. "He has to leave."

"At this hour of the night?" She looked at him suspiciously. "You're driving him off, aren't you?"

"No. Word of God," he could say with a clear conscience. "He's in a rush to get to a Tattersall's sale."

"You're not serious."

He nodded. "Aubrey's been waiting for Glouster's sale for months." What he didn't mention is that the Earl of Glouster's stable would have been beyond his reach prior to his meeting with Simon. "It's Tuesday next and the roads are bad as you know."

"Then, I'll come to say goodbye too." She half-turned her back to him. "Help me take off this veil."

They took their leave of the bishop a short time later, exchanging courtesies and offers to visit, as well as mutual thanks. Then Simon accompanied Aubrey to the coach, presumably to give the driver instructions.

Once Aubrey was seated inside, Simon handed him a note. "The driver will stop at Netherton Castle first. If you'll give this to Ian, personally, I'd appreciate it."

"Certainly." The bishop took the missive. "Will they come after Lady Caroline?"

"They shouldn't. I've explained as much as can be explained and we *are* married. I'm assuming that in itself will nullify anyone's objections."

Aubrey nodded, the duke's marriage was sure to make a strong statement concerning his sincerity. He didn't expect anyone in London would have bet a shilling on the duke's marrying anytime soon. "Your bride seems content . . . indeed happy," Aubrey said, perhaps needing justification for his role in so unorthodox an event.

Simon smiled. "She just required a bit of convincing. You needn't have misgivings. If Caro didn't have such a temper, we would have been married long ago."

Simon's dissolute life had given no indication of an ambition to marry, but Aubrey tactfully remained silent on that point. "Just so, Your Grace. My blessings on you both," he murmured. "Perhaps, we'll meet on the turf next summer."

"You can count on it. Caro and her father used to breed some fine racers. I expect she'll take a hand in my stable." Simon shut the carriage door, lifted his hand in salute and nodded to the driver.

As the carriage pulled away from the door, he ran his hands through his hair and slowly exhaled.

One hurtle down—the marriage was accomplished.

Two hurtles left.

Both of which would generate controversy.

He slowly turned to the door.

This time though, he wasn't going to let her run.

Caroline was waiting for him in the entrance hall, seated in the porter's chair, the skirt of her gown a pouf of lace and shimmering gold, its train trailing over the black and white marble floor.

"That didn't take long. Did you assure him I wouldn't sue him for his part in this marriage?"

Simon grinned. "I did, of course. He was relieved. Are you hungry?" he asked, opting for a less controversial topic of conversation.

"Starved."

He was surprised after she'd eaten half a cake, her answer not reassuring in terms of one of the hurtles facing him. But he smiled politely and held out his hand. "Come then, we'll sample the chef's work."

As she placed her hand in his, she met his gaze squarely. "Don't forget our wager."

"After we eat," he replied, pulling her to her feet. If she lost, she'd be sulky and if he did—that possibility didn't bear too close scrutiny. They might as well enjoy the food and champagne first.

And to that end, Simon dismissed the servants once they reached the dining room. They could serve themselves from the numerous dishes arrayed on the sideboard. And he was capable of opening a bottle of champagne.

While the newlyweds were partaking of champagne and the various specialities of the chef and sous-chef at Kettleston Hall, Ian was closeted in his study with the Bishop of Coultrip.

Everyone had been in bed when the servant had come for Ian. Fortunately, Jane hadn't wakened, twelve days of celebration having taken their toll. Ian met Aubrey in his study, the bishop immediately assuring Ian that Caroline wasn't being kept against her will. She and the duke were in fact, married. He handed Simon's note to the earl.

Ian read it quickly. "Married," he breathed. His gaze snapped up and he looked at Aubrey sharply. "Are you real?" He indicated the clerical collar with a flick of his hand.

"Yes." But Aubrey's voice indicated a small measure of his unease.

"Did he make you do this?" Ian challenged, taking note of the cleric's discomfort.

"No." If Aubrey were a religious man, he would have had to pray over the ambiguities in his answer.

"You say she wasn't forced?"

"She seemed very happy when I left," Aubrey replied, choosing his words carefully; there was no point in stirring up unnecessary debate.

Ian tapped the note. "He says I'm not to visit for a fortnight."

"Perhaps—I mean . . . their, er, honeymoon . . . might—ah . . ."

"She's fine now?" Ian dropped into a chair, a faint frown creasing his forehead. "You're sure?"

"I believe they'd planned to marry several years ago, but had some disagreement."

"Simon no doubt refused."

"I didn't get that impression."

Ian's expression registered surprise. "She refused *him?*"

"It rather seemed that way according to the duke."

"Good God! . . . er, beg pardon. But Simon *rejected?* As long as I've known him, he's been fighting off the ladies."

Aubrey cleared his throat delicately. "Perhaps fighting off matrimony would be more precise; his reputation reflects a rather different approach to . . . er, the ladies."

Ian suddenly smiled. " 'Pon my word. So, he was finally caught. I think that awe-inspiring event calls for a drink!" He came to his feet. "Care to join me, parson?"

"Perhaps a wee dram."

Ian looked back on his way to the liquor table. "You like our whiskey?"

"I grew fond of it while studying in Edinburgh."

"Our Northumberland stills are first-rate. Let's see," he murmured, surveying his choices. "Why don't we try the whiskey from Talbot vale first?"

Chapter

25

The wedding dinner didn't remain long in the dining room. Simon had more pressing interests on his mind.

Although, he was infinitely polite when he suggested, "Why don't we have the servants bring some of this food upstairs?"

Caro grinned. "You're afraid I'll spill on this gown."

He laughed. "I'm afraid *I'll* spill on your gown."

She slanted a glance his way. "You always were impatient."

It had been four weeks, three days, and twenty-one hours he wished to say, hardly an instance of impatience. "I've good reason," he said instead, rising from his seat. "I'll ring for the servants. Pick out what you want; I'll have some champagne."

The footmen were given their directions.

Picking up Caro's train, Simon draped it over his arm and offered her his hand. "So far, this marriage is going very well," he said, his smile affectionate as he led her from the room. "I'll have to write my mother and tell her she was wrong."

"Oh, Lord." Caroline made a small moue. "Do I have to take orders from Isabella? If so, I may consider an annulment." A not entirely facetious remark.

"Relax, darling. I won't let her touch you."

Her brows lifted faintly. "I'm not sure you have sufficient authority." Caroline knew Simon's mother. They'd both avoided her whenever possible during their childhoods.

"Remember who controls the exchequer, darling. She's relatively manageable."

"I hope you don't consider me in the same light."

His guffaw echoed through the high-ceilinged corridor. "Darling, you've never been manageable."

She flashed him a smile. "Thank you."

Once they reached Simon's apartment, Caroline suggested Simon wait for the servants in the sitting room. "Tell them to put all the food in here. I'm going to freshen up."

He glanced at her, her tone as odd as her mannered phrase. But maybe women had some esoteric rituals they performed on their wedding night—freshening up a case in point. "Yes, dear," he replied.

"What does that mean?"

Maybe they both were on edge. He kept his voice exquisitely noncombative. "It means, yes, dear, I will tell them where to put the food."

She looked at him. "That's all?"

He opened his arms. "I swear."

"Sorry." She exhaled softly.

He smiled. "Go. I think I can take care of this."

The footmen arrived a few moments later with the food, an extra table to hold it and several bottles of champagne on ice. Simon oversaw the disposition of the items and once the servants had withdrawn, he went to fetch Caro.

On opening the bedroom door, he came to a stop, a slow smile forming on his lips. "What do we have here?" he drawled.

"Am I a pretty package?"

She was lounging nude against a mass of pillows, all the jewelry he'd given her artfully displayed on her voluptuous form. Bracelets sparkled on her wrists and ankles, several necklaces were layered at her neck, her fingers glittered with rings, a long string of pearls was wrapped around her waist and the ruby tear-drop earrings shimmered in her ears.

He hung in the doorway, his hands braced against the door frame, his smile stretching from ear to ear. "Do you know how many years it's been since I've seen you like that?"

"But now this jewelry is mine, not your mothers."

"I always thought mother's jewels looked better on you than they did on her."

"Do you remember the ones you couldn't see?"

His eyes shut for a fraction of a second and when they opened again, a visible heat glowed in their depths. "I remember," he murmured.

"You can come closer. I won't bite," her voice dropped to a silky whisper, "unless you want me to. And if you find the hidden jewels, you win an additional prize . . ."

He didn't move or speak for a moment.

"Frightened?" she murmured.

"On the contrary." He smiled. "I was debating my options. Do you like your jewels?"

"I adore them." She adored more that he'd taken the trouble to care. Or had Gore selected these? Don't ask, she told herself. You may not like the answer. "Did you buy these?" She touched her earrings. "Or did Gore?"

"Does it matter?" He let his hands drop and stood in the door-way resplendent in full evening attire—including ruffles on his shirt front in honor of the occasion.

Be polite, some inner voice reminded her. "I suppose it does," she replied, ignoring her voice of discretion. "Actually, it does. Odd, isn't it, considering the manner of your proposal?"

His mouth quirked faintly. "I thought my proposal was courteous. Your acceptance on the other hand," his lashes lowered marginally. "And yes, I bought them," he added, understanding the answer mattered, like it mattered to him that they were married. "I knew you liked rubies and the rest"—he half-lifted his hand—"were for your amusement."

"When did you buy them?"

His brows arched as he moved toward her. "Why the catechism?"

She shrugged, her need to know as ambiguous as her feelings that fluctuated wildly.

"I bought them in London four days ago. I wanted you to have jewels of your own."

"You say that to all your paramours, no doubt."

His gaze went shuttered for a moment. "I've only said it to a wife once," he said in a deliberately casual voice, choosing to ignore her provocation in the interests of conjugal harmony. "And I must say, I find it enormously pleasing"—his hand came up in a lazy gesture—"looking at you so festively arrayed."

"I was hoping to impress you." She responded to his pleasantry with equal cordialness.

"And well you have."

"You have time, I hope."

"If I didn't, I'd damn well make time. But seeing as how it's my wedding night, you have my undivided attention." He pulled his cravat loose.

"Can you tell what's missing?"

He shook his head. He'd purchased whatever the jewelers had brought to Hargreave House and he'd not been attentive to the manner of her gifts when Caro had opened them.

"Would you like me to undress you?" she asked. "Sometimes you like it."

He dipped his head in deference to her allure. "When I can stand to wait."

"I'm glad I'm not the only out-of-control person."

For a man who had spent a great deal of time playing at love, he recognized one of the more pertinent motives behind his marriage. Only Caro made him frantic. She always had. "You noticed," he said with a smile. "But we have all the time in the world now. We needn't be out of control. Undress me if you wish."

"If I were your harem houri, I would *have* to undress you."

At her tone of voice, his gaze narrowed and he took in her sudden shifting movement. Rolling onto her side, she lay propped on one elbow, her plump breasts suspended in soft, elliptical mounds, the sweeping curve of her hips gently oscillating.

"You can feel something inside you." He watched her small rocking motion. "It must be large enough to make a difference."

"It's making a vast difference." She briefly shut her eyes. "I may not be able to undress you . . . after all."

"If you're incapable of carrying out your duties tonight, my sweet houri," he drawled, an undefined edge to his voice, "should I call for another of my harem ladies?"

How many times had she seen him like that—dark and handsome, ready for sex and play. And while he was not, in fact, some pasha or caliph with a harem, in his own way, he had one. Although his ladies were captive only to his great beauty and sexual expertise. "No, please, my lord," she said, breathy with need. "I didn't mean that. Please, let me stay. I haven't been allowed in your bed for months."

"I've been gone." His dark gaze holding hers was self-willed and commanding. "You know you're my favorite wife when I'm home," he said, a kind of disengaged promise in the mildness of his tone.

"You don't take me with you anymore," she noted with a small petulance.

He couldn't help but smile at her jeunesse dorée pose. "Perhaps, I may again."

"If I please you."

"If you don't *displease* me. You always please me with your body. It's your temper that often displeases me."

"I've changed, my lord. Ask anyone."

"We'll see. Come." He held out his hand.

She immediately rolled from the bed in a shimmer of jeweled light and delicious sensation and came to stand before him.

He ran his hands over the glittering necklaces resting on her breasts. "You do these justice."

"I'm pleased you think so, my lord."

His erection surged at the docility in her tone. "The eunuchs tell me you're progressing in your lessons." He took her nipples between his thumbs and forefingers and tweaked them lightly. "You've not had to be disciplined for your temper of late."

"I've been on my best behavior, my lord, so I could be admitted back into your good graces. You have but to test my accommodating nature, my lord, and you'll be gratified, I assure you."

With a gentle squeeze, he released her nipples. "Undress me, then, and we'll see if your temper has improved."

"You'll see it has, my lord."

"You must fold my clothes and put them away."

His instructions brought a momentary spark to her eyes, but as quickly as it appeared, it vanished. "As you wish, my lord."

"And you must be wet for me."

"I am, my lord."

"I'll see for myself. Later . . ." He pointed at the buttons on his waistcoat.

And she did as she was bid. His coat and waistcoat were removed and folded away, his shirt as well.

"Now, my shoes," he said. "Kneel."

That small hesitation again, but she obeyed, the descent to her knees, shifting the object inside her, bringing her to a breathless standstill.

"Are you capable of serving me?" He touched her bent head.

"Yes." She drew in a shallow breath. "Yes, my lord."

He lifted one foot and she slid off his evening shoe, each movement intensifying the throbbing ache deep inside.

"Look at me." He snapped his fingers. "Show me how wet you are."

With effort, she concentrated on his words, gazing up past his blatant erection to meet his eyes.

"Put your finger in and show me that you're ready." So might some satrap speak, with utter authority.

"Here, my lord?" Her voice trembled, all sensation focused on her pulsing need.

"Yes. There. On your knees."

Gently stroking her head as though she were a favorite pet, he watched her finger disappear between her legs, saw her shudder faintly, his erection rising higher in response. A moment later, having regained a modicum of composure, she raised her hand to him.

"Bring it closer," he commanded.

And she lifted her hand higher.

Her finger was drenched with glistening liquid. He touched it lightly, scooping up a dab of fluid on his fingertip. He raised his finger to one nostril. "I like your smell," he said, as though he were her vetting agent. "I always have."

"You used to say you'd know me in the dark, my lord."

He smiled. How many times had he inhaled her fragrance in the dark. "I'd know you anywhere." Moving his hand, he placed it near her nose so she could draw in the scent of herself. "You're in rut, I'd say. Are you ready for me?"

"I am, my lord. May I, in all humbleness, ask the same of you?"

He glanced down. "Open my trousers and see for yourself."

"Would you prefer me kneeling or standing, my lord?"

He felt his penis swell at the sudden image that came to mind. "Kneeling. So you can take me in your mouth."

"Yes, my lord."

How did she do it? Make him want her even more with that breathy acquiescence? Willing women were a norm in his life, so it wasn't the compliance, but rather, knowing how rarely Caro yielded her independence that brought him to rut.

All his senses were riveted on her touch as she slid his buttons free and eased his trousers down. Stepping out of them, he kicked them aside, suddenly past any obligatory folding of clothes. And when she fumbled with the small pearl buttons on his undershorts, he muttered, "I'll do it."

A second later he was stepping out of his shorts and a second after that, he sucked in his breath. She'd taken his penis between her hands and was forcing the stiff length downward to her mouth. As she touched the small slit in the tip with her tongue, his breath caught in his throat and when she slid the engorged head past her lips and into her mouth, he felt the silken friction jar his body like a hammer blow.

Tamping down a ramming speed mentality, he grasped her ruby earrings, exerted a slight pressure and tipped her face up so he could see her eyes. "So docile, darling. You *have* improved," he whispered, her eyes huge, her mouth stuffed full. "If you continue to please me, I'll send for you more often. Would you like that?"

Unable to speak, she nodded as any well-trained houri would.

Her meek submission perversely pleased him; he hadn't realized he was despotic. Or perhaps other women had never inspired his possessive impulse. "Take a little more, darling." He pulled gently on her earrings, drawing her closer and another portion of his erection disappeared into her mouth. "Do you like servicing me?" His voice was hushed, fresh blood pumping into his rigid penis with each powerful beat of his heart.

She nodded; she couldn't do more.

"Would you like me to come in your mouth?"

She shook her head, wanting him inside her.

His voice went soft. "Are you refusing me?" And he pushed in further, moving one hand to the back of her head to hold her in place.

She growled, a low, moody sound that vibrated along his turgid length as though in warning. Then she bit him. Not hard, but enough to gain his attention before pulling away.

"Are you refusing me?" he asked again, not in play this time, his voice oddly constrained.

She sat back on her heels, a ravishing surge of lust streaking upward with her heels pressing into her bottom. "I'm as selfish as you," she said on a caught breath. "And dying for you. You please me now."

"Why should I?" He smiled faintly. "If I'm your master and you're my houri."

Her green eyes were dark with passion, the rubies and pearls glittering bright. "You must do it for love," she said.

He hesitated, gazing down at the lush woman at his feet—his wife . . . strange, strange word. "For love," he murmured, uncertainty echoing in his words.

"If you oblige me, I might be induced to obey your orders on occasion as well."

He grinned; the Caro he knew had spoken. "If it's worth your while, you mean."

"You might find it worth *your* while to look for those hidden jewels. Have you thought of that?"

"You always were a little hussy," he murmured, intrigued and perhaps more remarkably, willing to defer to her. Bending down, he lifted her into his arms. "Very well, la duchesse mine, let's see what you're hiding from me."

She savored the beauty of the word, *mine,* feeling as though she was part of Simon somehow, as though she was no longer alone. And whether he knew or whether she fully knew what the future would bring, she was happy. She purred low in her throat from sheer joy and also from the luscious pressure of the jewels inside her. With her legs draped over her husband's arm and the slight jarring movement from his stride, enchantment was taking on another more tangible form.

If not aware of his wife's affectionate musing, Simon understood the physical manifestations that elicited that purr. "Maybe I should just walk around the room while you come."

Her gaze was heated. "What a marvelous idea."

"If I was grossly magnanimous, I might, but I'm as selfish as you."

"A fact well known in the world at large."

"One can only hope your selfishness isn't as well know as mine."

"If I wasn't so attuned to my sexual desires, I might take issue with your male double standard."

"But since you are . . ."

"And you as well."

"We'll fight later," he said with a grin, gently placing her on the bed. "Now do I get my prize?"

She patted the bed and the bracelets on her wrist glittered and sparkled.

But he didn't lie down beside her. He moved her legs enough so he could sit cross-legged between them, his knees brushing her thighs, the light-weight foretaste of his strength and power. But he touched her mons with a delicate brushing stroke. "Do I have to guess, or may I look?"

"Guess."

"Not the pearl necklace." He tapped the rope of pearls wrapped around her waist. "And it looks as though a great many rubies are accounted for." Leaning forward, he ran his palms over her throat and breasts, then down her arms so she felt the metal settings sink marginally into her flesh. "But there were some diamonds weren't there?" he said, softly, "with pearls . . ."

"Maybe."

"And if I were to press here, just a little," he placed his palm on her pouty vulva. "Would you feel that?"

It took her a moment to respond, for the strumming pleasure to calm enough for her to speak. "You're an excellent husband."

"How excellent?" he whispered, increasing the pressure of his hand.

She moaned softly and lifted her arms to him.

"Do you want me inside there, too?"

She hesitated briefly and then nodded.

"Are you sure?" The words were heated, bluntly sexual and perhaps not a question after all.

"Does it matter what I say?" She'd heard the surety in his voice.

"Maybe," he murmured. "Let me know." Spreading her thighs wider with a gentle nudging touch, he moved between her legs with a fluid grace, readying himself to enter her.

She watched his muscles coil and flex as he shifted his weight, his lithe power always a flagrant aphrodisiac—like his sexual talents. And she felt a renewed glow of happiness quite apart from the heat of passion scorching her senses. He was hers by some curious act of fate—at least now, this moment, she more practically reflected. Curling her arms around his neck, she ran her hands over his muscled shoulders and waited, aching and fevered.

He was fairly certain what was inside her, but preferred erring on the side of caution. Gore had liked the pearl and diamond bracelet enough to call his attention to it. He should fit if it was the pearls.

But he slipped a finger inside her first, just to be sure. This was his wedding night, after all. He intended to be up all night and for that, he'd want his wife unscathed.

"Pearls," he whispered, touching the bracelet that was strung with small diamonds separating the pearls. Looking up, he smiled at Caro. "We should manage with those. They're small."

"Soon, I hope," she murmured, trembling at his touch.

"Yes, dear, your servant, dear." His voice was low, his finger running the length of the bracelet, smoothing it straight along the length of her vagina. "Stop me anytime," he whispered, beginning to enter her, holding one end of the bracelet at the very entrance to her sleek passage. "I don't want to hurt you."

He moved forward slowly, the pressure of his penis forcing each pearl into his flesh and hers, the unreeling friction curling with tantalizing rapture through their heated senses one pearl at a time until he was lodged deep within her body.

"I'm moving back now." The pressure was so acute, he felt she needed warning.

"No, no . . ." She clutched at him. "Stay."

He did for a lengthy interval while she panted in little delirious inhalations and then he moved back just a fraction while she shuddered in his arms.

"Oh, God . . ."

Understanding that particular heated supplication, he moved marginally again and then once again, settling into a rhythm of limited penetration and withdrawal that took all his considerable restraint to maintain.

The first time Caro climaxed, she said, "Thank you," afterward with such breathless charm he was reminded of a young girl he once knew. And when she said, "More," brief moments later, he was reminded of a young lady he once knew. Perhaps he was in a particularly generous mood, because he even disregarded her fretful insistence when she clutched at his shoulders the next time and said, "Right now, damn it," like some spoiled bitch.

She was, after all, his darling little bitch.

After she climaxed numerous times, he finally gauged his hot-blooded wife sufficiently satisfied and withdrew for his own long delayed orgasm.

But as he pulled out of her jeweled interior, her eyes flew open. "What are you doing?"

It was impossible to speak, his orgasm already rushing downward.

She pounded on his chest in outrage.

But he only tightened his grip on her arms and held her down, his surging, shuddering climax impossible to staunch, all sensation centered in the fevered, orgasmic deluge. He poured his long-contained semen in spurting, gushing jets onto her stomach, gasping at each gut-wrenching spasm, heedless to all but consummation and lust. Until lengthy moments later, completely drained, panting, he slowly opened his eyes to meet her furious gaze.

"What the hell are you doing?" she hissed.

It took him a pulse beat to understand, to bring himself back from orgasmic paralysis. "Nothing," he muttered, rolling off her, shutting his eyes for a fleeting moment. He and his father had rarely agreed on anything, but on the issue of paternity they had. And after the warm embrace he'd interrupted at Netherton Castle, he was taking no chances on the paternity of his heir.

"Don't tell me nothing, damn you!" Surging upright, she swung at him, landing a vicious blow.

He winced, but he didn't retaliate, steeling himself instead for the inevitable confrontation. He rubbed his stinging jaw. "I thought it might be a good idea to wait."

"For what pray tell?" she spat, pulling out the pearl bracelet and flinging it at him.

He dodged it deftly and it hit the wall with a splat. "You know as well as I do, for what," he said, looking at the stain on the wall-paper.

"I'd like to hear it from you."

"All right," he said, gruffly, turning back to her. "I don't want any question about paternity. I thought it might be wise to wait for your menses."

"You don't trust me."

He didn't answer.

"I can see why someone like you wouldn't trust anyone. You've been telling charming lies to women for years," she said, tersely.

"Don't get righteous on me," he brusquely rebuffed. "I know you, and if that man only kissed you once, he must be a fucking eunuch!"

"It would be impossible for Will to simply be a gentleman?"

His glance was derisive.

"Did you ever consider I might not have *wanted* to kiss him?"

He snorted. "You?"

"Bloody bastard!"

"No, I'm not. And that's the point."

"And I have nothing to say about this?"

"Not at the moment." His voice was as adamant as hers.

"And when might I?" she inquired, rudely.

"I'm not arguing about this."

"No matter what I say, you won't believe me?"

"Jesus, Caro, consider our history," he returned crossly. "You don't trust me and I don't trust you."

"I not only don't trust you, I *despise* you."

"Fortunately for me, that never interferes with your fucking," he said with withering sarcasm.

"It certainly will now. You won't touch me," she snapped.

It was a particularly inflammatory phrase under the present circumstances; marriage had been an extraordinary undertaking for Simon. He wasn't likely to concede his conjugal rights. "I'll touch you when and where I wish," he growled.

Scrambling away, she tried to roll from the bed, but he caught her around the waist and swung her around. Dropping her on her back, he said, "Don't move," in so unyielding a voice, even in her defiance, she obeyed.

Ignoring her virulent gaze, he wiped her stomach dry and then cleaned himself with a fastidiousness she took note of with rancor, knowing what dictated his caution.

When he was finished, he shoved the sheet aside and leaning back on his hands, contemplated her as though debating the manner of his assault. "Tell me about Will," he said. "In case it should matter."

"I don't choose to. You're wrong. You'll find that out soon enough," she finished, fretful and sullen.

"How soon will that be?" Soft, dulcet words that belied the flinty harshness of his gaze.

"You'll have to wait and see, won't you?" she snapped, her temper rising. She was never docile long.

His jaw tightened. "I hope I don't have to wait nine months."

"For your information, everyone's not a gross libertine like you."

"You never had any trouble keeping up." His brows arched upward in derision. "Or setting the pace on occasion."

"I must have been crazed."

"That's one way of putting it," he jibed. "Let's hope you didn't become crazed too often at Ian's. Remember, I know what you're like." His smile was tight.

Overcome with a moment of discomfort, she wondered if Simon was more right than he knew. Would she have given in to Will at some point? Would she have succumbed to his affectionate advances?

Was her self-righteousness unfounded?

"You surprise me, darling. No biting retort? How many men *did* you fuck in the last five years?"

"Considerably less than your record with women, I'm sure."

"That's not a reassuring answer."

"If you were looking for a virgin, you should have thought of that before you forced me into," she half-lifted her hand, "this bizarre arrangement."

He didn't reply for a moment. Nothing remotely rational had entered into the compulsion that had brought him from Paris to this marriage bed. "Well, since I obviously didn't find myself a virgin and we *are* married," he murmured, not unfamiliar with impulse in his life, "we might as well take advantage of our un-limited opportunity for fucking."

"If only such a gallant invitation had put me in the mood," she noted with exaggerated sweetness.

His smile was insolent. "Would you care to make a wager on how long it would take to get you in the mood?"

"We already have one unfulfilled wager." Her gaze was chal-lenging.

"Ah . . . the one on fidelity," he remarked, as though he'd not been evading the issue all night. "Why don't I get the cards and then we can get on to more interesting wagers." And he left the bed without so much as a warning glance for her.

For a flashing moment she debated whether she could run. And if so, where? Rising on her elbows, she surveyed the room, looking for options.

He turned just before exiting the room, his mouth twitching into a grin. "Did I mention I have guards inside and out?"

He was gone before the pillow she flung at him reached its tar-get and all she could do was curse her stupidity. No wonder there had been a dozen footmen at dinner. The spectacle had nothing to do with Gore's organizational skills. And the familiar grooms who had greeted them when they'd arrived. They, too, weren't simply there to ease Simon's stay. Instead, he'd taken the pre-caution of bringing a phalanx of guards from London for his own express purpose.

To keep her captive.

To make sure she didn't run.

To play duenna during their sojourn at Kettleston Hall.

Which undisclosed period of time was no doubt carefully planned as well.

Damn his iniquitous soul.

Chapter

26

She was dressed in a man's navy-blue silk robe and seated on a chair when he returned with the deck of cards.

"You're fast," he murmured, taking in her attire. "Although I should have had Gore send up something closer to your size."

"Is this yours?" Loathing filled her voice.

"Sorry." He grinned. "Maybe you should take it off."

"And maybe I'm not a stupid ingenue. Just cut the cards."

He sat across from her, shameless in his nudity, his bronzed skin dramatically appropriate against the viscount's fashionable green, striped, silk-covered chair with gilded sphinx heads for arms. "Do you feel lucky?" he inquired, the tenor of his voice unabashedly cheeky.

"Perhaps if I weren't prisoner, I might," she petulantly replied, annoyed at his nonchalance. "What are we playing?"

He gestured at the deck of cards on the table between them, his wide muscled shoulders looking wider as he leaned forward. "Your choice, La Duchesse."

"Piquet."

"Your favorite."

She detected a hint of sarcasm and relished it. So he remembered her winning that night at Shipton. And Kettleston Hall proved as providential; she took the first hand by thirteen points.

Perhaps everything in this marriage wasn't completely biased, after all, she reflected, pleasantly.

But then Simon won the second hand.

Although, just barely.

"Let me shuffle before we cut for deal," she said, looking for whatever advantage she might considering the dead heat. Rolling up the sleeves of her robe, she gently flexed her wrists and shuffled.

They cut for dealer.

Hers was high, her advantage again.

Five minutes later, she was twenty points ahead and permitting herself to indulge in the smallest degree of elation.

Simon was about to lay down his last cards.

He glanced at her as he placed them on the table. *"Quartorze,"* he said, softly, spreading out four kings.

Sweeping the cards from the table in a rage, she jumped to her feet and stormed out of the room. It was a childish reaction of course; she fully realized it. But *fifty-six points! Four kings!* How bloody rare was that? she fumed. Must he *always* win? Would she always lose? Had he cheated? she suddenly wondered. And if it would have made an iota of difference, she would have stalked back into the bedroom and accused him.

But even had she won their wager, what were the chances he would have complied?

Certainly his past conduct gave her little cause to hope.

She stood in the doorway of the sitting room. Furious, inexpressibly frustrated . . . and—she decided, taking in the delicious array of sweets on the table—maybe just the tiniest bit hungry.

Dessert—actually, several desserts . . . and a great deal of champagne. That was what she needed. And then Simon could be as infuriating as he pleased. At least she wouldn't care.

Although, she thought, still highly exasperated, perhaps a modicum of revenge would be even sweeter.

Why not call for some of the guards to serve her? she decided, moving toward the apartment door, feeling a small gloating satisfaction for the first time since Simon's irritating and irrational stand on paternity.

"Don't bother."

His voice was amused and she turned from the door, her hand slipping from the latch.

"I'm not going anywhere." Her expression was one of cloud-less innocence.

"They won't come in."

"I don't know what you're talking about." she replied, virtu-ously.

He lounged on the threshold of the sitting room, bronzed, honed, male splendor in repose, one shoulder resting against the door frame. "I'm interested in exclusivity; the guards have been warned."

"I resent your insinuation." She smoothed the skirt of her robe.

"Let's just say I'm a cautious man," he murmured, taking note of her nervous gesture. "Or were you calling them in to discuss the furniture arrangement?"

"If you must know," she said, churlishly, wondering if she was to be constantly checkmated, "I was going to bring them in to ir-ritate you."

"No need to go so far. I'm already irritated by the fact that you fucked that man at Ian's."

Caroline scowled at him. "This obsession of yours is ridicu-lous. Why don't we simply bring Will over and he can tell you that we only kissed once?"

"I expect he'll say whatever you want him to say." Simon's tone was dismissive.

"Will is a man of honor." Each word snapped with indignation.

"Good. Fine. I believe you." He moved to the table and lifted a champagne bottle from the monteith bowl. "Do you want some of this?" He'd know soon enough if she was pregnant, and if she wasn't, he'd see that she was carefully guarded until she was. He didn't plan on sharing his wife.

She refused to answer. Did he think everything was resolved now that he had thwarted her again? That she wanted to share his champagne? . . . Or anything of his for that matter—*damn him!* But regardless of her annoyance, she found it difficult to ignore the perfection of his lean, muscled body as he moved about the room or more unnerving yet, to avoid looking at his magnificent penis—aroused as usual. Which fact was doubly annoying, considering both his dissolute past and the wager he'd just won.

"Are we sulking?" He shot her a glance before dropping into a chair. And then apparently indifferent to her humor, sulky or not, he raised the bottle to his mouth and drained half of it.

Caroline proceeded to deal with her frustration in the time-honored female answer to impediments and rage—dessert . . . in this case, a charlotte russe with pistachios, one of her favorites; a meringue with berry sauce; and two chocolate confections that would go a long way toward improving her mood. Picking up her own bottle of champagne from the bowl on the table, she took her restoratives to a chair as far away from Simon as the room allowed.

At her deft uncorking of the champagne bottle, her husband's brows drew together in a scowl. "Where did you learn to do that?" he asked, a surly note to his voice. In his experience, only females in the demimonde who waited on their client's every wish developed such skills.

"I believe you taught me." Her smile was treacle sweet. Having been on the fringes of the demimonde during her exile in Europe, she knew what was causing Simon's scowl. "It's been very useful on numerous occasions."

"Fuck you," he said, not at all agreeably.

And her sweet tone turned even more cloying. "There's no need to immediately bestir yourself, darling. We have a lifetime ahead of us to indulge in that activity. Although, with luck, you'll soon find interests elsewhere."

"You, however, won't." Each word was implacable.

"We'll see."

He looked at her from under the dark fringe of his lashes. "No, we won't."

"Do you think you can watch me every minute?" she purred, enjoying her piquant moment of retaliation.

"Someone on my staff of hundreds certainly can."

She didn't reply for the time it took her to put a forkful of chocolate mousse into her mouth and wash it down with a lengthy draft of champagne. "We'll see about that, won't we," she eventually said, her gaze angelic. "In the past you often spent a great deal of time in the brothels. That will allow me a certain—shall we say—freedom of movement? And your servants have always liked me, you know."

He growled deep in his throat, the sound too shockingly literal for his peace of mind. "God, Caro, you're going to drive me crazy," he muttered. "Although, I should be used to it by now."

Taking note of his less arbitrary tone, she paused with a forkful of meringue poised inches from her mouth. "Perhaps we could come to some amicable agreement. It's a common enough arrangement in the ton, is it not? Most fashionable couples lead separate lives and still manage to keep up appearances in the most civilized way."

"If by separate lives, you refer to sexual freedom, absolutely not."

"Are you speaking of your sexual freedom as well?" she remarked through the meringue melting in her mouth.

"You lost the wager, darling. Not I." His voice was unutterably bland.

She sighed in a blatantly theatrical way that put his teeth on edge. "Unfortunately, I've never taken orders well," she murmured, scooping up another portion of meringue before meeting his gaze. "You're aware of that minor flaw in my character I presume."

"And nobody touches what's mine," he drawled, each word underlaid with a steel inflexibility. "If you weren't previously aware of that unflinching principle in my character, consider yourself warned."

She lifted her forkful of meringue in salute. "It should be interesting then . . ."

He raised the bottle in his hand in a negligent gesture. "Take off that robe and we'll see . . ."

"You don't really think I'm likely to do that, do you?"

"Actually, I know you will."

"And why is that?" she asked licking the meringue off the fork in a particularly provocative way.

"Any number of reasons—most of them having to do with your unquenchable sexual appetite." He set his bottle down. "I could show you."

"Don't bother."

"It's no bother. In fact," he said, rising from his chair, "I look forward to your education."

"I'm not frightened, Simon. If that's what you're trying to do." But she set down her plate and fork.

"Nor would I want you to be frightened, darling." But his dark gaze belied the softness of his voice and he was steadily advancing. "On the other hand," he murmured, "you may need some schooling on your wifely duties."

"Do husbands have duties as well?" She refused to show fear, although she understood she was quite alone and well guarded.

"I'm not sure. We can discuss it later if you like."

"Why not now?" She had to look up because he was standing directly before her.

"Mainly because I don't wish to."

"Do you expect me to tremble before you?"

"Certainly not. Although you do tremble in passion on occasion, do you not?"

She wouldn't answer. He was annoyingly right, as he was annoyingly imperious.

"Are we sulking?"

"Don't press me, Simon. I'm not in good humor with you."

"I know the feeling."

"Even if it were true about Will and it's not, for you of all people to take issue . . ."

"I'd prefer not giving my title to a byblow."

"And I prefer you believe me."

"Time will tell."

"Lord, I dislike you righteous."

"I'll try to fuck you in a different frame of mind. Take off that robe."

She gazed at him, hot-tempered and sullen. "You're the last person I want to have sex with."

"I'm the only person you're going to have sex with. Take off that robe or I will. I'm not in the mood to play."

She didn't move.

Leaning forward, he nimbly opened the robe tie and slipped it from around her waist with a light jerk of his wrist.

As she moved to rise, he pushed her back, looping the silk tie around her wrist in the same smooth motion.

"Simon!" In vain, she pulled on the tie.

He had already secured her wrist to the chair arm. "Just a minute, darling," he murmured, as though she'd been speaking about something innocuous and sweeping the tie once around her waist, he held her against the chair back with his forearm while he tied her other wrist to the chair arm.

Only mere seconds had elapsed.

He stepped back to admire his handiwork.

Speechless with rage, she glowered at him.

"You look very pretty."

"Trussed up like a Christmas goose?"

"No, like a succulent, lush, alluring wife who I expect will soon be in a much improved mood."

"Not likely," she snapped, although against her will, her gaze was drawn to his erection—very near and very large and lamentably a magnet to her treacherous cravings.

"Do you like it?" he murmured, taking note of her gaze.

"Not at the moment," she muttered, wrenching away her gaze, her perfidious sensibilities responding to his swelling erection with a surge of desire.

"Maybe we could induce you to think of us with more fondness," he said gently, leaning near to slide his robe down her shoulders. The fabric caught at her bound wrists and shifting his attention, he opened the front of the robe, pulling it away from her body so she sat nude before him—framed in navy silk.

"Your nipples are hard."

"It's cold."

"You don't look cold."

She was flushed pink, her breasts noticeably rising and falling, her breathing agitated.

"I could warm them."

"No!"

"Don't say no to me, darling." He touched one nipple with a light flicking touch. "Lesson one in wifely duties." And taking a pink crest between his thumb and forefinger, he compressed the pliant tissue, delicately rolled it against the pads of his fingers, stretched it slightly, forcing her to sit up straighter. "Can you feel that?"

She sucked in her breath. "No." But there was no longer vehemence in her tone.

"Is that so," he murmured. Dropping to his knees, he moved between her thighs, forcing them open. "See if you like this better." Cupping one of her breasts in his hands, he lifted it as he bent his head, and taking her nipple between his lips, he drew it into his mouth. Gently kneading her breast, he sucked on her taut nipple with unerring pressure, tugging it slightly as he suckled so she felt the tingling rapture ripple down to her heated core, down her thighs, into the heavy, aching flesh of her vulva.

She felt it most intensely, where her engorged clitoris and unsated lust waited for surcease.

He didn't have to ask again whether she liked what he was doing to her. He could tell. And when he moved to her other breast, she arched her back against the exquisite pleasure and pressed into his mouth.

"You want more?" he whispered, lifting his head.

"Please," she breathed, beyond questions of sovereignty, aroused and ravenous, aching to feel him.

"Are you ready for me? A wife must be ready when her husband wants to have sex with her."

"Yes, yes."

He dropped his hands from her breast and sat back. "Will I slide in easily? I can't have my wife unprepared to receive me."

"Yes, yes . . . please, Simon—I'm more than ready."

"I think that would be for me to decide. Open your legs wider."

She instantly complied and he slid three fingers into her pulsing core with unimpeded ease. He gently stroked the sleek flesh while she panted and strained against his hand. "Very nice." His voice was velvety. "Are you ready to perform your wifely duties?" He slid his fingers deeper.

"Yes, yes," she gasped. "Whatever you want."

He kissed her lightly. "I'll untie you then."

"Thank you—I mean it, Simon—thank you very much."

He smiled faintly, withdrew his fingers and came to his feet. "Get into bed and wait for me," he ordered as he began to untie her.

Her lashes came up, her eyes filled with entreaty. "Will you be long?"

"I don't know. You must wait. Dutiful wives wait. I'll come to you when and if I decide to fuck you."

As he pulled the last knot open and she was suddenly free, she lunged forward and seized his testicles in a punishing grip. "I'm not in the mood to wait," she said, fretful and peevish and strongly averse to further delay. "Perhaps," she added, very, very softly, "this would be a good time to discuss husbandly duties."

"If you squeeze much harder," he murmured, standing utterly still, "you're going to lose whatever chance you have for sex tonight."

Her brows arched upward. "If you don't oblige me, what do I have to lose?"

"Compromise?" he breathed, every muscle taut with restraint.

"I'm open to compromise," she replied, dulcetly.

"Sex now?"

"Here?"

"It's up to you."

She grinned. "You can be so agreeable, darling. I think it's your most charming trait. Would you like to sit or stand or lie?"

"How about all three?"

In answer, she released her hold and winked at him. "Perfect."

He could have retaliated had he wished, and for a brief moment, he considered the possibility.

But more pressing, overwrought urges impelled them both and issues of conjugal duties were abruptly dismissed in favor of orgasmic bliss. Very frenzied, heart-stirring, unbridled orgasmic bliss.

Caro even overlooked Simon's cautious withdrawal at climax.

And Simon overlooked the fact that his wife appeared to be disturbingly insatiable.

Chapter
27

The next few days were an unrelenting contest of wills, the battleground confined predominantly to the bedroom. Sometimes Caro won and other times Simon prevailed, both equally stubborn and uncompromising on issues of independence. But when it came to sex, they grudgingly came to the conclusion that they shared an astonishing compatibility.

Which considerably muddled the other areas of contention.

On the fifth day, late in the morning, while they were still abed, temporarily reconciled on their treaty ground of sexual gratification, Simon withdrew for his orgasm, glanced down and suddenly smiled.

He'd not realized how profound his misgivings until he was struck with the full force of his relief.

Lying beside her a moment later, his heart still beating furiously, exhilaration inundating his brain, he murmured, "It started."

There was no need to question the unspecified phrase after the contentious nature of the last few days. Sitting up, Caroline looked down, saw the minute streak of blood on the sheet and turned to her husband. "You owe me an apology." Rapping him on the chest, she put a hand to her ear. "I'm waiting . . ."

"Yes, dear." Which was all he was capable of saying with the image of Caro kissing that man at Netherton Castle still inciting an ungovernable jealousy. In his experience, grown men and women didn't exchange single kisses. In his experience, Caro *certainly* didn't exchange single kisses—regardless of her protestations. And her insatiable sexual appetite of the last few days hardly induced him to change his mind. "Get dressed," he ordered, throwing his legs over the side of the bed. "We're off to London. You need some clothes. I need to get back to my life. And I haven't fucked you in a carriage for years."

"And you're not likely to now, either, unless I hear an apology," she retorted, not moving.

"You think I and my guards can't throw you in the carriage?"

"I think I need an apology. And then I'll consider whether I want you *or* your guards to touch me."

He was standing beside the bed, his smile benign, all suddenly right with his world. "Your father has much to answer for, darling. I've never known such a difficult, obstinate female."

"My hearing is very good, however." She put her hand to her ear once again.

"Good God, I apologize. Now, may we leave?"

"Why should I?"

Because he had no intention of allowing her out of his sight, he wished to say and he no longer had reason to stay. The unknown Will was now free to fuck whomever he pleased. It wouldn't be necessary to kill him. "I thought you might like to pay Daphne a visit," he said instead, his grin a flash of mischief.

"You do know how to tempt a woman," Caroline murmured, a sportive light in her eyes.

"And then there's mother. You two could discuss the disposition of the Hargreave jewels."

She laughed. "Perhaps for that, I'll harness the horses myself."

"And as an added fillip, I could introduce you to the publisher, Bothwick. Gore knows him well."

"Bothwick! You don't mean it! If you're teasing me, Simon, I'll never forgive you. Do you know how many wonderful authors he publishes?"

"I have no idea, darling, but I'm sure Gore will know. Are we agreed then?"

"I don't really have to see your mother, do I?"

"Not without me for protection. I promise."

"Will you come with me to Daphne's?"

"If you wish."

"Why are you being so cooperative?"

He was quickly dressing. "I'm always cooperative," he said with the perverse presumption of a man who bent the world to his will. "Do you want me to send up a maid?"

"I haven't been to London in five years."

"It looks the same." He glanced at her. "You're not worried about"—he made a dismissive gesture—"what would you be worried about?"

"Nothing, everything . . . I don't know."

Moving to the bed, he sat down and drew her into his arms. "You'll enjoy yourself, darling. And I'll keep the Daphnes away if you're worried. And mother too."

"I don't know if I'm worried or not."

And he didn't know why he couldn't live without her. But he couldn't so he understood a measure of her incomprehension. "We'll see Bothwick first thing," he promised, offering her an indulgence sure to please. "What do you think?"

She nodded, jettisoning her apprehensions about the viciousness of the ton, and Simon's patterns of amusement. He was offering her a lavish world and a place by his side. She'd be foolish to refuse on principle. And Bothwick. She couldn't help but smile.

Twenty minutes later, they were traveling south.

Chapter
28

The news of Simon's marriage had raced through the ton within hours of their arrival at Hargreave House. But all the curious callers were turned away until the new duchess had a suitable wardrobe—a process much accelerated by Simon's wealth.

In the meantime, though, as promised, the publisher, Martin Bothwick was sent for immediately. And for the occasion, Simon presented Caroline with an at-home gown he'd had the modiste who made her wedding gown deliver to Hargreave House in his absence.

"How did you know I'd be coming back?" Caroline asked, her life one of uncertainty and transience for so long, she still didn't think in terms of the future.

"I was hopeful, of course." The ultimate politesse from a man who would have abducted her from the dungeons of hell. "Try it on. We can have some adjustments made before Bothwick arrives if need be."

"Bothwick is really coming here today?" she said, still in awe. "Do you know how important he is—how influential?"

"He must have had time in his schedule," Simon replied casually, more aware than she perhaps of a wealthy duke's position in the hierarchy of influence.

The moss green silk gown fit well, as did the matching kid slippers; and the cashmere paisley shawl that was all the rage was so delicate and fine it could be drawn through a ring.

"You look good enough to eat," Simon said with a wolfish grin, lounging in a chair in Caroline's dressing room while she finished her dressing with the addition of beaten gold earrings. "A shame we don't have time." He glanced at the clock. "Although . . ."

"Don't you even dare think of it," Caroline interjected, shaking out the folds of her shawl so they draped over her arm properly. "I'm not going to meet the important Mr. Bothwick with my hair all atumble and my face flushed from lovemaking." She pointed a finger at him. "You stay right there."

"Yes, ma'am. And if I behave, will you lift up your pretty green skirts for me later?"

"I may if you don't embarrass me with Bothwick."

"Yes, ma'am, thank you, ma'am," he murmured, grinning.

Her look was one of reproof. "I mean it, Simon. This is very serious. I don't want any of your sardonic or disparaging comments."

"Me?"

"Simon!" She turned back from the mirror. "Promise me this instant or you'll have to stay in your room."

He laughed. "Now that I'd like to see."

Her answering smile was seduction incarnate. "And I know just what to offer you to have you oblige me."

His mouth quirked. "I suppose you do at that. Very well. I promise to behave." He had something to say to Mr. Bothwick as well, although his conversation would be by necessity, private.

The duke was extremely kind to their visitor when he arrived. He went to meet Bothwick in the entrance hall and personally escorted him into the drawing room to meet Caroline, a mark of distinction that didn't go unnoticed by the publisher who was never invited to ducal homes.

Martin Bothwick was a plump little man, clearly nervous despite Simon's amiability, but as he and Caroline began discussing several of the authors he'd published, his disquietude subsided. They spoke at length of various books that he'd brought to prominence; Caroline had read them all. They spoke of plots and dialogue and pacing through several cups of tea while Simon listened and occasionally offered a comment. Caroline was surprised Simon was so well read in terms of the newest fiction; she would have considered him too busy with carousing.

Martin Bothwick was equally surprised. He hadn't thought the Duke of Hargreave dedicated to intellectual pursuits. But apparently, he'd read a great deal of contemporary English literature as well as that of France and Germany. There was absolutely no doubt he knew the best tailors. Even a man of Bothwick's background who professed no interest in sartorial matters found his gaze returning to the duke's elegant lounging form. He might have such a coat made for himself, he thought, sitting up a bit straighter to hide his paunch. Black would be slimming too.

Sometime later, when Simon brought up the subject of Caroline's manuscript, she immediately blushed. "It's not in the least ready yet, Simon. Really, Mr. Bothwick, it's in the very earliest stages."

"When you've finished it, Lady Hargreave, please allow me to have the first look."

"There's no need to be polite, sir. I'm the most rank amateur," she protested, all her dreams of writing paling into insignificance against this man's accomplishments.

"Nevertheless, I'd be remiss as a businessman if I didn't take advantage of this meeting with you. You understand, writers from the ton are very rare. And of great interest to the world."

"There, you see, darling," Simon interposed. "Mr. Bothwick has a point. And who better than he to know the literary landscape?"

"Thank you very much." Caroline could scarce catch her breath. "I'm thrilled, of course."

"The manuscript is in Yorkshire at the moment, but we'll have it brought to London," Simon remarked.

"It's not at all ready, though," Caroline quickly noted.

"When it is, Lady Hargreave, I'd be delighted to read it."

And for the remainder of their visit, Caroline was floating on air.

The men spoke briefly once again as Simon walked with the publisher to the front door. And whether His Grace could actually read minds or whether Bothwick's inspection had been too obvious, the duke said, "Let me send my tailor to you. You'll enjoy him. And it would give my wife pleasure."

The publisher attempted to refuse, but the duke was ingratiating and winning and Bothwick was ushered from the house, quite charmed.

Hargreave was in love with his wife, Bothwick understood as he paused curbside a moment later, waiting for a footman to open the door of the duke's carriage that was there to drive him home.

Although he wasn't sure His Lordship realized it.

Perhaps he'd been the byword for vice too long to recognize the gentler emotions.

Simon's reputation gave pause to many in the ton as well, when at the end of the week, the duke and duchess were finally at home to visitors. The shock of Simon seated in the drawing room beside his new wife was almost as astonishing as news of his marriage.

Many might understand a man's eventual need for a wife. Or more pertinently, a man's need to marry an enceinte lover, but for the Duke of Hargreave to actually make an appearance at tea was definitely in the nature of a miracle. Not that he went so far as to actually drink tea—the brandy at his elbow his preferred choice—but his mere presence spoke volumes.

His choice of Caroline Morrow for his wife caused enormous tittle-tattle and rumor. Was she not already married? Although certainly, the duke had enough money to buy off a husband or two. But five years wasn't so long and everyone recalled the circumstances of their parting. That scandalous little story had spread through the ton like wildfire.

So, where had he found her?

And where was her other husband?

And more important, why had he married her?

No one ever contemplated he'd married for love. Hargreave's profligate manner of living rather nullified any such fantasy. And while the duke and Lady Caroline had grown up together, friendship, too, was hardly a reason for marriage.

Which left only the likelihood that Simon had sired a child.

But if Caroline had been married, whose was it?

Not only would everyone be counting on their fingers, but the entire ton would be waiting with bated breath to see the child.

Simon, of course, was aware of all the rumors. Gore and all the servants had their ears to the ground and news traveled faster below stairs than above. But he'd forbidden any of the gossip reach Caroline. It was pointless to worry her.

Now that they'd finally reached a measure of emotional compromise.

It helped that he'd been home with her since their return to London. Although truthfully, he didn't know how much longer he could continue playing the cicisbeo.

Neither spoke of his altered stance on having a child.

His reasons were too brutally possessive.

And Caroline couldn't bring herself to voice the extent of her attachment and affection for a man who didn't understand either emotion. But she quietly wished and hoped and considering the frequency of their lovemaking, judged the possibility of a child as highly likely.

They had made love repeatedly since their marriage, their journey to London, more leisurely than anticipated when they found themselves more interested in sexual amusements than travel. And while they'd been incommunicado at Hargreave House, waiting for Caroline's wardrobe to be finished, their days and nights had been a carnal feast for the senses. In fact, Caroline found herself in a constant state of raging desire, as though she were perennially in heat. She had but to look at Simon and she melted in longing. He had but to smile her way and she was wet with desire.

It wasn't as though Simon was unaffected by ravenous lust. He was in an ungovernable state of rut as well. And while he didn't understand the finer points of love, he understood carnal desire. He quickened at the mere sight of his wife, and when she welcomed him into her body with the wild, tempestuous passion that was so much her nature, he was always reminded how intensely he'd missed her. And during those glorious moments of fierce, fanatical delirium, he would have gladly relinquished all his worldly goods.

That first afternoon at tea, they were forced to ignore their ready passions and close proximity and present the face of composure to their callers. Their guests had all come to ask pointed questions in as oblique a manner as possible and watch their hosts' every move as though such close scrutiny would uncover the unimaginable reasons behind their marriage. Or at least lend a piquant authenticity to the reports that would come from this afternoon teatime. The whole town would be dining on the details of this mysterious marriage for weeks.

Throughout the afternoon, Simon was dealing with feelings he hadn't experienced since he was fifteen. Not since then had he been so aroused by lustful cravings. At times he only half-listened to the banal conversation, consumed with desire. All he wanted to do was push Caro down on the settee, toss up her skirts, plunge into her and fuck himself to death. Glancing at the clock, he swore under his breath. Would these people never leave?

Caroline wondered if the heated flush on her cheeks was visible. Simon was much too close. It had been a mistake to sit side by side on the settee. She was wet with desire, the throbbing between her legs increasing in intensity, while she was having more and more trouble concentrating on the conversation. She moved away fractionally, so Simon's thigh wouldn't touch hers.

He shifted position, following her and she glanced up at him in panic.

His dark gaze was hot with lust.

She quickly looked away.

But not before everyone in the room had taken note of the shocking display.

Daphne was one of the visitors and her mouth tightened in resentment. "Do you ever see Louvois, Caro?" she asked in a silken tone, eaten with jealousy, wanting to draw blood. "Or shouldn't I mention your former husband?"

Daphne was very blonde and very beautiful and not showing her pregnancy at all, a fact everyone in the room had observed the moment she had arrived. Another of Daphne's ruses, everyone had concluded. Or she'd rid herself of the stable boy's child, Simon more cynically reflected.

"Actually, I saw Louvois last," Simon interposed, better able to withstand Daphne's barbed tongue. "He was in fine spirits, as was his new wife. They seemed very happy. How is Blessington?" he inquired blandly. "Still in Ireland?"

"Charles is very busy with his estates."

And his Irish mistress, Simon thought. "Charles has found a new calling, I hear. Although, farming? I wouldn't have thought him a devotee."

Daphne's mouth firmed for a moment. "He's quite involved, actually. Will you be visiting Monkshood soon?" she shot back.

As capable as Daphne at dissembling, Simon turned to Caroline and smiled. "What do you think, dear. Should we go and visit mother?"

"I'd love to."

There was an audible gasp. Isabella had been heard to tell Caroline on more than one occasion, that she would never allow her son to marry a woman with a drunken father and no money.

"Mother may be off for Florence soon, Gore tells me," Simon noted with a smile. "Perhaps we'll drive down before she leaves and bid her adieu."

If the visitors hadn't known better, they might have thought

Simon actually talked to his mother other than on those instances when their business affairs required it.

The visit was turning out to be more entertaining than a performance at Covent Garden.

"Will you be staying in London long?" The young Earl of Dalhousie asked.

And those friends of Simon's who had come today to see the rare wonder of Simon married knew Dalhousie was asking—*without your wife.*

Caroline glanced at Simon. "I'm not sure," she said. Although she would have left for the country tomorrow if Isabella were gone. The pettiness and insincerity of society held no appeal.

The duke smiled at his wife and then cast his gaze on all the expectant faces. "It depends," he said. On how long he could stand to play the husband. On how long it took his wife to get with child. On whether either of them could truly withstand the day-to-day obligations of marriage.

"Brookes isn't the same without your high play," Dalhousie noted.

Simon knew what Douglas had been asking the first time. "Perhaps after the honeymoon," Simon murmured.

Caroline blushed furiously.

"Did I mention Caro has taken on the task of redesigning the gardens here?" he smoothly interposed. "You must all ask her about Villa d'Este, which is her favorite. Tell them, darling, about the grotto you've planned." And he placed his arm along the back of the settee and leaned toward her slightly.

It was a protective gesture. He was telling them all to be kind to his wife or risk his wrath. A strange new role for a man who had always been charming but relatively indifferent to the woman on his arm.

The afternoon continued apace, with probing questions and temperate answers, the avid curiosity seemingly boundless until finally Simon had had enough. Coming to his feet, he bowed faintly to the visitors. "Thank you all for coming to welcome us back to the city. But my wife and I have a pressing engagement."

Drawing Caroline to her feet, he slipped his arm around her waist and then kissed her gently not on the cheek, but on the mouth. After which he escorted his wife from the room.

The guests were left wide-eyed with shock.

The duke's fondness for his wife, and more titillating, his sexual ardor was undisguised.

It was the most delicious scandal.

Imagine, the infamous Duke of Hargreave in love with his wife!

Everyone tumbled from the room in haste to spread the news.

Chapter

29

Within another fortnight, Simon was visibly chafing at his bonds and the naysayers were smugly quoting the old saw about a leopard's spots. He'd escorted Caroline to countless entertainments in the weeks past, attended several plays with her, had even gone shopping with her in Bond Street on numerous occasions. He hadn't once visited his clubs, nor any of his usual haunts and the constraints on his life were taking their toll.

He was edgy and short-tempered.

Even Gore, who was the most mild-mannered of men, found himself the object of Simon's displeasure one afternoon.

Immediately apologizing for his outburst, Simon flung himself into a chair and swore under his breath for a lengthy interval.

"Is there anything I can do, sir?" Gore inquired once Simon had stopped cursing, although he cautiously stayed near the door.

"Thank you for asking, but no." The duke sighed. "Now give me the bad news. What's on our schedule for tonight?"

"A dinner at the Eustices, sir."

Simon groaned.

"Thalia tells me Lady Hargreave is resting now though—a headache, she thought. Perhaps Lady Hargreave may not wish to dine out tonight."

Simon looked up, his gaze examining. "Really," he said, coming to his feet. The faintest of smiles played across his mouth. "Thank you, Gore. That will be all for today."

As he entered their bedroom, Simon took note of the drawn shades and stood for a moment in the doorway, a look of concern creasing his brow. Moving quietly, he walked to the bed.

Caroline's eyes came open.

"Gore said you had a headache." She looked pale, he thought. "Do you want me to call a doctor?"

"It's just a stomach upset. I haven't felt well all afternoon."

"Grantley's wine was poor last night. Do you think it might have affected you?"

"Perhaps."

Her tone struck him as odd. "Something *is* wrong." Sitting down beside her, he gently stroked her hand. "Tell me now and if I can't help, surely we can find someone who can."

"I didn't want to say anything before . . . that is . . ."

"Good God, Caro," he exclaimed, seized with trepidation, her pallor suddenly looking more pronounced. "If something's amiss, you must tell me."

"I don't think it's anything serious . . . like—er—an actual illness."

"Well, something obviously is wrong when you're lying abed looking peckish."

She took a small breath. "We're going to have a baby."

At first he thought he must be mistaken; she'd spoken so softly. Or perhaps the statement was so foreign to his life, he couldn't immediately comprehend its significance.

"A baby, Simon."

Her words suddenly hit him like a hammer blow. He drew in a breath, a dozen possibilities racing through his brain, none of them benign.

His freedom was restored.

He no longer had to play guard to her virtue.

Or protect the Hargreave dynasty.

His former way of life beckoned, lured, tempted . . . the siren song of dissipation ringing in his ears.

He'll be gone soon, she thought, back to the freedoms he missed. He'd been like a tethered animal of late. No one in his presence could have been unaware of the hindrance marriage had become for him.

And said or unsaid, spoken or not, she'd always understood the reason for his flagrant possessiveness, for his not allowing her out of his sight.

But she'd wanted a child too.

For reasons as selfish as his, although their motives had differed.

"Are you pleased?" he asked, sitting very still, his gaze watchful.

She nodded and smiled. "And you?"

More than you know. "Yes," he said. "I am."

Tears welled into her eyes. "I'm glad."

"Don't cry, darling. I'll take care of you both," he said, gently. "Always."

And he would, she knew, although he may not be able to give them his heart. But who in the ton was granted their husband's heart? she reminded herself. "I'd like to go to Monkshood as soon as your mother leaves."

"If you wish, I'll have her out tomorrow."

Caroline shook her head. "There's no need to make her life difficult."

"I don't want her near you."

"I know."

He inhaled, looked away for a moment, trying to decide how honest he should be. His mother had written to him twice since they'd returned to London; neither note had contained good wishes on his marriage. "Why don't I have Gore go down and see that mother leaves in a day or so." He'd buy his mother the very expensive villa in Florence she'd been wanting. With the stipulation she stay away from Monkshood. He'd throw in all the belongings she'd taken from his house in the bargain. "We could plan on driving down the end of the week? How would that be?"

"Perfect. Thank you."

"You've been wanting to get away, haven't you?"

"I so dislike society," Caroline murmured. "I always have."

"As do I."

"You've been very patient, escorting me about."

"My pleasure, darling," he replied with the effortless charm that was his hallmark. "Now, tell me, how do you feel? How do you know for certain we're having a baby? And what can I do to help?"

Stay with me at Monkshood, she wished to say, but knowing better, she said instead, "Once this nausea has passed, I would very much like a—"

"Piece of chocolate cake, no doubt," he said, grinning.

"Actually, a dish of macaroni."

His grin broadened. "Am I going to be obliged to hire an Italian chef?"

She shook her head. "Bessie knows the kind of macaroni I like."

"And Mrs. Tiffen knows how to cook it, I suspect." As children, they'd spent a great deal of time in the kitchen at Monkshood when their parents were away.

"She makes the most perfect creamy macaroni with the local cheddar and lots of butter . . ."

He heard the note of longing in her voice. "I'll have mother out by nightfall. Just say the word."

"No . . . no, I can wait."

He laughed. "As long as I find you that perfect macaroni."

"And perhaps just a very tiny piece of beef roast, sliced very thinly . . . no fat—or I'll throw up . . . with maybe a very small dollop of horseradish sauce on the side."

Simon was chuckling as he rose from the bed with his commission. "And I suppose by the time I return, you'll have some other item of food on your mind."

"A servant can do this, Simon. You needn't fetch and carry for me."

"I don't mind, darling. Now rest. I'll be back directly."

But on the way downstairs, he found himself thinking about the play at Brookes and then the play afterward that had nothing to do with cards. Quickly repressing those images, he descended the stairs to the main floor, but there was a new lightness to his step.

Chapter
30

Caroline was welcomed with open arms at Monkshood, all her servants from Maple Hill along with Simon's staff lined up to greet her. Rose and Bessie hugged her first with tears in their eyes. Then Caroline and Simon moved down the ranks of servants, exchanging words with each member of the household, the full measure of happiness at the duke's marriage evident in everyone's smiles.

"I knew you'd be back, my lady."

The phrase was repeated so many times Caroline felt as though her exile abroad had been no more than an intermission in her life. "It's grand to be here," she'd reply each time, truly feeling as though she were back home.

But the moment the last greeting had been exchanged and the final expression of good wishes had been delivered, Rose and Bessie—exerting their prerogatives as long-standing family retainers—dismissed Simon and bustled Caroline upstairs to bed. Fussing over her like mother hens, they took over the tasks they'd long performed for her, helping her undress and put on her nightgown, brushing out her hair, helping her into the large four-poster bed.

"There, now, dearie, you're back where you belong," Rose murmured, tucking in the coverlet around Caroline.

"And we're here for any little thing you need," Bessie affirmed, shaking out Caroline's gown.

Rose smoothed the hair back from Caroline's forehead, like she'd done countless times before. "Everything's going to be right fine now."

Rose had helped raise Caroline since birth, while Bessie had offered her a home away from home at Monkshood.

The old duke—perhaps motivated by dislike of his wife—had allowed Caroline the run of his house. Simon's mother had always objected to the little girl next door, wanting a more illustrious marriage for her son. Although, in truth, it was more often the servants who were in charge of the young Hargreave heir and Caroline. The duke and duchess were rarely at Monkshood and more rarely together. And while Caroline's father was devoted to her, as prisoner to his addictions, he wasn't always able to discharge his fatherly duties.

Simon and Caroline had been hoydens of sorts, although there were tutors aplenty at Monkshood and Maple Hill who encouraged the youngsters to explore their intellectual interests. And outside the schoolroom, the thousands of acres on the two estates offered outdoor amusements in all seasons to the two wild children.

It was an unconventional life, but not an unhappy one.

They had each other.

Simon was reminded of those carefree years as he waited in his study for permission to visit his wife. Relaxing before the fire, he smiled over his brandy. Now that his mother had vacated the estate, it was good to be home. And between Bessie and Rose, Caro would be coddled and cosseted to the point of obsession.

No doubt, he had become relatively insignificant, he reflected, drolly. Having done his part, he was expendable—being shunted off to his study a case in point. He glanced at the clock, drank another brandy and then feeling he'd been lenient enough, rose from his chair. Surely, they had Caro settled in bed by now.

But he was forced to wait outside in the hall for some minutes more before Bessie finally ushered him in.

"Now, I don't want you upsettin' her," she said, speaking to the duke as though he were eight. "It's a right long drive from London and the sweet girl is almost done in."

"It's twenty miles, Bessie. Not halfway to Egypt."

"Humph, as if you'd know anything about how it feels to be in the family way. Didn't I just say as much, Rose?" she noted, huffily, glancing at her cohort who was fluffing the pillows behind Caro's head.

"Men!" Rose snorted, the single word impugning the entire gender. "Drink and gamble too much, they do, and that's not the worst o' it."

Caroline and Simon exchanged glances but held their tongues until the two ladies had fluffed the last pillow and poured the last glass of water and were finished arguing about Caroline's preferences in food.

"And stay off the bed," Bessie ordered at the last.

When the door finally shut on the housekeepers, Simon dared move from his position just inside the entrance to the room. "I can see that I'm going to have to reassert my authority here at Monkshood," he said, amusement in his gaze. "I was very much afraid Rose was going to sound a peal over my head on my drinking and gambling habits."

"Not to mention those unspeakable ones," Caroline noted, lightly.

He grunted in reply, not likely to respond to that rejoinder. "And I hope you don't mind, but I have no intention of staying off your bed."

Caroline grinned. "Thank God. I didn't relish having to become celibate."

"Not likely that," he murmured, beginning to strip off his coat as he moved toward the bed.

She nodded at the door. "You might want to lock it."

"I'm thinking it might be more prudent to attempt personal contact in small stages." Tossing his coat on the chair, he began unbuttoning his vest. "I'm trying to avoid being sent to bed without my supper," he added, with a roguish grin. Dropping his vest atop his coat, he kicked off his shoes and sat down on the bed beside Caroline. Although, not too near.

She measured the space with her gaze and grinned. "You're afraid of Bessie."

He looked at her, a waggish light in his eyes. "Damn right."

"Does that mean I have to wait until dark?" she asked in a pouty little whisper. Rising to her knees, she leaned across the small distance separating them, placed her hands on his shoulders and lowered her head until their eyes met. "I don't know if I can wait until dark," she breathed, nibbling on his bottom lip.

"We probably should, though." His voice was taut with restraint.

"Don't want to," she purred, bending closer, her breasts swinging slightly beneath her nightgown, brushing against his chest.

Through force of habit, perhaps, his hands seemed to come up of their own accord, his fingers splayed over her soft, pliant flesh and he filled his palms with the weight of her breasts.

She softly moaned, the pressure of his fingers sending little sparking tingles down to the pulsing tissue deep inside her. "Please . . . I want to feel you," she implored, breathy, eager. "It's been so long . . ."

He shut his eyes against the spiking lust, resisted for a millisecond more while he debated whether three hours was indeed too long. Then he muttered, "I'll be right back," and left the bed.

There were cardinal moments and this was one where rank was useful, he decided, moving toward the door. Striding out into the hall, he swiftly traversed the plush Uzbek carpet to the head of the stairs and without hesitating, shouted, "I do not want to be disturbed!" His voice thundered down the stairwell, past numerous Hargreave forebears staring out from their portraits to the front hall servants at their posts.

The footmen looked up in surprise. The duke never raised his voice. But then again, he was half-dressed in the middle of the day. They glanced at each other and smiled. And when they looked up again, he was gone.

Returning to the bedroom, Simon locked the door and quickly stripped off the remainder of his clothes to an appreciative audience of one.

"Is that all mine?" Caroline purred as he walked toward the bed, her gaze on his magnificent upthrust penis.

"It's all yours," he murmured with a smile.

"What if I want it inside me always . . ."

His heated gaze turned hotter. "I'll see what I can do. You're not too tired, now."

"Au contraire. I'm very much awake." And so saying, she lifted her nightgown over her head in one fell swoop and flung it away.

He laughed. "It looks as though your nursemaids might have misdiagnosed your condition. Instead of bed rest, you have other things in mind."

"Sex with you is rather constantly on my mind. I feel as though I should apologize," she added in a genuinely contrite tone.

He smiled. "That won't be necessary. I doubt I'll find it inconvenient."

"Oh, good," she exclaimed, like a child allowed a special treat. "Do you think you *could* stay inside me for a very long time? I seem to be insatiable."

"I'll do my best," the man who held all the records for continuous sex in the brothels of London replied, mildly. Climbing into bed, he lay back against the pillows.

"I absolutely adore when you come in me." Her voice held that same note of breathlessness. "I wonder if other women feel that way, like some primordial female fertility figure waiting to be implanted with male sperm. All expectant and fruitful and yielding. Is that strange?"

He smiled, his gaze flicking to his erection. "I don't know, but it's making me horny as hell."

"Oh my God..." she breathed, watching his penis surge higher. "May I lick it just a little?"

"Be my guest." It was his turn to offer up a supplication of his own—in his case a prayer of thanksgiving.

Kneeling over him, she held his stiff erection upright with one hand, guided it to her mouth and ran her tongue over the swollen, sensitive head as she massaged and gently pulled on the soft skin of his testicles with the other hand. She tested the weight of the balls in her palm, ran her tongue up one side and down the other of his stiff length, around and around the engorged head, wetting all his turgid flesh until his penis was glistening. "Look, darling. It shines ever so nicely. Oh, dear, I missed a spot." And bending low once again, she set to rights the small unlicked area of skin. Looking up through her tumbled curls, she smiled. "How much do you think I can get in my mouth?"

Her question added new dimension to his arousal and she uttered a soft muffled cry. "How do you do it?" she whispered, rocking gently on her knees, liquid heat pulsing between her legs. "Get so big?"

"Looking at a delectable little wanton like you," he murmured, gently stroking her hair.

Her smile was seductive. "Watch me then."

He watched his erection slide in and out of her mouth, its length swelling even more with each caress of her lips and tongue, his pleasure so great he didn't know if he was going to come in her mouth or wait to fill her with sperm or whether he was capable of controlling his orgasm at all. She was luscious, pink, and curvaceous—like the earth mother, the fertility deity she'd mentioned. Her breasts were noticeably larger, full and plump, hanging like ripe fruit. And the flare of her hips was more exaggerated than before, adjunct to her new sexually ravenous mood. She was more wanton and eager, more irrepressibly tantalizing and cupping her head in one palm, he pushed his erection deeper into her mouth. She didn't mind. She sucked on him with all her power as though she were starved and famished for the feel and taste of a man.

But just before he was about to come, he jerked away, wanting to sink into her soft body more. Lifting her mouth to his, he kissed his tangy flavor from her lips. "I may just keep you locked away in here; screw Bessie's orders," he whispered against her mouth.

"I'd lie in bed waiting for you to make love to me. You'd let me come and come and come," she said on a little caught breath, rubbing her breasts against his chest. "My body would always be wet for you and wet from your sperm. I would be your receptacle for sperm."

It was too much even for a man of his restraint, or maybe he'd never had a wife before, a woman who was his. Maybe that sense of possession, of ownership heightened the avaricious nature of sex. "Open yourself," he said, his voice rough with lust. "And we'll see if your body is ready for me."

She lay back against the pillows instantly; she spread her legs. Her pubic lips were swollen, distended, the moist fluid of desire gleaming on the soft flesh. "Is that wide enough?" she whispered, her expression diffident and so unlike Caro he glanced again at her face. "I'll do anything to feel you inside," she breathed, shuddering with need. "I can't help it."

Jesus . . . he'd never seen her so necessitous, so overcome and he wondered if her pregnancy was cause and agent for her new wellspring of burning desire.

"Please, Simon," she sobbed, her vagina quivering, swimming in glossy lubricant, her thighs spread wide so the little runnels of pearly liquid oozing from her cleft were visible. "I know I've said please before, but, I really, really mean it this time . . ."

"Hush, darling," he murmured, quickly moving over her, taking her in his arms, gliding into her body, widening her passage, filling her, impaling her as she arched up in desperation to meet him. "I'm here . . . I'm here," he whispered as she clung to him, whimpering. "I'm right here inside you for as long as you need me . . ."

Her hips were writhing, pumping, drawing him deeper and deeper, her need for consummation a fiery, hot hysteria.

And he gave her what she wanted, what she yearned for and craved, staying deep inside her, satisfying her greedy desires with indefatigable patience and skill, indulging her unbridled lust over and over, filling her with come an astonishing number of times.

Enjoying in full measure his first day in the country.

Chapter
31

For almost a month, the duke and duchess resided in a state of pure undiluted sexual bliss. While they disagreed on much in life, sex was not an area of contention and the days at Monkshood were as close to paradise as carnal passion allowed. Until one morning, during breakfast, Simon handed Caroline a letter from the mail he'd been perusing. "This looks like a command performance. One of Prinny's last minute affairs. Do you care to go?"

George IV was having a dinner party.

Caroline wrinkled her nose. "Not in the least," she murmured, barely glancing at the engraved note.

"Even if I see that Prinny keeps his hands to himself," Simon noted, drolly, aware of the king's interest in Caroline.

"The last time you said that, I was forced to fight him off myself because you'd disappeared into the card room. I'd rather not be put in that position again, thank you."

"Well, one of us has to appear." Pulling the card back, he perused it again, his mouth pursed.

"Give Prinny some excuse. Others do."

Simon frowned faintly. "The dinner is in honor of some new decoration the king is awarding Wellington."

"If you want to go, go."

He looked up at the pettishness of her tone. "It's not that I *want* to go. It's just that all Wellington ADCs will be there."

"I'm sure you're right." Even as she realized how unreasonable she sounded, she couldn't desist. Perhaps she was more thin-skinned than usual. She'd noticed recently how occasionally Simon would seem to be making a particular effort to amuse her, as if he were playing the dutiful husband. She should be grateful; instead, she was mortified and provoked.

And as if she wasn't already irrationally jealous of his past, he was looking much too handsome lounging in his chair, his dark hair ruffling the collar of his partially opened shirt, a portion of his bare chest exposed, his shirt cuffs unbuttoned. He had that indolent look of a man who had dressed haphazardly after leaving his amorous play.

Which he had.

"I am right and you know it," he said, evenly, taking issue with her pique over a dinner with the king that was unavoidable. "Don't be difficult."

"I wouldn't think of it. Go and see all your *dear friends*," she murmured, her biting emphasis on the last words indicative of her feelings as to their gender. "I expect they're all wondering why you've tarried so long in the country anyway."

His nostrils flared for a moment, but he controlled his urge to respond.

"Speak up. I won't tell Bessie or Rose that you dared argue with me."

His housekeepers had warned him endlessly about the volatile emotions of pregnancy. Heeding their words, he'd been on his best behavior. As he continued to be now. "I'll go up to the city later today and be back in two days," he said, each word deliberately impassive. "Do you want anything from London?"

"No. I'm fine."

The clipped, crisp words were considerably less than fine, but he did have to go. This wasn't an occasion where an excuse would suffice. "I'll see if Bessie and Rose need anything."

"Maybe Daphne needs something."

A small silence fell.

"What the hell does that mean?" he asked very softly.

"Exactly what I said. I've seen you looking bored."

"Jesus, Caro. Sometimes it's quiet here. That doesn't mean I'm bored."

"You mean *too* quiet—say it."

"No I don't," he replied, curbing his temper with effort. "And I'm not going to fight over something ridiculous."

"My concerns are ridiculous?"

"If they're about Daphne, they sure as hell are."

"I suppose she bores you too."

He pushed away from the table. "I'm not taking part in this stupid conversation." He came to his feet. "I'm going for a ride."

"Because I can't go riding."

"Fine." He sat down again. "I won't go riding. Would you like to play cards?"

"Don't talk to me in that tolerant, long-suffering tone. And, no, I don't want to play cards."

He slid down in his chair and shut his eyes.

"And don't shut your eyes on me!"

His eyes came open. "I give up. What the hell do you want?"

Don't go to London; stay with me; want to stay with me. "Why don't you go to London right now!" she said, petulantly.

He came to his feet, his face a mask. "Thank you for your permission," he said with cutting sarcasm. "I'll give your fond greetings to the king."

The door closed on him brief seconds later and she burst into tears.

The dinner for Wellington was the usual affair with all the usual crowd—people Simon had known and amused himself with all his life. It was easy to fall into the familiar patterns of entertainment and association. He didn't openly flirt, but women surrounded him as they always did and he was charming as he always was . . . and hospitable. When the orchestra began to play after dinner, he refused the first few invitations to dance, but it was impossible to refuse them all and eventually he succumbed to the pressure of his admirers.

But he didn't dance with Daphne. Even in these most casual of circumstances, he knew better than that.

Afterward, when the party was over and he was being cajoled by his friends to join them in their revelry, he had no trouble declining their invitations. He was content to go home.

And were it not for Dalhousie, he would have gotten there.

It was a pleasant night for a stroll. Simon was only a block from Hargreave House when Dalhousie's carriage stopped at the curb and several of Simon's friends manhandled him into the carriage.

He could have resisted. He knew how to say no as well as anyone.

Perhaps he was tired of being the brunt of their jokes, or maybe he was tired of saying no to amusements when he seldom had, or perhaps he was wondering if it was worth the effort when no matter how dutiful he was, it wasn't good enough for his wife.

He accompanied his friends to a small house on Half Moon Street where he'd spent considerable time in the past. Although, on principle, he still remained aloof from the intimacies of the private rooms, restricting his entertainments to gambling and drink. It took considerable willpower, however, to withstand the persistent invitations of the ladies of the house who had sorely missed Simon's talents in bed.

But he did.

It was daylight when he found his way back to Hargreave House.

And when he came awake late that afternoon, he was greeted by Dalhousie and several other of his friends who had made themselves at home in his rooms.

His head hurt; he shouldn't have drunk so much the previous night. Compensation perhaps.

When Dalhousie handed Simon a brandy-laced coffee—another familiar ritual from the past—his headache was soon gone. His scruples were considerably compromised by the third brandy and coffee. And in time, Simon and his friends moved on to Brookes.

He won at the tables—another familiar ritual.

As was the later excursion to a smaller club known for its excellent chef, discreet staff, and luxurious private rooms.

He was at ease in the unconstrained world of male pleasures and merrymaking. All his friends were delighted to have him back in the fold and he smoothly slipped back into the habits of a lifetime. He had no one to please but himself. Self-indulgence was not only permitted, but encouraged. There were no expectations or obligations beyond purely selfish ones. And there wasn't an unreasonable woman in sight.

Chapter
32

Simon was still in London three days later when a groom from
Monkshood arrived at Hargreave House.

The man had ridden hard. He was out of breath, muddy,
soaked through from the rain and clearly indifferent to the fact
that the duke was still abed. Shoving past the footmen without so
much as a word of explanation, he raced up the stairs and entered
Simon's darkened bedroom without knocking. Jerking open the
draperies, he shook Simon awake roughly, gasped, "You'd best
come home," and thrust a note in his face.

Simon came awake instantly, realizing nothing but the most
tragic of circumstances would bring this man so unceremoniously
to his bed. Quickly reading the few lines Bessie had written, he
immediately understood what everyone at Monkshood knew—
including this groom. "I'll be out in five minutes," he said,
throwing back the covers. "Have Templar saddled."

"They already be doin' that . . . sar."

Simon took note of the grudging courtesy. He waved the man
out, needing a moment alone. But he saw the look the groom
gave him before he turned away. They all blamed him.

It was all her fault, Caroline silently bemoaned as she lay in
bed at Monkshood. She should never have fought with Simon

over something so nonsensical. She shouldn't have let herself become angry. Hadn't Bessie and Rose constantly warned her against becoming upset? Hadn't they insisted she be serene and even-tempered for the sake of the child? Hadn't they told her all the gruesome stories about babies being harmed by their mothers? looking at something grotesque or thinking bad thoughts?

She never should have pressed Simon over some silly invitation. He'd been like a saint since their marriage. Couldn't she have been more grateful? More understanding? Less quick to take offense?

Had she been, perhaps God wouldn't be punishing her now for her stupid jealousy.

The spotting had started almost the moment Simon left, as though it was divine retribution for her ingratitude.

Like an implacable eye for an eye.

Why couldn't she have been satisfied with her life?

She had a husband who had been kind and gracious and obliging. Hadn't he brought her home to Monkshood because she wished it and stayed with her even when he was obviously chafing at his confinement?

And even without Simon's benevolence, wouldn't the glorious hope of a child have been more than enough to bring her happiness? Hadn't she wanted a child with Simon for as long as she could remember?

Why had she pressed him on such a ridiculous issue when she knew Simon was the last person in the world who was likely to acquiesce to a demanding wife?

Oh, please God, please let the bleeding stop, and she'd never be ungrateful again.

In her dizzying grief, she promised a thousand good faith promises, and a thousand more abject penances if only her plea would be granted.

She was frantic with fear, desperate for hope. She hadn't moved since the morning disaster had struck. She'd lain completely still as directed by Bessie and Rose. She'd drunk the restoratives they brought to her, vile concoctions of herbs and roots. She'd drunk every drop without once complaining.

Hoping God would notice her new meekness.

Simon was riding dangerously fast, using whip and spur, forcing Templar to foolhardy limits. The roads were a quagmire, rough going even for riders not intent on breaking their necks. But Simon was heedless of all but his need to reach Monkshood and his massive thoroughbred seemed to understand, pounding through the treacherous mud and muck with phenomenal, unfaltering strength.

The two riders thundered through the villages between London and Monkshood, shouting villagers out of their way, not slowing for man or beast. When the driver of a pony cart was unable to pull off the road quickly enough at the entrance to a narrow bridge, Simon lashed Templar and the powerful horse cleared the cart in a high soaring leap. The lighter groom, up on the second best horse in Simon's London stable followed like a leaf in the wind.

Throughout the perilous run to Monkshood, the catastrophe Simon was about to face took center stage in his brain, a chaotic jumble of emotions jostling for position—fear, anger, frustration, sadness . . . guilt, too, for his part in what had transpired when last he spoke with Caro. He could have handled the situation better that morning; he *should* have. And an inchoate sense of melancholy at what might have been, overwhelmed him.

How could something like this happen? Was it normal or abnormal? Was it avoidable? Then his brain would loop back to the niggling unease that persisted beneath the labyrinthine disorder of his thoughts, the intangible damning resentment spurred by the contentious pattern of their marriage.

At base, he didn't trust his wife.

And during the whole of that maniac, headlong sprint to Monkshood, the obsessive question remained: Had she done this in retaliation?

Both horses were lathered, and beginning to falter as Simon reached the drive at Monkshood. Templar's great chest was heaving, the groom's mount a quarter mile back barely able to walk. But when Simon called on his racer for one last effort, the black thoroughbred dug in with gutsy heart and turned on an additional burst of speed up the incline to the house.

Whispering his thanks to his gallant mount, Simon jumped from the saddle before Templar had fully plunged to a stop. Standing in the entrance hall a moment later, dripping water on the floor, he stripped off his wet gloves and growled, "I want Bessie," to those servants unlucky enough to be within range. Sweeping his wet hair back with both hands, he bit out in a voice as cold as the grave, "This instant."

Everyone scattered before his wrath.

Ignoring the puddle forming at his feet, he didn't move, not sure he might not explode with rage if he took a single step. Not sure he was equipped to deal with the answer to the damning question burning through his brain.

When Bessie came running down the stairs, he waved away the servants who accompanied her and waited, his nostril flaring with impatience, until they were alone. Then he turned to the only person he knew who would tell him the truth and asked, harshly, "Did she do this to herself?"

"No! No!" Bessie cried, wringing her plump hands in anguish. "She didn't! She's terrified!"

The duke's gaze was murderous, a convulsive tick pulsated over one stark cheekbone and the young boy she'd rocked on her knee was entirely absent from the towering man with icy eyes who seemed not to have heard her. Taking a small breath, she forced her tone to one more reassuring and calm, hoping to mitigate the fury in the pitiless gaze. "Lady Caro would never do anything to harm the babe. On God's oath, she wouldn't."

"You're sure?" As if God wasn't guaranty enough.

The small, elderly woman nodded. "Yes, yes . . . I'm sure."

"Very well."

The sound of his voice was wholly forbidding. He could have been the old duke, speaking in that unrelenting tone. And while she knew he wasn't likely to take kindly to advice, she courageously spoke from her heart. "Please, Your Grace, don't frighten the dear child. She's pitiful scared."

His gaze came up. Bessie had never used an honorific when addressing him. "You believe her."

"She wants this child. By all that's holy, it's the truth."

An uncomfortable silence fell, the duke's scrutiny abrasive, as though the rasp of his anger was an audible friction in the air. And then he sighed. "Can the child be saved?"

The bitterness had lessened in his voice, although a faint echo remained and Bessie debated how best to reply. Did he want the child or not? "We've had Lady Caro take some herb potions that may help." She watched his reaction.

"I'll go and see her now."

It was impossible to read his thoughts. His gaze was shuttered, his words restrained. "I'll take you," she said, knowing she had to be there to protect Caroline whether he approved or not.

He looked at her, his head tipped in a quizzical way she recognized from his youth. He smiled, faintly. "Don't you trust me?"

She exhaled in a great rush of air. "Now I do."

She once more recognized the man before her and back on familiar ground, Bessie's trepidation vanished. When she left Simon at the door to Caroline's bedroom, she gave him warning. "That sweet child has always loved you," she declared. "I don't want you to forget that when you get your temper up," she added, firmly. "In fact, you're not even allowed to have a temper until this babe is out of danger. Understand?"

He grinned. "I sort of miss that, 'Your Grace.' "

"Humph. As if your arrogance needs any further bolstering. Just mind your manners now. She's right scared."

"Yes, ma'am." But beneath the mockery, he was pleased Bessie had been there when Caro needed her. Reaching down, he put his arms around the rotund little lady who always had been there when he needed her too, and gave her a quick hug and a kiss.

Turning ten shades of red, Bessie gave him a sharp look. "We won't be havin' any more o' that madcap behavior. I can still give you a good spankin' if need be."

He grinned. "I've been able to outrun you since I was six."

"Well, that may be, but—" Tears suddenly filled her eyes. "You just be good to her, Simon. Promise me, now."

"Yes, ma'am." His voice was solemn this time, as was his gaze.

"You always were a good boy," she whispered, patting his arm.

Bessie watched him open the door and walk inside.

And when the door closed on him, she said a little prayer.

Chapter

33

"I'm so sorry . . . so very sorry," Caroline sobbed, her voice choked with emotion as she caught sight of Simon. "It's all my fault and I understand . . . if . . . you don't want . . . to ever see me again . . . oh, God—I'm not supposed to cry, or get upset," she cried, tears streaming down her face. "Bessie and Rose said I mustn't . . ." she added with a stifled wail.

Simon was across the room in three long strides, but he came to a sudden stop by the bed. "I don't know if I'm allowed to touch you," he whispered, reminding himself grown men didn't cry.

"I don't care," she sobbed, lifting her arms to him.

And hoping Bessie wouldn't crucify him or he wasn't harming the baby somehow, he sat down on the bed, soaking wet and lifted Caro into his arms. "Everything's going to be fine," he said. "And it's not your fault. I shouldn't have gone. It's my fault."

"What if we lose the baby?" Her eyes were huge with despair.

"We won't. You and the baby will be safe."

"Truly?" Her voice trembled with hope.

"I promise," he said, vowing to move mountains or hold back the tides if necessary.

"You don't hate me?" she whispered, her eyes wet with tears.

He shook his head. "And I promise not to fight with you anymore."

Her smile was shaky. "You must be sick."

"No," he said, very softly. "Just glad to be home."

As though Simon were the antidote Caro needed for perfect health, the bleeding slowly diminished and then stopped completely. But no one was taking any chances. For the next two weeks, both she and Simon obeyed Bessie and Rose in all things. Caro drank the ghastly potions, barely moved and thought only happy thoughts—a simple enough task now that her husband had returned. Simon had a trundle bed set up, so he could sleep beside his wife and he spent every minute with her. All the servants walked about the house on tiptoes and spoke only in whispers until the duchess was finally pronounced cautiously healthy once again and allowed out of bed.

That first afternoon Caro was released from her sickbed, she and Simon moved to the solarium to enjoy the winter sunshine and their newfound sense of well-being. Simon almost immediately began rummaging through drawers and before long he held up a deck of cards. "Are you up to a few hands of piquet?"

"You don't have to be solicitous, darling. I needn't be amused."

"I was thinking about a repeat of our game at Kettleston Hall. I'm afraid I took advantage of you when we played for our wager. The viscount's deck had a few nicks in it."

"Did you really cheat?"

He didn't answer. He only smiled. "Do you feel lucky?"

"I feel like the luckiest woman on the face of the earth."

"Then you might win today. Three hands? Same rules?"

She grinned. "You're being awfully nice."

He shrugged and winked. "I expect I'll be rewarded some day."

She laughed. "You'll have to talk to Bessie about that."

"I already have my orders in that regard. I'm under strict control."

Caroline's eyes widened. "Did she actually . . . I mean, did she—"

"In no uncertain terms. I didn't know I could still blush."

"Show me, show me!"

And at recall of that very stilted conversation, a slight pink glow was evident beneath his tan.

Caroline's laughter rang through the room while Simon gave her a jaundiced look. "I'm glad you find it so amusing." He shoved the cards at her. "We're done with this embarrassing conversation. Cut the cards."

Caroline won the first hand by thirty points, the second by fifty, the third by forty. "You're not even trying," she grumbled.

"Consider it a gift."

She glanced at him, then her gaze narrowed and she looked at him more quizzically. "Are you saying what I think you're saying?"

"Did you think I'd forgotten how to play piquet?"

"You mean it?"

"I mean it," he said, softly. "If you want a faithful husband, you have one."

"I've never had someone for myself alone," she whispered.

"Speaking of that—I have a small request myself."

She looked frightened. "Is this some trick?" She had won too easily.

"No. No trick. I was just hoping you would do something for me as well."

"Of course." But her voice was tentative.

"I don't want you to run . . . if you should get angry—like you have," he took a breath, "before . . ."

She had to take a deep breath too, because she had always run when her life was in chaos. She'd learned the art of avoidance from her father. But Simon was waiting for her answer, looking grave. "I won't run." It was much harder to say than she thought. "I promise," she added with a soft winsomeness.

The warmth in his eyes could have melted the glaciers at the poles. "You've always been the only family I could count on, you know."

"I know." She smiled. "Along with our servants."

"Do you think Bessie would mind if I kissed you?"

"Kiss me now and we'll ask her later."

He moved the table aside, lifted her from her chair as though she were weightless, placed her on his lap and kissed her gently, chastely, with tenderness and love.

But very soon, he abruptly lifted her off his lap, set her on her feet and rose from his chair. "I can't be this close," he muttered, moving a safer distance away.

"Don't stop, darling, please . . ." She followed him. "I'm feeling so-o-o wonderful."

Quickly barricading himself behind another chair, he put up his hand. "Stay there."

She stopped, but reluctantly. "I'm feeling perfectly fine. Why don't I talk to Bessie and Rose?"

He groaned. "I can't believe this is happening to me."

"Would *you* like to talk to them?"

His eyes flared wide. "Christ, no."

She moved to the chair and leaned forward while he backed up as far as the wall would allow. "We could just wait until the baby is born I suppose," she said, her voice a delectable soft purr that had nothing to do with waiting.

Drawing in a deep breath, he exhaled in a whoosh of air. They needed a diversion or at least he did before he lost control. "I've something to show you first," he abruptly said, easing out from behind the chair. "Come into my study." He stepped back and waved her past him.

"Are we not allowed to touch?" she murmured.

"No!" He smiled ruefully at his explosive reaction. "Lord, Caro, I'm going crazy here. Humor me."

"If you promise to humor me afterward—in your own very, very special way . . ."

"Jesus," he said on a suffocated breath. "You're making this very hard."

"I'm *glad* it's hard," she whispered, feeling ravenous.

"Caro, for God's sake. I've never been celibate for so long"—
he grimaced. "Sorry . . . I didn't mean—" He decided it was safer
not to explain. "Forgive me, it was a slip of the tongue."

"Ummm, did you say, tongue? . . . Ummm . . . just the word
makes me feel all tingly and—"

"Damn it, Caro, don't!"

"You're adorable when you're rattled."

Her smile was tantalizing, a temptress's smile. "I'm not
adorable, nor have I ever been," he said, firmly, understanding
the urgency of taking charge of a situation that could easily get
out of hand. Quickly approaching her, he swept her up in his
arms and keeping his gaze averted, as though one glance at her
might turn him into a pillar of salt, he strode through the adjoin-
ing door into his study. Setting her down before a table covered
with documents, he commanded, "Sit," and pointed to a chair
with a jab of his finger.

"Yes, sir." Sitting down, she half-turned to him so her lush
bosom—even more showy now in pregnancy—was thrust out in
a most beguiling fashion. "Will this do?" she queried, with
feigned innocence.

This was drawing his gaze as she knew it would and she deliberately shifted in the chair so her heavy breasts swung faintly.

"I may have to spend the next few months in a cloister,"
Simon muttered. "Or put you in one, if you don't stop misbehaving."

"You never called it misbehaving before."

Her breathy little voice was so theatrically seductive, he
stepped back in self-defense. Moving to the other side of the
table, he cleared his throat in an attempt to focus his thoughts.
But, *damn*, she was an enchanting little witch and had it been
possible, he would have given her what she wanted until she
begged for mercy. "I have something for you," he said, gruffly,
quickly repressing the illicit images that came to mind.

"And I have something for you." She slowly ran the tip of her
tongue over her plump bottom lip, leaving a glistening wet trail.

"Caro, fucking behave," he growled, his voice hoarse with restraint. "I don't know how to be a monk and I'm not about to hurt you."

"I'm sorry." The agony in his voice was so stark, she was immediately stricken with guilt.

Inhaling deeply, he released his white-knuckled grip on the table and dropped into a chair opposite her. "As soon as we're done here, I'll talk to Bessie myself," he murmured, understanding there were limits to his willpower and he'd damned near lost control a moment ago. He shoved a number of papers toward her. "Here, take a look. I thought you might like something to keep you busy in the country."

"I rather thought you and our babe would keep me busy." A sudden suspicion entered her voice. Was he leaving her here?

"Would you mind adding the care of Maple Hill to your duties?" he asked, grateful to have something other than sex to discuss, already feeling a modicum more relaxed.

She glanced at the numerous heavily scribed sheets and then at him, her gaze incredulous. "Maple Hill? How—I mean . . . Maple Hill?" she whispered.

He smiled. "It's all yours."

"Mine? You don't mean it! I couldn't—"

"Of course you could. I want to give you something for the child you're giving me, although," he added, his dark eyes warm with affection, "my gift is not so splendid by half."

"How—when . . . I mean—tell me how it came about that you have Maple Hill?" Her father had lost it to his creditors two years before his death.

"After you left England, I made the new owners an offer they apparently liked." He shrugged. "I missed you I suppose, although I'm not sure I knew it. But I wanted Maple Hill. That I knew."

"You never said anything . . ."

He gazed at her from under half-lowered lashes. "There was a great deal of . . . uncertainty in our relationship," he said softly.

She smiled. "But, now, I'm not going to run anymore."

"And I've changed my priorities," he added with an answering smile.

She softly laughed. "Do you think this means we're all grown up?"

"Probably as grown up as we're likely to be," he replied with a cheeky grin. "But don't change. I like you just the way you are."

She winked. "For my part, I'd like you *just* a little bit closer. So, thank you from the bottom of my heart for Maple Hill—I'd love to share it with you . . . but right now . . . Are *you* going to ask our wardens for permission or am I?"

"Two hands out of three?" he offered, thinking perhaps those wardens would save him from himself.

"Loser asks?"

"Done."

"You know I always win," Caro murmured.

"I always let you win, you mean."

"No, you don't."

His brows flickered. "Yes, dear . . . I'm sure you're right."

Epilogue

It was questionable who let whom win that afternoon with their skills so evenly matched. In their new harmonious accord, however, they compromised, going hand in hand to ask what had to be asked, embarrassing not only themselves in the process, but Bessie and Rose as well.

After a constrained and stumbling interchange between the two parties, the duke and duchess were given a "proceed with reservations" answer that they observed with diligent caution and considerable bliss in the months that followed.

In the fall, to the delight of the young couple, a healthy, robust heir was born at Monkshood. He was plump and pink, had all his fingers and toes in perfect order, sparkling green eyes like his mother, a charming smile like his father, and the sweetest of dispositions.

And any latent fears the parents may have had concerning the health of their child were instantly dispelled.

With the birth of their son, the lives of a young boy and girl who had been first, the best of friends; in time, lovers; and now as man and wife, the most celebrated and captivating love-match in the ton, were brought full circle.

And life was again as it had been in their youth.

Carefree and bright with hope.